Mann Alone

Philip Kelly

First published 2020

Copyright © Philip Kelly. All rights reserved.

ISBN: 978-1-83808-452-3

Chapter 1, Monday 5 April 2027

"Are you crazy? You are saying that we should impose an immediate indefinite embargo on goods or people entering or leaving the island? Do you remember how difficult it was just stopping the movement of people in or out seven years ago, and it didn't stop Covid 19 getting here anyway. I can't ask the Minister to try selling that to the rest of the Council of Ministers." This was David Quayle speaking. His title was Chief Executive of the Health and Social Services Department. This meant he was the top official in that department of the Isle of Man Government. He was talking to Dr Vihan Singh, who had followed him into his office at 8.30 that particular Monday morning. David knew that Dr Singh was the senior consultant at the Pathology Department at the main hospital, and that he had been a rival candidate for his job. But he had had very little previous contact with him.

Dr Singh, feeling very agitated, said, "Look, have you been following the news at all? There are very few signs of life left on Madagascar. This ultra pneumonia virus will appear soon on the continent of Africa, because people will have been taking flights to Johannesburg from Madagascar. Luckily, flights to Paris from Madagascar stopped about four weeks ago, because of some industrial dispute in France, so it may take a little longer to get to Europe. But it seems nobody who gets this virus is surviving. It might be too late already, but we ought to at least try to save the people on this island."

David Quayle replied, "I think you are exaggerating the threat. We have had new diseases before which created some alarm, Aids, Sars, Ebola and of course Coronavirus, or Covid 19. None of them did or should have had much impact here. We obviously had some Aids cases amongst our LGBT community. Oh yes, I think we had what, about twenty five to thirty Covid 19 deaths in the end, but the main problem with that was the economic damage done by the shutdown. And now you want to repeat that? In my experience, it is much too early to take such extreme measures."

Dr Singh said, "What do you mean 'in my experience'? You are just a jumped-up social worker, whereas previous chief execs in this department have at least come from a health background. I am a very well qualified and experienced microbiologist, and I have never seen or heard anything like this. All the people in this field I have spoken to over the weekend are absolutely terrified. And, with flights linking nearly everywhere these days, ultra pneumonia is going to spread rapidly. It seems to be extremely contagious, and with a 100 per cent fatality rate. But, with 14 days delay before there are any symptoms. As I say it may be too late already. I feel absolute dread to be honest. My son Matthew is still in London, after a weekend conference, and I am expecting him back this evening. From a selfish point of view I would like the port and airport closures to happen after he has got back, even if the right thing to do is to close the airport and ports immediately. Look, apart from hoping for the best, we could all pray for deliverance I suppose. I have rejected all religion personally, as lacking any rational basis and pandering only to human weakness, but if anyone else wants to pray to God, or any other deity, that this virus somehow does not spread through Britain, Europe and the rest of the world, even with no vaccine, that is fine by me. And, if their prayers achieve such a miracle, that would be great. In the meantime, let's have a complete embargo on all contact with the outside world. And if praying does work, then we can say sorry for all the fuss, and reconnect ourselves to the rest of the world."

Dr Singh was red eyed and shaking slightly. David had not tried to interrupt him. He felt a chill as he realised, not only that Dr Singh was absolutely serious, but that he was probably right in predicting the doom of most of mankind.

After a short pause David said, "Okay Dr Singh, I know that you are the well respected Senior Consultant in Pathology at Nobles Hospital, our main pathologist in other words. Whilst I may be a jumped-up social worker, I like to think I take Public Health very seriously, and obviously we have to listen to your concerns. And maybe you are right. Oh, and just for the record, I do have a religion. My particular weakness, as you put it, is Christianity, even if I don't go to church except on Christmas Eve. We will both go and see the Minister of Health and Social Care, as soon as we can get hold of him. He might be in his office already, because there is a Council of Ministers meeting at 10am, and I know he wants a quick run through some budget figures with me first. His office is on the same floor as the other ministers, although I used to be next door to him. Things are always being reorganised, mainly to give the impression of improving efficiency, although most of the time it has the opposite effect. Anyway I digress, when urgency seems to be what is required. I think your first name is Vihan, isn't it?"

Dr Singh had calmed down a bit, "Yes but most people call me Vin. I am sorry about the jumped up social worker remark."

David replied, "That's alright Vin, call me David. Don't worry about the remark; I like to know what people think about me, even if usually they don't tell me to my face." He smiled at Vin in a friendly way, and went on, "But I think I will do most of the talking, because we want to get the Minister on our side if we can."

Vin responded, "Oh I don't know; I seem to have been persuasive with you. Perhaps I will call the Minister an old fool, and see if that does the trick." Vin smiled weakly at David.

David said, "Well yes I am 53, and the Minister must be at least 5 years older than me, but he is a bit vain, so I don't think you should try that! Anyway, you must be about 60 yourself?"

"61 actually, but feeling a lot older sometimes," Vin replied.

David said, "Tell you what, you wait here, whilst I go up to his floor to see if he's in his office and will speak to you as well as me. He wouldn't like it if if I take you in unannounced."

David's office was on the 2nd floor of the main Government offices in Bucks Road, in Douglas. Douglas was the key port and main town of the Isle of Man, or just Mann as it was sometimes called. The island was a Crown dependency in the Irish Sea, about 30 miles long roughly north to south, and about 13 miles wide, in the shape of a badly damaged rugby ball. In the 2026 Census it had a population of 84,000. This would have been the same sort of size of population as a fairly small local authority would have had in England, but being a Crown dependency meant that the Isle of Man Government, even then, had complete internal responsibility for all aspects of life. Only Defence and Foreign Representation were provided by the UK Government.

A few minutes after he had disappeared David returned, and he took Vin with him up to the Minister of Health and Social Care's office on the 3rd floor. The Minister, Adrian Kelly, sighed and frowned, "Look David, I know you said this is urgent and vitally important, but I am meeting the rest of the Council of Ministers at 10am, and the budget for health spending and hospital services, which we've both worked on, is first on the agenda, so you and I are being distracted from that. Anyway, sit down both of you."

Adrian was looking at David, so he decided to speak, "Minister, you must be aware of this new virus, possibly a new strain of flu, ultra pneumonia?"

"Yes, doing a lot damage in Madagascar, but how does that affect us?" Adrian replied.

David said, "The thing is Minister, any kind of flu is very hard to contain. In theory, when it is airborne, it can only spread a few feet through the air, before it starts to perish outside a host body. However, the incubation period is about fourteen days, so that the infection is spread by people who do not even realise they have the infection."

Vin thought that, to be having such a damaging impact, the ultra pneumonia virus must actually be carrying considerable distances in the air, but he was warming to David, and decided not to comment.

Adrian said, "Okay, I still don't see how this affects us, when the virus is restricted to Madagascar."

David answered, "Well the trouble is that this particular virus seems to be very contagious, and to have pretty much a 100% fatality rate. Dr Singh here, who has good contacts with other microbiologists around the world, has advised that no one who has manifested its symptoms seems to have survived. There seems to be very little sign of remaining life in Madagascar. Almost certainly, infected people will have already flown from there to Johannesburg. All strains of flu are generally very adept at being spread to other passengers on an aeroplane, and aeroplanes link nearly everywhere in the world these days. It might have got to Britain already!"

Adrian replied, "So basically you are saying that it could spread to the Isle of Man. Well how can we stop it? I recall we tried sort of quarantining, or embargoing, the island from outside contacts with the Covid 19 pandemic, and it didn't really help much."

David said, "Well let's look at the precedent of the Cornavirus pandemic. Luckily that did not ultimately kill more than about thirty people, I think. And no one seriously tried to stop us from closing our borders. Our problem was that we did it too late, and we allowed some of our fellow islanders back in, even though they were in so called isolation in a hotel for a while. It might cause quite a stir this time if we close, without any notice, all access to Mann for all traffic – sea and air, passenger and freight. And, we would have to exclude fellow islanders trying to return home. It would be dangerous not to. With someone, such as yourself, arguing the case for principled and decisive action, we might be in time to save the people of this island. The Manx people will eventually come to appreciate the actions of those involved."

David paused briefly. He knew that Adrian's twin sister was married to the British Prime Minister, and he decided to mention it, "I hesitate to mention your relationship with the British Prime Minister, but is it possible that you could persuade them to lend their Coastguard and military support to our own Coastguard and police, in keeping our ports and coastline closed to outsiders? That is assuming our Government decides to implement an embargo."

Adrian said, "Okay I hear what you are saying. I would just like to get my own bearings on things from Google." He started clicking on the mouse of his PC, whilst Vin restrained a strong urge to shake him. After a few grim minutes of netsurfing, Adrian looked at Vin and said, "Dr Singh isn't it? Is there anything you would like to add to what Mr Quayle has said?"

Vin replied, "Minister, I think Covid 19 was nothing compared with ultra pneumonia. The embargo for Covid 19 was too late. Even so, and even if we had had no lockdown or social distancing of any kind, it still was never going to kill more than, say, two or three hundred people, with an average age of dying from it being 79 years. With ultra pneumonia, if it gets here, it will simply kill everyone. So we must give the people here a chance, and close the airport and ports to all traffic as soon as possible." Vin looked him in the eyes as he spoke, "If you persuade the rest of the Government to agree, when people look back, you will be seen as a hero."

David winced. Adrian's lip curled. Adrian said, "There is no need to insult me, by suggesting I am mainly interested in some sort of ego trip. I want only to do what is right and necessary. I am persuaded that this matter should be raised urgently with the Council of Ministers. As I said, we are meeting this morning, and I will see if I can get it included in the agenda. David, after we have run through the budget figures, I would like you to come with me to the meeting. I will join you in my secretary's room, after I have made a quick phone call."

David and Vin left the room. Vin looked at David and said, "Sorry, I don't think that last remark about the Minister becoming a hero helped."

David replied, "Don't worry. Your sincerity seems to override your occasional crass remark, even with our vain Minister. Anyway, he is vain – don't tell him I said so – so it probably didn't hurt. I am not sure who he is calling, probably organising purchases of supplies for himself, which will soon be in short supply. He clearly doesn't want you anywhere near the rest of the Council of Ministers, but I have an idea. I have a good relationship with the Chief Medical Officer of England. If I give you his phone number can you ring him, tell him what is happening, and try to get ideas and support from him."

Chapter 2, Monday 5 April 2027

Tony Sharp, Chief Medical Officer for England was in his office in Whitehall in London. His personal secretary put his head round the door. He said, "I am sorry Tony but I've got someone on the line, who insists that it is important that he speaks to you. He says he is Dr Singh, the senior pathologist on the Isle of Man, and he needs to talk to you about the ultra pneumonia virus."

Tony thought to himself, "I think I know of a Dr Vihan Singh. I am sure I read a paper by him once about treatments for pneumonia."

Tony said to his secretary, "Okay, well that is the topic that we are worried about. Put him through."

Tony's phone rang. He picked it up and said, "Hello, you are through to me now, Dr Singh. I am Tony Sharp, the Chief Medical Officer. How can I help you? We have a bit of a crisis on, so, sorry to appear brusque, but can you be brief?"

Vin said, "David Quayle, the Chief Executive of the Health and Social Services Department here on the Isle of Man, suggested I ring you. I am the Senior Consultant in Pathology at the Nobles Hospital, and a lot of my training was in microbiology. We are very concerned about the ultra pneumonia virus which is going to spread from Madagascar."

Tony asked, "Is your first name Vihan? I am sure I saw a paper by you about the distinction between viral and bacterial pneumonia, and the best treatments for them."

"Yes my first name is Vihan, or Vin for short and I did write such a paper a few years ago."

"Well I am bit surprised that you are based on the Isle of Man, which must be a bit of a backwater. Anyway, you are not telling me you have any suspected cases of ultra pneumonia on the Isle of Man, are you?"

"No not yet, but it is only a matter of time before it spreads everywhere, don't you think? It seems to be very contagious and with 100% mortality. It looks to me like there is no-one left alive in Madagascar, yet we first heard about this virus less than a week ago."

"Well that virus is a major concern. My own office has been gathering what information it can. I am already speaking to the Prime Minister and other Ministers about what they should do to protect Britain. Since the Coronavirus crisis seven years ago, the holder of my post seems to get much better access to Ministers, and to have more influence. So they do listen to me. It looks like we are going to impose major restrictions on access to the UK. Possibly this will be a ban on all direct flights inward from anywhere outside Europe, no admittance to any non-European passport holders, and no admittance to anyone admitting recent travel to Africa, or with a recent stamp on their passport showing travel to Africa."

"Do you really think that will work? Do you actually know about viruses and how they can spread?"

Tony was amazed. People did not normally challenge his medical knowledge. He said, "Listen Dr Singh, I am the Chief

Medical Officer for England. I know a lot about public health. Of course I know quite a lot about the spread of viruses."

Vin said, "Sorry, I didn't mean to upset you. It is just that this virus looks to me like pretty much like the end of mankind, and I think the kind of restrictions you are talking about won't change that."

Tony said nothing for a few seconds, as he reflected. Nobody in his department, or within his contacts, had spelt it out as starkly as Dr Singh. But, given what he himself had learned, he felt Dr Singh could be the first soothsayer of doom for mankind actually to be right. The thought made him shudder. He said, "Okay, but my job is to protect public health in England, whilst I can, even if mankind is doomed. Have you any positive suggestions, because I need to get on?"

Vin replied, "Well I am not sure I can help much in England, or the rest of the UK. But, if we think about saving mankind, I think we need to concentrate on a smallish island that might not yet have had anyone travel into it with the virus. An island that can be completely isolated, with resourceful people, who will have to become completely self-sufficient, but that could do with some immediate help with supplies, and with enforcing an embargo preventing others getting access to the island."

"Call me psychic, but the island you are talking about is the Isle of Man. Well I can see all sorts of problems. Even if its people did survive, and the rest of mankind is wiped out, you would have no trade of any kind. No food imports, no imported fuel, no imported clothes, medicines, electronics, vehicles, just nothing at all."

"Well basically you are right. Although, on the subject of fuel, I know we have recently opened a gas pipeline to the island, from our own territorial waters in the Irish Sea. I think we would just have to adapt. So, are you saying you won't help then?"

"Yes I will help. Maybe you are right, and this virus will spread as an irresistible completely fatal pandemic. In which case when I lie dying, gasping for my last few breaths, at least I will be able to think I did my best to save humanity. Okay, humanity will be mainly Manx, but I suppose that's better than everyone being Scousers for example. That's a joke by the way, and I'm allowed to say it because I'm a Mancunian, and the Scousers are rude about us. Anyway, it will be up to your Government to close its airport and its ports, and embargo all movement in and out of all people. And freight as well I would say, or else you will still get it from lorry drivers, and the crews of boats and planes. Has your Government decided to do that?"

"David Quayle and I persuaded Adrian Kelly our Health and Social Services Minister to bring it up, at the Council of Ministers meeting, being held this morning. David has gone as well. I think David is convinced that an embargo is necessary, but I am not sure Adrian is. So I am not really sure whether my Government will or not."

Tony commented, "Adrian! Oh yes he is brother in law of our Prime Minister Keith Hardy isn't he? Keith married Kathy Kelly, Adrian's twin sister. If your Government decides it wants an embargo, it wouldn't surprise me if Adrian contacts our PM today. That won't hurt. And, as I said, I seem to have influence, so I will make your case as well - humanity's case if you like - for support from the British Government, should your Government decide to go ahead. In fact, I will try to get the Minister of Defence onside in particular. It can't hurt to give the MOD a bit of advance warning. The MOD should be able to get supplies flown in via your Isle of Man Airport at Ronaldsway, and to organise Royal Navy and RAF patrols to deter people trying to breach your embargo, especially if, or when, ultra pneumonia spreads in Britain."

Tony was also wondering whether the UK Government might also see itself relocating to the Isle of Man, but he decided against saying that.

Tony spoke again, "Look, you are the probably the best mind on Mann for understanding the issues around a pandemic."

Vin replied, "Yes I am. But I am not an epidemiologist."

"Well even so, it might be useful if we can contact each other at short notice, without going through hospital switchboards etc. So, let's swap a few contact details. Perhaps you personally do not have any decision making status on the Isle of Man, but it sounds like you are having an influence. You seem to be on good terms with David Quayle, who is a good chap, even if he does not have any medical or health background. And you will definitely know what is going on, on the island. I just ask that we are honest with each other, and I will try to help all I can."

"That's good. Honesty in a situation like this is important. I am always completely honest with other doctors, when advising them about the results of pathology tests on their patients, even if they perhaps are less so, when talking to their patients. So, do you think the British Government will acquiesce about the Isle of Man Government imposing a complete embargo on the island, assuming that they screw up the courage to do the right thing in time?"

"Yes I am pretty sure the UK Government will be fine with that. As we have discussed the two key things are stockpiling supplies, and enforcing an embargo. I hate to suggest delay in closing the island but, if you are to survive on your own, you need a good start with a stockpile of supplies, that you will not be able to replenish from outside ever again. So, assuming we can get my Government to agree to the MOD transporting supplies in, your Government should perhaps delay for one or two days in closing the ports. As for enforcing an embargo, I know you have police and a few of your own Coastguard vessels these days. Even if we do we get Royal Navy and RAF patrols, your own Government is going to have to put whatever resources it can into securing the complete coastline and airstrips."

"Well, every fresh plane or boatload of people who arrive now increases the risk that we will have acted too late to isolate ourselves from ultra pneumonia. But you are right of course about the supplies. And, even more importantly we need to make the embargo secure, as just one infected person breaching it could result in everyone on the island dying too."

"There is something else." Tony hesitated, and then went on, "I am sixty, but I still don't want to die. I don't suppose many in the UK Government are actually indifferent to their own fate, and I know of several Ministers with young children. I am worried that the UK Government might decide they are justified in relocating to the Isle of Man at some stage. It probably would not happen, until there are confirmed cases of ultra pneumonia on the British mainland. Your Government might not agree, but could it stop it happening? The British Government control the military forces. But, I am willing to tell you that I would do my best to thwart this."

"You're a good man," said Vin. "I wish you well. I just hope we are proved wrong about the spread of this virus."

Chapter 3, Monday 5 April 2027

Adrian Kelly asked David to wait outside, whilst he went into the meeting of the Council of Ministers in a conference room, next to the Chief Minister's office, on the 3rd floor of the Government Offices. He muttered in the ear of Henry Smith the Chief Minister. David was invited to come into the room, and took a seat in a set of chairs set back from the main table.

Henry said, "I know this is not in accordance with our agreed agenda, but Adrian has an urgent matter which I have agreed can be dealt with first."

Adrian rose from his seat and said, "Some of you may be aware of the ultra pneumonia virus, which has had a devastating impact in Madagascar. I have been advised by one of our Consultants at Nobles Hospital, that this could actually threaten us on the Isle of Man, unless we take preventative measures now. In particular, he is suggesting we should close our ports and airport straight away. In fact that there should be a complete embargo of all movements of people and goods onto or off the island."

At this point several Ministers all talked at once. One of them was Jack Coyle, Minister for Environment, Food and Agriculture. He said, "This is all a bit premature. It does seem to be a nasty virus, but it is contained in Madagascar, so it won't necessarily be getting here any time soon. Anyway, we had a lockdown with Coronavirus didn't we, which didn't actually stop a lot of people getting it. But most people recovered didn't they. I think it was about twenty-five or so who died in the end. And we didn't stop supplies coming in then did we. So, I am not with you on this one."

Adrian responded, "Well, I am not really an expert, so perhaps we could ask David Quayle here, my department's chief executive to explain?" He looked towards Henry who nodded his assent.

David stood to speak, but Jack spoke first, "David, am I right in thinking you have no medical training, or any expertise of any kind in epidemics?"

David smiled at Jack and said, "You are absolutely right about that of course, Minister. But my lack of expertise does not alter the seriousness of the situation. We have been advised by Dr Vihan Singh, who is the Senior Consultant in Pathology at Nobles Hospital. What is more is that he is a microbiologist, who is well respected internationally, and we are lucky to have him working for us here on this island. We may even count ourselves very lucky to continue living thanks to him, if his advice is correct. I don't pretend to understand why this virus is so deadly, but it seems clear that it is currently leaving no known survivors. Oh, and it has almost certainly spread to Africa because there have been flights from Madagascar to Johannesburg."

David looked at the Ministers in the room, and saw frowns and heads being shaken slightly. He went on, "I get the impression from your reactions, that you are not persuaded to take any action at this stage. Could I make two requests? One is that you have another meeting this evening, in which Dr Singh is allowed to give you the data, and explain why he thinks action is necessary. And secondly, please can you keep what has been discussed confidential to only those in this room now."

Henry said, "Adrian, you have spoken personally to Dr Singh haven't you?"

Adrian replied, "Yes."

Henry asked, "And do you feel action is urgently needed?"

Adrian hesitated, not being sure which way to go. But he knew that David was waiting for his reaction, and that there would be no way of ducking the blame if this went wrong. He said, "Well, as I said, I am not an expert either, but to be fair Dr Singh is. I think, on balance, it would be as well for you all to hear from him, and form your own judgements."

Henry made up his mind, "Right, we need more information, and it seems urgency may be important. I am calling a meeting for 6.30 this evening to discuss this. If Dr Singh really thinks it is as serious as Adrian and David are suggesting, I am sure he will make himself free to speak to us here this evening. But, right now let's carry on with business as normal. So, Adrian, first item on the agenda is the Budget for health spending including the two hospitals. As always, we seem to be asking for an increase in this area exceeding inflation..."

Chapter 4, Monday 5 April 2027

David finally got through on the phone to Vin in his office at Nobles Hospital, late in the afternoon. He said, "I think the Council of Ministers were a little bit shaken, by what Adrian and I were telling them. The trouble was that Adrian didn't seem able to convince them that this would be any worse that the Covid 19 pandemic, or that an embargo would work any better this time. He often fails to get a grip with his subject, even with his vain self regard. I tried to explain too, but, as you pointed out, I don't have the professional knowledge and expertise, so they weren't convinced by me either. But the Chief Minister Henry Smith did arrange another meeting for this evening, so I think they are definitely worried. And he wants you there to talk to them. There will be no embargo otherwise if you are not there, I am sure. Sometimes, expressing points in polite measured language only gets you so far. I am not trying to say that you don't use reasoned argument, but maybe a bit of passion and blunt speaking is sometimes required. It was your blunt speaking that made me convinced that an embargo is necessary."

Vin responded, "I suppose I will take your comments as a compliment. I also suppose I should have expected dithering and delay, but at least we can give it another go this evening. I am about to go off to a meeting at Ramsey Hospital. What time, and where, is the Council of Ministers meeting?"

"It's the same building as my office, and it's 6.30pm on the 3rd floor near the Chief Minister's office."

"Well, I will just have to leave Ramsey in time I suppose. I am going to be talking to various medical staff there, about services available from the Pathology Department, but clearly I think trying to convince the Ministers about the urgency of the ultra pneumonia situation is much more important. I will make sure we are finished by 5.45."

"I have asked the Ministers not to say anything to anyone else at this stage, as we obviously want to avoid any excess numbers coming to the island in panic. By the way, how did your conversation with Tony Sharp go?"

"It seemed to go quite well. I think I convinced him how deadly ultra pneumonia is. He said he would urge his own Government to support us, not just with supplies, but with Navy and RAF patrols. If we are going have an embargo, it is going to have to be completely watertight. It would take just one person with the virus to get on the island to wipe us all out. But, I don't know how much influence Tony will have."

"Well that sounds promising. And, notwithstanding my own poor opinion about Adrian Kelly, I am pretty sure he does get his brother in law's ear when he wants to, and I think he does understand how serious this is, so he will help with the UK Government too."

"As you say this is serious. It is very serious. I am now convinced, especially with more people knowing about our plans, that we need to shut our ports down from tomorrow, if possible. Supplies can still be flown in by the RAF for a short while afterwards, with strictly no contact between their personnel and anyone else."

"Well, let's hope you can be convincing this evening then. See you later," David said in conclusion.

A few minutes later, Vin phoned his wife Martha on her mobile. Vin said, "Hello Martha. I know I said I would be home by about 6.30 this evening, but something has cropped up. I have to go to a meeting this evening with the Council of Ministers. You know I was getting agitated about the ultra pneumonia virus over the weekend?"

Martha said, "Yes. Is it something to do with that?"

"Yes. I am trying to get them to make preparations, in the hope of stopping the ultra pneumonia virus getting to the island, and I have been asked to speak to them."

"Well good luck, and try not be too rude to them, even if you think they deserve it!"

"By the way, I know that Matthew took Emma off to London with him over the weekend, but he did promise to bring me back a book from Foyle's bookstore. I think he said they would be back on the evening flight today." Vin was concerned not to mention an embargo, but did not want his son to be stranded in London, if such an embargo were to be imposed.

Matha responded, "Yes that's what he told me as well."

Vin breathed a silent sigh of relief, "Okay sweetness, I don't know when I'll be home, so don't wait up if I am very late."

Martha told Vin, "I have just left a client, and I am on my way home. I should probably have gone back to the office, but I think I have got a migraine coming on. I am glad I don't get them very often like some people do. But I will probably be in bed whatever time you get in."

"Okay, I am sorry to hear that. Take something for it. You know you are okay taking 2 paracetamol and 2 ibuprofen tablets together?" said Vin sympathetically.

Martha said, "Yes Vin, my wonderful personal physician, I think you have told me that before!"

"Well, take care Martha. Bye!" said Vin.

Martha said, "You take care too Vin."

Chapter 5 – Monday 5 April 2027

All nine members of the Council of Ministers, together with David Quayle, two other departmental chief executive offices and a minutes secretary, were sitting ready for their additional meeting at 6.30pm. Vin had not arrived. At 6.40pm Henry demanded of David, "Well we are all waiting for Dr Singh. He does know where and when this meeting is, doesn't he?"

"Yes he does. I know that he had an important meeting in Ramsey, but I am sure he must have been held up, or else he would be here," David replied.

Adrian spoke up, "Well everyone else is here. I have had to give up my bridge night to be here. Perhaps we could reschedule it for our next regular meeting next Monday? I could probably still make it for bridge, if I leave now."

Henry was feeling that the Council were not being shown much respect by Dr Singh. At the same time, he felt sure that action about the ultra pneumonia virus was needed. He said, "I am reluctant to put it off, but we really have no idea when or if Dr Singh is going to show up. Let's give it another five minutes."

Five minutes later Henry was looking at his watch. Adrian said "Right I can still make it." and stood up. At that moment Vin walked in the room. Vin was below average height, he looked his age of 61, and he also looked flustered.

David said, "This is Dr Singh everyone." To Vin he said, "Are you okay?"

Vin replied, "Yes I am fine. My meeting was dragging on, so I had to tell people in Ramsey that I had no time for any more questions. Then there was a furniture lorry unloading on the main road out of Ramsey; and then there was a three way traffic control for road repairs at the Bungalow. Still I am here now!"

Vin looked around, and counted thirteen faces apart from his own. He thought that if an embargo was not put in place straight away word would spread, and people could start flooding onto the island. Henry said to him, "Dr Singh, please can you sit here, next to me."

When Vin was ready Henry said, "I think we should start by asking Dr Singh to tell us about ultra pneumonia, and why he seems to think that we need to basically shut off the Isle of Man from the rest of the world indefinitely."

He turned to Vin, saying, "Can you confirm that you are the Senior Consultant in Pathology at Nobles Hospital, and that you know all about microbiology?"

Vin responded, "Chief Minister, yes I am the Senior Consultant in Pathology at Nobles Hospital. I don't think anyone knows everything about microbiology, but it is my speciality. I have made a point of keeping up to date with the more serious research in this field. The key point here is that the ultra pneumonia virus does not seem to be conforming to the pattern of other viruses, in that everyone seems to become infected, and nobody seems to survive."

This caused a few comments. Henry said, "Surely not, not even the Black Death did that. And even if everyone who is infected dies, what about anyone who keeps themselves completely isolated?"

Vin replied, "I will tell you what I know, and also what no-one really understands. I do know that in Madagascar there is a tradition of digging up relatives periodically, and running around with their remains for a while. I can see how this could spread a bacterial infection, but I have not heard any definite link with this ultra pneumonia virus. Perhaps the virus was living in bacteria, and transferred from the bacteria to human cells. By the way, a lot of scientists say that viruses are not alive, but that is a bit academic. The important point is that viruses can only reproduce themselves in the cells of living organisms. But they depend also on being able to transfer to other organisms, people in this case, because otherwise the host organism kills them with antibodies and other responses, or they kill the host, and then the virus dies because the host cells all die. Normally a virus only survives about 24 hours outside its host organism. So, normally it needs a live host. But viruses can travel through the air a short distance on droplets, if the host sneezes or coughs. Also, they can be transferred onto hands or handles or other surfaces, and then onto mouths or noses. Usually you could avoid infection indefinitely, if you completely avoid any contact with anyone else. But with ultra pneumonia, my guess is that the virus is capable somehow of getting itself transmitted further through the air. There are what are known as airborne pathogens, which can attach to tiny dry particles, and carry much further than a normal flu virus. Perhaps that it is what is happening with the ultra pneumonia virus. It is lasting longer and carrying much further than other viruses. So, if you are anywhere that the air is circulating nearby to an infected person, you will get infected too. As I say, exactly how and why the virus is so easily transmitted is not at all certain. But, it does seem absolutely clear that it is also unusual, unique even, in killing everyone. All we can do, our only hope, is to embargo the rest of the world completely, and hope nobody has brought it in already."

Jack Coyle interjected, "Look we know you a pathologist, and you are an 'expert' microbiologist, even if you don't really seem to know that much about this particular virus. But what you are talking about – how diseases spread and how to stop them – is called epidemiology isn't it? And I don't think you are an epidemiologist are you? Its just crazy talking about closing down all contact with Britain and the rest of the world, whilst this disease has only affected one backward island country off the coast of southern Africa thousands of miles away."

Vin responded angrily, "Well Mr Coyle, I don't suppose you have any relevant qualifications in environmental sciences of any kind, which hasn't stopped you becoming Minister for Environment, Food and Agriculture has it? Of course I am not an epidemiologist; a small place like the Isle of Man won't have any specialists in that field. And I have not seen this particular pathogen under a microscope. But, I do know that this particular virus is much more rampant and deadly than any ever seen before. I am absolutely convinced, if it gets to this island, we will all start dying within two weeks and nobody will be left within three to four weeks."

Vin looked at all the faces looking at him. He thought Adrian and Jack were glaring at him. Everyone could see him shaking slightly, and sweating. He felt at least they had to realise that he was utterly sure of what he was saying.

Vin went on. "Normally with a virus, temporary protection is given against infection by remaining isolated for a time. To reiterate, this has not worked with this virus. Everyone anywhere near anyone who is infected becomes infected, and everyone dies. At the time of the Coronavirus crisis, I was not consulted about how the Manx Government should deal with it, although obviously I was involved in supervising the testing of tissue and blood samples, and in post-mortem examinations of some the population who died as a result. But I do know that our attempts to embargo the island then were too late, and inadequate. And even then we allowed returning residents entry following a period of quarantine, and I am confident that some of those returnees then caused additional infections."

Vin paused briefly and took a drink of water. He looked at all the Ministers again. He continued, "Please, I am begging you. Close the ports and airport. Have a complete clampdown on everyone and everything, moving on or off the island. If just one infected person arrives on the Isle of Man, it will be too late. We know that people have flown from Madagascar to Johannesburg. An infected person may have already flown into say Heathrow from Johannesburg, or maybe from another South African airport. They might be about to fly to the Isle of Man next. Or maybe they have infected someone in London, who is about to fly here. Don't let anyone in at all. Do it tonight. Do it because you want to save humanity. Or just because you want to save your families. If I am wrong, we can lift the embargo later. But if I am right, and we have stopped ultra pneumonia getting to us, then maybe we will have saved everyone on Mann."

Vin sat down. He looked at David who just nodded slightly at him. Henry said, "Thank you Dr Singh. That was a more emotional, and less factual, contribution than I was expecting, Perhaps you were short of details about this virus, but, I think we all felt your passion."

Henry turned to the others, "Some of you know that I asked Adrian to sound out the British Government about how they would feel about our imposing an embargo on all contact, and whether they would be willing to help us in any way. Adrian, what can you tell us?"

Adrian started, "I spoke to the Prime Minister..."

Peter Corlett, the Minister for Home Affairs interrupted, "And how are your brother in law and your sister?"

Several Ministers suppressed a chuckle, and Adrian gave Peter a filthy look.

Henry said, "I don't really think we need childish interjections, thank you Peter. Please go on Adrian."

Adrian continued, "Basically he said they had been advised about the gravity of the threat by their own Chief Medical Officer for England. They would be imposing serious travel restrictions of their own, but his Government would be likely to accept any embargo the Isle of Man wished to impose, and would assist with flying in supplies and running naval and air patrols." He gave Vin a short stare.

Henry spoke, "Thank you Adrian. That sounds very helpful. I don't know that there is any point in discussing the principle of closure of our airport and ports any further. So, I am going to ask all of you Ministers to vote on whether you agree to this, or not. And, if we do agree, we can then discuss all the things arising, such as the wording and timing of the Emergency Proclamation by the Governor in Council, under the Emergency Powers Act 1936. In fact, this Act will probably be needed to implement a lot of the other measures we might need to take, if ultra pneumonia really does sweep through the rest of the world."

Henry went on, "Okay, I will ask you, one at a time, whether you support immediate action to close our borders." He looked at Jack.

Jack said, "This is crazy. No."

Adrian said, "I know I brought this up in the Council this morning, and we will have the co-operation of the UK Government, but I think maybe we should wait for a bit. I can't vote 'Yes' but I won't oppose it either."

Henry said, "Well we will call that an abstention," and then added with a slight hint of sarcasm, "Thank you, Adrian."

Henry thought to himself, "Yes, that's pretty much how I thought those two might vote."

He went on, "Just so you know, this has got my backing, and I am counting myself as a 'Yes' but I could do with some support here."

Henry turned to the Treasury Minister, Eddie Moore. He asked him, "Which way are you voting?"

Eddie replied, "This is going to damage the economy and Government finances. But, assuming our businesses can still keep serving their overseas finance and gambling clients, via the internet or telephone, then I say yes."

Henry turned to the only female Minister, Gemma Cain, Minister for Enterprise, who said, "Well, Eddie is right about the economic damage, but a big part of our economy these days is international finance, insurance, internet betting, none of which should be too hampered by a temporary embargo. So, yes!"

The Education, Sports, and Culture Minister Mike Brown spoke next, "Huh, it sounds like the only chance our schoolchildren have, of having a future, is to close our borders in time. So, a definite yes from me."

The Minister for Policy and Reform, John Quayle said, "My cousin David, sitting opposite me, doesn't get a vote, but I always respect his opinions, and I am with him on this one. Yes."

Peter Corlett spoke next, "I think some people living here don't like other people coming here anyway! But seriously, it has to be yes."

Lastly Daniel Clague, Minister for Infrastructure spoke, "I am a bit concerned that we are being guided by hysteria, rather than by any science. And if the rest of humanity is extinguished, do we really want to survive alone? But, I suppose we should do the right thing. A reluctant yes."

Henry said, "Thank you everyone. That was seven votes to one, with one abstention, that we immediately close the ports and airport, and prevent anyone at all from coming onto or leaving the island. A complete embargo in other words. We are going to put this in place as soon as possible, without giving any notice. Now, that a decision had been made, my view is that any disclosure of this decision, before the port and airport closures take place, would be a breach of the Official Secrets Act. So, everyone is this room is required to keep this decision secret. I personally will take charge of the text of the draft Emergency Proclamation, and before that I will contact Government House, to see if I can get an urgent meeting with the Lieutenant Governor. The proclamation needs his signature. Let's have a break, and I'll make that call."

During the break Adrian came up to Vin and told him, "I would like a private word. We can use my office."

In his office Adrian said, "You are quite a pushy character really, aren't you? Getting yourself involved in political decisions, even though you haven't been elected by anyone. Everyone is now wondering who is in charge in my Department. And, who said you could make representations to the British Government? When I spoke to the British Prime Minister..."

Vin interrupted, without considering whether it would be helpful, saying, "Your brother in law, Keith Hardy."

Adrian bristled, and continued, "I am an elected Member of the House of Keys. I am a duly appointed Minister for Housing and Social Care. I was acting upon a request by the Chief Minister to contact the UK Prime Minister, Keith Hardy. And that is what I did. And yes, Keith does happen to be my brother-in-law. He told me that you had already contacted their Chief Medical Officer for England. He said that our Government was thinking about an embargo, and might ask if the British Government could possibly fly in some supplies, and mount sea and air patrols. It made me look foolish, not knowing that you had already made contact. Alright the PM was helpful, but who do you think you are? I will tell you. You are just a pathologist, whose job it is to cut up dead people, and to tell the Coroner's Office how they died. Leave politics and diplomacy to the politicians."

Vin retorted, "Actually, my Pathology Department also makes a major contribution, by helping other doctors assess what is wrong with their patients. But, when I phoned Tony

Sharp, all I was trying to do was to save humanity, while others dither. Your abstention just now amazed me. You are more worried about loss of face, than whether we all live or die! I am going back to join the others."

The meeting resumed thirty minutes later.

Henry announced, "Well I did manage to speak briefly to Sir Hugh Whitlock, the Lieutenant Governor. You know that we have a lot of say in who fills that position these days, but even so, Sir Hugh does take his responsibility to the Crown seriously, and he interprets that as avoiding, if possible, any conflict with His Majesty's Government in London. Anyway, he said he was in the middle of a dinner party, meeting his son's fiancee's parents for the first time, so he would not be prepared to see me until 11.30pm. I did manage to tell him it concerned emergency arrangements to do with the ultra pneumonia virus, and that we had been given expert advice by Dr Singh."

Henry looked at Vin and said to him, "So, he said he would like you to come at 11.30pm, as well. I hope you are okay with that, Dr Singh?"

"Well, if that is what is needed to get an embargo in place, then of course I am," responded Vin.

"I imagine you know where Government House is. Just tell them your name on the intercom at the gate, and you can drive in. If we both aim to get there at 11.20pm we can go in together," Henry told him.

Henry then spoke to everyone, "Well, we need to take advantage of the British Government's offer to fly supplies in. I am just wondering if we would get more stuff in through Douglas harbour."

Vin raised a hand and said, "In terms of minimising risk, I think it would be safer just to use the airport."

A few people looked quizzical. Daniel Clague said, "I think I know what Dr Singh means. It would probably be fairly difficult to segregate the crew of a ship from any contact with port workers. Whereas, when a plane lands down at Ronaldsway, or the Isle of Man Airport if you prefer, it can stop on solid ground hundreds of yards from airport buildings, never mind residential areas. I expect the RAF have some expertise at airlifting supplies to all sorts of places. We could check that they would bring their own fork lifts, and get them to do their own unloading. We could allocate some sheds and hangars to store items. I think there are even refrigerated and cold storage units, but we would have to check on capacity. Maybe certain drugs and medical supplies would need those. We would have to keep all airport personnel away. What do you think Dr Singh?"

Dr Singh responded, "I think your support for the embargo was reluctant, but you seem to understand the risks. What you are saying about segregation at the airport means we can justify the small risk that the RAF personnel have already been infected, against the benefit of extra essential supplies. But, I would like to restrict it to just the one day after the embargo starts, so just Wednesday."

Henry was satisfied. He said, "Well that all sounds like good sense. Daniel, as Minister for Infrastructure, you are responsible for the airport. If we ask Adrian, with his contacts, to get the RAF flying stuff in all day on Wednesday, you two can liaise about how it is all going to work. And let's hope we can get as much in as possible on just the

Wednesday. Okay everyone?" and Henry looked in particular at Vin, who nodded.

The meeting finally broke up just before 11pm. Nobody had asked Vin to leave, so he had stayed. Henry said to Vin, "We had better go straight to Government House, now. I'll wait for you in my car outside the gates, so you can follow me up the drive."

Chapter 6, Monday 5 April, and Tuesday 6 April 2027

Henry and Vin were outside the front door of Government House at 11.30pm. To their surprise, Sir Hugh himself answered the door. He said, "Let's go into my own lounge. You must be Dr Vihan Singh. Can I offer either of you a malt whisky?"

"Yes, but I will just have a small one please Your Excellency, as I am driving," was Henry's reply.

Vin's response was, "Not for me thanks, but have you got a lemonade perhaps ...err Your Excellency?"

Sir Hugh poured the drinks and said, "Okay, it is just the three of us, late at night. Let's stick to first names. Call me Sir Hugh, and shall I call you Vihan?"

Vin replied, "Just call me Vin please, everyone does."

"Okay Vin it is. Now Henry, let's get down to business. I know you want me to sign an Emergency Proclamation, under the 1936 Emergency Powers Act. So, if you have prepared one, I would obviously like to read it first," was Sir Hugh's request.

Henry passed over the unsigned Proclamation, and Sir Hugh read it. Then he said, "I recall we had serious travel restrictions during the Coronavirus crisis, but this goes a lot further. Constitutionally, I know I am expected just to sign it, but I think there is no point in my signature being required on a Proclamation, if I cannot at least discuss the need for the Proclamation. I know that Vin is a well renowned microbiologist. Also that he isn't an epidemiologist..."

Vin interrupted "Yes but..."

Sir Hugh raised his eyebrows, and kept talking, "I was going to go on to say, that I expect an understanding of microbiology is more relevant that epidemiology, given that that epidemiology is probably just a strange kind of actuarial guesswork anyway. So Vin what can you tell me about ultra pneumonia?"

Vin was willing to contradict anyone. He said, "Sir Hugh, I think there is a lot more to epidemiology than you suggest, but we don't have the luxury of having the time to get an epidemiological assessment. And, although I like to think that I am well respected for my microbiological expertise, I have to admit, like everyone else, to only having a limited understanding of the ultra pneumonia virus. You would be the fifth person, or group of people, I have had to explain the situation to today. Can I just put it like this? For reasons nobody else understands either, this virus seems to be 100% contagious and 100% fatal. It takes 14 days for symptoms to manifest themselves, and local isolation away from infected people does not work. If just one infected person gets on this island we will all die. It will be too late to take action, after we have found out that that person has arrived. The time to close the ports and airport is now."

Sir Hugh was unused to being contradicted. He also felt that Vin's explanation was fairly minimal. Neither of those points, though, altered the seriousness of the situation. He asked Henry, "Do you accept that what Vin has said justifies an embargo, closing the ports and airports, and not letting anyone in at all, even returning residents who have, perhaps, just been away on a short break?"

Henry replied, "Well we have not been given graphs, statistical tables, or even any great detail about ultra pneumonia, but really you only have to look at the news. I sort of admire Vin, for being so bold and outspoken about this. The Council of Ministers supported this Proclamation by 7 to 1."

"So you didn't vote yourself then presumably. There are nine Ministers including yourself. I think I am right about that?"

"I did vote actually, and I told six of them my vote before they spoke, to encourage them to vote Yes. The first two had been a No and an abstention, naming no names."

"So just to reiterate, you are completely convinced personally of the need to do this?"

Henry looked at Vin, and felt a moment's doubt, before saying to Sir Hugh, "Yes, I am convinced of the need to do this, but not because I am certain the virus will get to Mann otherwise. It is just that the risk of not taking action is so enormous. If this virus gets to the Isle of Man, it could make Covid 19 look like the proverbial picnic by comparison. Even if no action at all had been taken with Covid, we were never going to lose anywhere near one per cent of our population from it, and those being mainly the very elderly. With ultra pneumonia, the risk, of not taking immediate action, is that all 84,000 of us die. We just can't afford that risk!"

Sir Hugh asked, "Has anyone spoken to Her Majesty's Government in London about this?"

Henry replied, "Our Minister for Health and Social Care, Adrian Kelly, has actually spoken to Keith Hardy this afternoon…"

Sir Hugh interrupted, "Wait, isn't Keith married to Adrian's sister? It must be useful having Adrian in your Council of Ministers."

Henry said, "Uh, yes indeed, to be candid, his connection can be useful. I was going to say that Adrian reported that the British Government were very concerned about ultra pneumonia reaching Britain, and would be imposing their own travel restrictions, but that they would quite understand us imposing our own complete embargo of any physical contact with the island. Further they would provide support, if required, with the RAF flying supplies in for a short time, and with Royal Navy and RAF patrols to deter and detect anyone trying to get to the island."

Vin gave a slight cough.

Henry noticed Vin again, and added, "Oh, Vin has also been in unofficial contact with the Chief Medical Officer for England. These sort of contacts can be useful in a crisis like this. You know, Vin might be able to get more technical information about ultra pneumonia from a fellow professional; he might be able to get pharmaceuticals and other medical supplies included in the RAF deliveries. That sort of thing."

Sir Hugh pronounced, "Right, I will sign this Proclamation, and I will time it to come into effect at 2pm," He looked at his watch, "which is later today now. We are supposed to give at least 12 hours notice, although, in this case, we won't tell anyone in advance."

Henry commented, "Good. I'll get onto the Chief Constable, Terry Corps, in the morning. I will ask him, and his top ranking officers, to deliver a copy of the order to the Harbour Keepers, and to the Airport Duty Manager, shortly before 2pm. So, there should be no question that all incoming and outgoing traffic will be required to cease, at that time. The ports and airport all come under the control of the Minister of Infrastructure anyway, but delivery of the Proclamation will give this legal force. I will ask Daniel Clague, the Infrastructure Minister, to brief all his key Ports Office staff at the same time."

Henry and Vin left Government House a short while later. Vin got home within 10 minutes, to find just the porch light on. He crept into bed at about 1am.

Chapter 7, Tuesday 6 April 2027

Vin was showered and dressed by 7.30am, at his house in Baldrine. Baldrine was a fairly small village about four miles north of Douglas, on the main coast road connecting Douglas with Laxey. Baldrine was actually about half a mile inland from the coast. Vin and Martha's house was a 3-bedroom bungalow, down a quiet lane, with great countryside views, as well as a distant glimpse of the sea. It was not the same house where he and Martha had brought up their only surviving child, a boy. That had been in Onchan, essentially a northern part of Douglas. In many ways, they had been happier there. For one thing Baldrine was also the village where Patrick Quinn lived. Patrick was the leader of the Mann First party, whose policies included making the Isle of Man a republic, and stricter control of immigration. Vin had bumped into Patrick in the local convenience store in Baldrine several times. Patrick had made it obvious he was not just mildly ambivalent about other cultures, but that he felt contempt for him, as one belonging to a visible ethnic minority. So, Vin and Patrick did not get on, although Patrick was well liked in the village. Vin was very glad that the Mann First party had only one Member of the House of Keys (MHK), who was Patrick himself. His constituency did not include Baldrine.

Martha and Vin spoke to each other across the kitchen table, between mouthfuls of toast and sips of coffee. Vin remembered that Martha had confirmed, on the phone, that Matthew was getting back to Mann the previous evening. He said, "Martha, have you heard from Matthew, since they got back last night?"

Martha replied, "He left a recorded message on the house phone, whilst I was in the bathroom, just before going to bed. He said that he and Emma had decided to extend their stay in London, by a couple of days. He said that their boss Simon had told them in advance that, if they wanted to extend their trip, a couple of days annual leave wouldn't be a problem."

She looked at Vin, and could see that he was agitated by this news. She said, "What's wrong Vin? Something has happened hasn't it. You went to a meeting with the Council of Ministers yesterday. Wait a moment. God, I can be so dim! You've got them to close the airport and ports, haven't you? That's why you asked about Matt wasn't it? Why couldn't you have rung him, and told him what you were going to initiate? And why didn't you tell me what were trying to do? God, will we ever see him again?"

Vin spoke, as Martha started crying, " Yes the airports and ports are being closed to all traffic today. Any ships or aircraft, freight or passengers, that haven't docked or landed by 2pm will be turned away. That's except for the RAF on Wednes..."

Martha interrupted, "You said 2pm. That means the airport is still open, so if Matt and Emma get a flight this morning, they will be back in time."

"But they probably won't be able to get a flight. And, anyway, they won't want to come back this morning, unless we tell them what's happening," said Vin, feeling flustered.

Martha raised her voice, "We can't just let Matt die, because his kind father has helped close the island, but has decided not to tell him, so he can't get back in time. I'm going to ring him now." She grabbed her mobile off the table.

Vin reacted, "Wait I will ring him. I will tell him that you have been in a car accident. He's very fond of you. He's bound to come back straightaway, if we tell him that you might not live. Let me do it this way. Then Matthew can tell anyone who asks, that I did not tell him about the embargo in advance, and he can say that he was due to come back anyway, even that he was anxious about you. That would all be true. Quick, you get on the Vannin Airlines website and check that there are seats on the 10.30am flight today, while I ring him."

Vin went in another room, whilst calling Matthew. After about six rings, he heard Matthew's voice, "Hello Dad, nice to hear from you for a change, even if it is a bit early for a tourist in London, still in bed with his girlfriend."

Vin swallowed hard, and thought to himself we've just got to get him on a plane this morning. Vin's anxiety helped with the lies he had to tell, "It's your Mum, she was in a bad car accident yesterday, coming home from one of her social work visits. She had to have transfusions. She has asked to see you. To be honest, I really don't know if she is going to make it. Please get a flight back this morning. There's a Vannin Airlines flight from Heathrow at 10.30am. Can you please both get dressed."

Vin heard Emma's voice, "What's up Mattie? Who's that? What's happened?" Then Matthew was asking him questions, between telling Emma what Vin was telling him.

Vin said, "Okay, you get yourself organised, and get a taxi straight to Heathrow. I'll sort out booking seats on the plane, and I'll get back to you." He disconnected, and went back into the kitchen.

He said to Martha, "Well they are coming, if we can get them seats."

Martha was crying again, and saying she couldn't get the 10.30 flight up on the screen. Vin said, "Well I will phone the Airline."

Vin got through quickly, and spoke to a female voice. She was saying sorry nothing available on the 10.30 flight, but several seats were still available on the 7pm flight. Vin said, "What about first class?"

The reply was, "Sorry sir, normally we would have spare seats in both economy, and in the business class seats at the front, especially on a Tuesday. But not today for some reason. But, as I say, there are seats on the 7pm. And we don't do stand by. If the seats aren't claimed, they just remain empty. Wait a moment. My screen's now showing a late cancellation of two seats on the 10.30. So, we can do it after all."

Vin practically wept. He had to ask Martha for Emma's surname, and was told it was O'Hara. He gave his credit card details over the telephone, and made a note of the reference number. Now, I am going to have to lie to my son again, he thought.

Martha said, "So have you got them on the flight then? They should definitely land well before 2pm, shouldn't they?"

She looked at Vin, and saw he looked very shaken. She went on, "Please Vin, I know we had a big setback in our life together, but that was a long time ago. Matthew is very precious to me, and I think he is to you too, although you don't show him how you feel. Please, just let me know what is going on, next time you are planning something." She stroked his head, and walked out into the back garden.

Vin called his son fifteen minutes later. Again, he went in another room to make the call, in case Matthew could hear his mother come back in from the garden. Matthew said, "We are just getting in the taxi. Do you know any more about Mum?"

Vin replied, "No I had phoned the hospital, just before I phoned you 15 minutes ago. I am going to the hospital now, and I will give you a ring before you take off. I did manage to get both of you seats on the 10.30 Vannin Airlines flight. Have you got pen and paper, and I'll give you the reference number, in case you need to quote it at check in."

An hour later Vin was rung by Matthew. Matthew sounded angry, "Dad, why have you been lying to me? I'm at Heathrow, and I have rung Nobles Hospital. They have no record of a Mrs Martha Singh having been admitted. You would think they would know if the wife of a Senior Consultant had been admitted, wouldn't you? Also I have googled for any local news of a car crash. There's nothing. What is going on?"

Vin replied, "Listen, I just can't tell you, but you have to trust me. I may not be the most sensitive chap alive, but I have always done the best I can to support you. And I love your mum very dearly, although it might not always be that obvious. I would not have made up such a worrying story for you, if it wasn't absolutely essential that you get that plane."

"Okay Dad I will trust you, but you must explain all this to me when we get back. Just tell me now. Is Mum okay?"

"Yes Matthew, she's fine. I'm really sorry to have lied to you. Just make sure you get on that plane."

"We've checked in. But apparently there is bad fog over the Midlands, and our flight is delayed."

Vin was shaken by that information. He said, "How long for, do you know?"

Matthew replied, "They are saying expected departure 12.30pm. It might have to have fly a longer route, if the fog has not lifted."

Vin knew that the scheduled flight time from Heathrow to Ronaldsway was 55 minutes, but that it could be up to 10 minutes quicker, if there were no headwinds. That day though, the weather was fog, not wind. If the diversion added 20 minutes to the scheduled flight time, the plane had to take off by 12.45pm, to beat the secret deadline of arrival by 2pm. "I'll be at Ronaldsway waiting for you," he said to Matthew.

Chapter 8, Tuesday 6 April 2027

Adrian walked into David's office, at about 9.30am. He said to David, "Henry has just asked me to chair an Emergency Advisory Committee, to deal with all the issues arising from the pandemic and the embargo. Obviously I will be looking for your support. Getting supplies from the RAF is a high priority. Can you consult Nobles Hospital about medical supplies, and consult other Government departments, so we can draw up a detailed list. And then can you suggest names for inclusion on this Committee, please."

David thought to himself that Henry had made a bad choice of chairman there, and that Adrian would be passing on to him even more problems to deal with than normal. He said, "Minister, presumably you would want to contact the London Government yourself, as soon as possible, to confirm to them that we do actually want RAF supplies. You and Dr Singh have already sounded them out about this."

"Yes, but first we need a full detailed list of exactly what we require," reiterated Adrian.

David said, "Minister with respect, time is of the essence here. If we did draw up a wish list, there would then be negotiations about some items not being available, the quantities of each, and so on. Really, we need it just to be a one day blitz, tomorrow. Isn't Daniel, I mean the Minister for

Infrastructure, dealing with making sure the airport is ready, and that the general public and all airport personnel including flight controllers are kept away? Do you remember that this was because Dr Singh agreed that this would be an acceptable risk, given the likely benefit of extra supplies."

"We seem to be jumping a lot to Dr Singh's requirements," responded Adrian.

"Well, that point seems sensible," David said diplomatically. He went on, "So, I am suggesting we leave it to the RAF to supply what they can. They are fairly used to flying emergency supplies to places, and I think we could leave it to their hierarchy to work out what is desirable and possible at such short notice. I have spoken to Daniel, I mean the Minister for Infrastructure, already this morning. He told me he was making sure that we have as much covered and refrigerated storage available as possible at the airport, for the RAF personnel to put the supplies in. In fact, thinking about security at the airport, I wonder if it would be a good idea if I phone the commander of the Isle of Man Army Reserve. I think there are about 30 of them in the Reserves. He would be a useful chap to have on your Committee. I could ask him if he could assist about securing the airport at the same time, and to liaise with Daniel about doing that, but obviously keep his men and women well clear of the RAF personnel."

"Yes that is a good idea about using the Army Reserve, and co-opting its senior officer onto the Committee, thank you. Can you find out who the senior officer is and give him a ring, and check it out with Daniel as well, and then bring me up to speed."

"I have heard his name mentioned before. He is actually a Major. Major Peter Quinnel, although he is really a farmer."

"Yes okay, so ring him, ask him to join the Committee, first meeting in this building Thursday morning, and get him to sort out the airport business with Daniel. In the meantime, I will see if I can speak to the British PM or someone to get these RAF flights. Just tomorrow only?"

"Just tomorrow, yes."

"Oh, and as I mentioned, after you've spoken to this Major farmer chap, please can you draw up a list of names and their posts, of people you think should be on the Committee. That would be very helpful."

"Well, another name would be Terry Corps, the Chief Constable. It would probably make the task of enforcing the embargo easier, if he and the Major are working together."

"That makes sense. So let's get on, shall we." And Adrian walked out of the office.

Chapter 9, Tuesday 6 April 2027

David Quayle tracked down a telephone number for Major Peter Quinnel. Peter was talking to his farm foreman, Dave, in the milking sheds, when his mobile rang. David persuaded him it was urgent, so he left his foreman to get on with cleaning the sheds, and he walked back to his office, just inside the back door of the farmhouse he lived in with his wife Amanda. He had his PC there, which was used mainly by him and Dave to run the farm. The PC also had bits of information about the Army Reserve tucked away on it. Information about the Army Reserve was also in a notebook he kept in a drawer, which was supposed to be locked, even if the only other people who went in the office were Amanda and Dave.

David and Peter reconnected on his landline. David said, "Peter, I need to confirm that you are still the Major in charge of the Army Reserve on the Isle of Man?"

Peter replied, "I am the senior officer here on the island, yes. And sorry, who are you again?"

"I am David Quayle, the Chief Executive in the Health and Social Services Department of the Government. Before I explain my call, I need to point out that I am going to tell you something that will be an Official Secret for about four hours."

"That is mysterious, but yes, I am fine with that."

"At 2pm today an embargo will commence which will prohibit indefinitely any person or any goods entering or leaving Manx territory. That has been approved by a Proclamation signed by the Lieutenant Governor, under the 1936 Emergency Powers Act."

"Gosh! Nobody and nothing allowed in or out! Let me think, that Emergency Powers Act had not been used until 2020, when it was used in conjunction with the Covid 19 pandemic. So, I think this must be related to that ultra pneumonia pandemic in Madagascar?"

"You are right, of course."

"So, is the Government really thinking that it could get here and cause a serious problem? Actually, I suppose Covid 19 started a long way away, and that got here eventually and killed about 30 people, didn't it?"

"The Government is very concerned that it could, indeed, get here. In fact, it is a lot more serious than Covid 19, which killed fewer than one in a hundred of its victims, whereas ultra pneumonia seems to kill 100% of them, and nobody seems to avoid being infected."

David gave Peter a few seconds to think about that. Then he went on, "So, you can see this embargo could be vital to preserving life on this island?"

"Yes, I suppose so," replied Peter.

"Well, would you and your men be able to help in enforcing the embargo, do you think?"

"Possibly, but can I just explain a bit about how we are set up. I am only in charge locally. There are 31 of us, and we meet on Wednesday evenings, which is drill night. Some of the lads are, like me, part of a part-time artillery regiment, spread over 5 locations in North West England, as well as here. The whole unit on the Isle of Man were all gunners, that is artillery, for a period, but the Army went back to offering different trades or training, about two years ago. Normally, if the gunners are involved in serious exercises, it is in combination with the rest of the artillery regiment from the mainland, under the command of my Colonel. The others, engineers and so on, also go off with other units for exercises as well."

"Sorry, I don't know much about military affairs, at all. It is just that it has fallen to me to try to enlist your help. Would your men be able to carry out armed guard and patrol type activities?"

"Five of the non-artillery reservists are women actually. Women have been included ever since this unit was formed in 2015. One of them is a Sergeant. But yes, everyone is trained in the use of a personal weapon, and they are expected to be able to hit a stationary target fairly reliably, at a range of up to 200 metres. We even have one 105mm artillery gun over here, which takes a crew of three gunners to use it."

"So will you be able to help?"

"I am assuming you want them officially mobilised, which means they will be available full-time, and will receive pay from the MOD to cover loss of earnings. This should be at a month's notice, but I am confident that they will nearly all sign in within a day or two, if you can convince me it is authorised. I say that because it would not normally be my decision, or the Isle of Man Government's decision. That would come down through MOD and British Army orders."

"So, if we get an order passed down through the right channels to your Colonel, that would do the trick?"

"In a word, yes. Can you do that?"

"I think we probably can. My Minister has his uses, because he has contacts. But, even if it had to be unofficial, I would appeal to your local patriotism as a Manxman. I have been convinced that we definitely need this embargo, and that it has to be secure."

"Actually, I was born in County Down in Northern Ireland, but I do feel loyalty to Mann as well as to Britain. Maybe I will contact my Colonel, and see if he can get the communication channels working upward, as well as down. He is quite a good sort really. Okay, let's assume, somehow or other, we are going to help. Do you have some immediate task in mind?"

"Yes I do. The airport will close at 2pm today. Ideally it would be secured straightaway, but we definitely need to keep everyone away tomorrow. The plan is that the RAF will fly in supplies on one day only, just tomorrow. They will bring their own forklifts, and their personnel will unload everything, and put it in designated warehouses and storage. Daniel Clague, Minister for Infrastructure, will be making sure all his airport staff stay away, including the tower control staff. The reasoning is that, even if say one or two of the RAF personnel have the virus, we should all be far away enough not to be infected. It is still a risk, but we think it will be worth it. It is only one day after the embargo will have started. I will ask Daniel to contact you, so that you can liaise with him."

"David, if we really want to make things as secure as possible down at the airport, it would make sense to close the perimeter roads, the A5 between Castletown and Ballasalla, the A12 from Castletown to Derbyhaven, and to close off Ballasalla Road. We could do road blocks at the road junctions in Castletown and Ballasalla. We would probably have to let a few residents through, but would it be okay to stop all the commercial traffic going along Ballasalla Road? It would only be for one day."

"It sounds like you are getting enthusiastic, which is good. Let me make a note of that, and I will see if I can get it included under the emergency powers. Otherwise, would your men and women be okay with the BS Act? So long as they don't actually shoot anyone, of course."

"Yes, I know the Act you mean. My farm actually produces BS every day. I think for most people, seeing is believing. If you see a group of armed soldiers blocking a road, you tend not to argue too vigorously."

"And it would help to reinforce the message on the island, and elsewhere, that the embargo will be seriously enforced."

"Did you say that the air control staff are being kept away as well?"

"Yes, I would expect RAF pilots to cope, wouldn't you? The weather forecast is good, and there won't be anybody else's planes using the airport."

"Okay, I have got to speak to my Colonel, speak to your Daniel Clague, rustle up some troops, brief them, and make sure my foreman Dave can manage the farm tomorrow. Was there anything else?"

"Just one small thing. My Minister, Adrian Kelly, is chairing an Emergency Advisory Committee to deal with everything. It is all a bit ad hoc, at the moment. I am sure we used to have proper contingency planning and designated officers to deal with emergencies, but I think that all disappeared with the financial cutbacks. Anyway, the point is Adrian would like you to be on this Committee, as security of the embargo will obviously be vital."

"So, that will be on top of running my farm, and organising my Reservists. Yes, I suppose so."

"Good, the first meeting is at the Government offices, in Bucks Road Douglas, this Thursday 9am. I will be there as well. In the meantime, if you need to discuss anything, give me a ring."

 Peter said goodbye, put down the phone, and swivelled in his chair, to find Amanda his wife standing there. She said to him, "Do you know what day it is today?"

Peter replied, "Yes, it would have been Gemma's 16th birthday." He thought she looked angry, and he didn't know what to say.

"Well, it shouldn't bother you. It sounds like you are going to be extra busy," she remarked.

"Gemma was a lovely girl, and we both miss her. But, she would have wanted us to carry on as well as we can, I am sure. And being busy certainly helps."

"Well, you will be alright then."

"You will be busy too, because I will be relying on you, when I am not around. You know Dave will be coming to you for decisions. But, I expect my role in this emergency will diminish, after a few weeks."

Amanda turned and walked away. Peter muttered to himself, "I had better start ringing round," and started scrolling down his contacts list, on his mobile.

Chapter 10, Tuesday 6 April 2027

Vin was at the Isle of Man Airport by 1.30pm. He had asked his secretary just to reschedule his appointments, and he had left the hospital. He knew that the other Consultant in Pathology, Philip Patterson, would not be impressed. Luckily, he did not have a post- mortem to do himself that day. He arrived at the airport, at the same time as he saw the Chief Constable, Terry Corps, in uniform and cap, getting out of the passenger door of a BMW. He was holding an envelope in his hand, and was accompanied by the driver, a uniformed sergeant. Vin assumed that the envelope contained a copy of the Emergency Proclamation, requiring closure of the airport.

Vin went into the airport terminal building, and saw the police officers disappear through some doors marked "No Entry". He looked at the scheduled arrivals board, and noted that Mathew's flight was just shown as "Delayed". Suddenly this changed to an estimated time of arrival of 13.55. At 1.45pm, Vin decided to go the observation area, which had previously been a low control tower. He could see, from the east-facing window, any aeroplanes approaching the airport. Normally, aeroplanes approached from the east and landed, so that any coming from London, for example, would not have to go around the airport. At 2.01 pm, by his own watch, Vin could see an aeroplane approaching. This particular aeroplane dropped fairly low, before it deviated north. Vin could see on it the telltale triskelion marking, that Vannin Airlines had been allowed to adopt, when the airline was formed 3 years previously. Vin presumed that the pilot must have been instructed to turn away. He felt tears come to his eyes. Then, Vin noticed that the plane had flown in a full anticlockwise circle, and was going round again a second time. Then, he saw it sweep into the airport from the east again. The aeroplane descended and landed. Vin looked at his watch, which showed a time of 2.08pm, and wondered if the plan to close the airport had just been cancelled, for some reason. He walked back into the Arrivals area. He became aware of voices being raised, and looked up at the Arrivals board. The other 3 flights that had been showing on it, were now all saying "Cancelled".

About 15 minutes later, Matthew and Emma emerged into the Arrivals hall. Vin gave Matthew a hug for the first time for 23 years. Vin said to Matthew, "I thought they weren't going to let you land. All landings have now been cancelled."

Matthew said, "You knew they would be stopping flights didn't you? And you weren't supposed to tell anyone? I suppose we were lucky, that one of the passengers went into labour, whilst we were over the Irish Sea. I recognised her and her husband. He is Oliver Coyle, you know the son of the Government Minister, Jack Coyle. Oliver and I were at school together. Emily and he had moved permanently to live and work in the Reading area. I think if she was over 7 months pregnant, she was not supposed to fly. But, if she was desperate to get back to the Isle of Man for some reason, she would have lied about that. The pilot actually said, over the speakers, that the airport had just closed, and he had been refused permission to land. He was going to circle the airport, whilst he considered his options. Second time around he said that, unless it would be dangerous to land, an airport is obliged to allow any aircraft to land in an emergency, and, in his view, an emergency included having a passenger in labour on board. So, he was going to land anyway. So Dad, what is going on?"

Vin took Mathew and Emma to a quieter corner of the Arrivals hall. He said, "You must know about the ultra pneumonia virus?"

Matthew understood straightaway. He exclaimed, "Good God! It really is desperate then. You have helped persuade them to close access to the island, because you, and others, are convinced it will inevitably spread to Europe and Britain. And I very nearly got left in England by my kind father, to face that fate. You are either mad for doing this, or evil for nearly abandoning your own son."

Vin said, "Look I didn't realise, until the weekend, how desperate this virus is. I had to concentrate on getting authority here, and on the mainland, to take notice and do something. I thought you were coming back yesterday. And I did get you back, a small favour not given to any other islanders, who are off the island right now. Except for Jack Coyle's son and daughter in law, whom it looks like were told by Jack. Not that I have any right to complain, considering that I persuaded you and Emma to..."

Emma interjected, "My sister Sophie is on holiday in Tenerife, at the moment. I am guessing nobody told her to get back. Let me check if I have got this right? All flights, and presumably ferries, to the island are cancelled indefinitely, and you are expecting her and the rest of the world to die, sooner or later, from this virus. And, in the meantime, is she supposed to carry on staying in the hotel in Tenerife. Or, is she supposed to fly back as far as Heathrow, but with nowhere to stay in London? And what happens to her, if her money runs out? Is the Manx Government going to pay her hotel bills perhaps?"

Vin replied, "I am sorry, I am not sure what will happen. It is possible she won't even be able to get as far as London, from Tenerife. At least your parents have you back. I understand your anger, but I didn't create ultra pneumonia. All I am trying to do is give one tiny sliver of humanity, the population of the Isle of Man, a small chance to survive this catastrophe, which is spreading from Madagascar right now." He went on, "Look, let's get out of here. I've got my car. I'll give you both a lift back to your house."

Ten minutes later, as Vin was driving, Matthew said, "I'm sorry I got angry. But can we talk about this now, please? Now that the airport appears to be closed, it won't be a secret any more anyway."

Vin said, "Matthew, this will be fairly desperate. And it all hinges on no one on the island having already contracted the virus. I know that the British Government is being very co-operative. What I am hoping is that we can get supplies flown in by the RAF for a day, tomorrow, if all goes to plan. The idea is that the RAF will bring their own fork lifts, and use their own personnel to do the unloading. The virus must be able to drift considerable distances in the air, so there is some risk to this, but by our shutting off the airport to everyone else, they will be a fair distance away from everyone. But, as I say, it all depends on ultra pneumonia not being here already. For example, if just one person, on the plane you were on, has the infection, then I think we are basically doomed."

"Dad, how is this embargo going to be enforced, even with the UK Government playing ball? People are going to complain, even if it is a matter of survival. And I am sure some will attempt to make illicit trips, by small boat or light plane. It won't just be Emma's family who have been separated."

"Well we do have resources. The Government's own staff control the ports and airport. We've got the police, and probably a few special constables. Civil Defence was abandoned in Britain decades ago, but we still have a unit here. We have our own Coastguard these days. I have just been reminded this morning, a few years back an Isle of Man Army Reserve Unit was formed. They are all locals, and trained as soldiers. It sounds like they are being mobilised, so to speak. Even if their command structure, above the local officer, will be serving the interests of the UK Government, I don't think there should be any conflict. I learned a bit yesterday, about Government on this island. There is an Emergency Powers Act of 1936, which I expect will be used to establish all sorts of controls over people's lives, and over businesses, which would seem outrageous normally. It would not surprise me if people could be shot on discovery, for doing anything that threatened the complete isolation of the island. There will probably be rationing of food and fuel for example. Even if we do get these supplies flown in by the RAF, we are going to have to fairly rapidly adapt to living without any trade with the rest of the world. It is hard to imagine. For example, we all use computers and smart phones, but there will be no electronic imports. Will the Internet servers all crash, as the virus spreads? No clothes or food imports. We might have gas still from our pipeline, if we can keep it working, but there will be no petrol for those cars that still need petrol, or oil for our older power station. No medicines. Just nothing, or not enough of most things."

"It won't be the Stone Age, but it will be pretty hard?"

"Well life will be very much harder than we are used to, but I think mankind is very adaptable and resilient. We won't lose all our knowledge or expertise. Even if we have to do without some technology for a while, we will still know what is possible. Strangely, I feel more optimistic now than I did two days ago. Two days ago I thought we were doomed, and that there was no chance of saving mankind. I did not really expect both the Isle of Man Government, and the British Government, to take decisive action in time. I was glad to actually witness the airport being closed."

Vin then noticed that Emma, who was sitting in the back, was crying. He thought he would try to be sympathetic. He said to her, "I am sorry Emma, for sounding so callous about the fate of the rest of the world."

" 'The rest of the world', including my poor sister Sophie," responded Emma. "Can you tell me what it is like dying from ultra pneumonia? Do people suffer as they are dying? She won't have her family with her. Everyone around her will be dying at the same time, by the sounds of it."

Vin answered, "I am sorry, Emma. The main symptom is increasing breathlessness, which is unpleasant, but I think it is not painful. They finally die in their sleep, or lose consciousness and then die. I am sorry."

Emma began to feel angry, "Well, I am not sure you have got this right. How do you know it isn't just a disease that affects blacks?"

Vin forgot that he was trying to be sympathetic. He said to her, "Do you think it would affect Asians? And what about people of mixed race, like Matthew?"

Emma replied, "I'm not sure about anything, but aren't some groups of people more susceptible than others? Isn't Ebola confined to Africa? And isn't it just gays who get Aids? And Covid 19, that was really just very old people. And do you really know much? If you were any good, why did you come from London to a backwater, like the Isle of Man? I'm going to speak to one of my MHKs. One of them is Patrick Quinn. I think he sticks up for Manx people. The least we should be doing is allowing our own people to come home, if they want to."

Chapter 11, Tuesday 6 April 2027

Matt and Emma lived in a 1970s bungalow, surrounded by other 1970s bungalows, in Glen Vine. Glen Vine was a residential development, just off the Douglas to Peel main road, 3 miles west of Douglas. Vin dropped them off at about 2.50pm. They got inside, and put their bags in their bedroom.

Emma just went and sat in silence, in the lounge. Matt said to her, "I'll make you a cup of coffee. I think the milk should be alright. It's only 4 days old."

Emma didn't say anything, and waited until Matt had given her a mug of coffee. Then she burst into tears again, saying, "This is awful!"

Matt took the mug away from her, and then he took her in her arms. "You haven't even tried it. It's not awful; it's just my normal standard coffee!" he joked.

Emma said, "You know what I mean, idiot!" and she pushed him away. "Let's assume that your father is right, and that ultra pneumonia kills everyone worldwide, except us here on Mann. That would mean I am never going to see Sophie again. My Mum and Dad are going to be devastated. They will be finding out soon, even if we don't tell them. And it is all your father's doing, that Sophie can't get home. And if he is right, it will be a frightening world to bring our baby into, won't it?"

"I suppose so. But we want to give our baby a chance don't we? Oliver and his wife obviously wanted to give their baby that chance. They don't even have a job or a house here. And my father is just trying to give everyone on Mann a chance. He, almost certainly, didn't know that Sophie was away."

"I am sorry I was rude about your father. But, I am going to do what I said. I am going to speak to Patrick Quinn, and see if he can get the embargo lifted for Manx born people who are just away on holiday or business."

"So you think this disease is just for inferior blacks? And Asians as well maybe?"

"Look, I am carrying a mixed race baby aren't I? But diseases do affect different groups differently don't they, like I said. I don't really know anything about diseases, but in the Coronavirus pandemic I am sure we let residents return, even when we were keeping everyone else out. And most people survived who got that, anyway."

"You just said, you don't know anything about diseases. Well my dad does. I suspect he is right. In which case, it would be very foolish of the Government to reopen the ports and airports to anyone. And suppose he is wrong, that ultra pneumonia never reaches Europe or Britain, or that a cure is found, well, then they will open the ports again. It might only be a few weeks." Although Matthew said this, he actually thought that the disease would spread unstoppably, but he hoped this would give Emma some comfort.

"Nope. I have got to do what I can, to help Sophie now," said Emma. "Even if it means we all get ultra pneumonia here. I don't really want to bring a baby into a world which just consists of a small island, where there might not even be enough food to eat. I wonder if I am too late for an abortion. But, right now, I am going to see if we've got Patrick's number on the board in the kitchen."

Matt felt a lump in his throat, and he took Emma's hand. He pleaded, "Please Emma don't talk of abortion. We are going to love our little boy or girl. I think we can survive and still be happy. In fact, I think we should get married, so we know that we really are in this together."

Just then the house phone rang. Not many people called them on that number.

Emma said unhappily, "That's going to be my Mum. God, this is terrible." She looked at Matt who didn't move, so she answered the phone, "Hello, Emma O'Hara speaking."

As predicted by Emma, it was her mother, Beryl O'Hara, on the phone. Beryl said, " Hello Emma, thank goodness you're there. I thought I would just try your number. Are you alright? We thought you would still be in London. That's what you told us yesterday evening."

"Hello Mum. Something came up. Last minute rechange of plan," Emma told her. Emma was looking at Matt, who shook his head, as if to say not to tell her Mum what happened. Emma said to her Mum, "Just a minute Mum," and then said to Matt, "Look I am not keeping secrets from my family, but were you serious about getting married?"

"Oh yes, definitely!" replied Matt.

Emma tried to continue with her mother, "Mum, I..."

Beryl interrupted, "Emma, I've just heard on the radio that the airport, and the ports, on the island have been closed to all traffic indefinitely, because of the ultra pneumonia virus in Madagascar. But, that will mean Sophie will be stuck in London. She was going to be flying back from Tenerife to

Heathrow today, and then getting the evening Vannin Airline flight home."

Emma responded, "Oh I didn't know Sophie was due back today. We were fortunate that Matt's Dad phoned us, with some pretext to get back urgently. We were on the last flight that landed. He picked us up at the airport about an hour ago, and admitted that he knew all about it, and had asked the Government to do it. He is convinced the ultra pneumonia virus is pretty much going to spread worldwide, and kill practically everyone. So we should, perhaps, be grateful to him, if it means we survive here, on the Isle of Man. But we must see if we can get Sophie and others repatriated. It, surely, should not be too late to do that. I am going to get on to our MHK Patrick Quinn. Could you or Dad get on to him too, or any other MHK, or anyone you know with influence too."

Beryl had become angry and upset, "Perhaps you should get on to Matthews's Dad. He seems to have enough influence. And tell me something Emma, because I never wanted you to move in with Matthew. Whilst he might have a nice house and a well-paid job, he's not really our type is he? Surely, you are not going to continue living with Matthew, after what he and his father have done to Sophie?"

Emma protested, "Matt had nothing to do with it. And his father was only trying to do what he thinks is right. I am not sure what type you mean, unless you mean that he is mixed race. Matt is a good man, and I love him. I am having his baby, and we are going to get married."

The phone went dead. Emma looked at it blankly a moment, and Matt tried to take her hand. Emma said to him, "Well, it looks like we are getting married, as well as having a baby if we survive, but in the meantime I really must do something for my little sister."

Emma disappeared into the kitchen, and came back with Patrick's number on a slip of paper. She rang the number. There was no answer, and she started to leave a voicemail message, when Patrick interrupted. He said, "Hello, it's Patrick Quinn here. Sorry, I was just dealing with something on the other phone."

Emma said, "Hello Mr Quinn..,"

Patrick cut in, "Just call me Patrick, my dear. You sound like a nice local girl. What can I do for you?"

"Have you heard that the Government has just closed the airport and ports indefinitely?"

"Yes I have. Nobody consulted me about it, at all. From what I hear, some foreign doctor at the hospital decided it would be a good idea, and the ninnies on the Council of Ministers nearly all went along with it. Whilst there are definitely people we shouldn't let in, and equally there are some who have come here we could do without, our own people should be free to go away on business or holidays, and come back afterwards, without our idiot Government closing the border behind their backs."

"That is what has happened to my sister Sophie. She is getting back to London from Tenerife..."

Patrick interrupted, "Oh yes Tenerife. I suppose you can't blame a girl for wanting a holiday where it is a bit warmer than here, although there are things there to lead you astray. When I was there a few years back, the natives all spoke English, because our friends across the water, the Brits, like it there so much. My own weakness there was the cheap booze. Hmm. Sorry my dear, what you were saying about your sister?"

"I was saying that she will be in London about now, but unable to get home from there. There must be other Manx people not able to get home. Surely, we could arrange a special flight for them in the next few days? I mean, maybe the virus is coming to Britain, but it is not there yet. Just restrict it to, say, one or two flights from London and Manchester. Obviously, the main thing I want is for my sister to get home, and make my parents happy, and perhaps they will feel better about my fiance too and...Sorry, I am beginning to gabble a bit. It is just that I am really upset and worried."

"Okay my dear, you know, I think this epidemic is probably the work of God, in some way. I am sure He is not always pleased with us; sometimes, when I get a hangover, I feel I have probably offended Him. But, there is a lot of much worse sin in Africa, and that is where the epidemic is. Well, in Madagascar anyway. But I am sure He also helps those who help themselves, and each other. So, I quite agree about laying on some repatriation flights. Sorry, what did you say your sister's name was? I will start a list."

"Her name is Sophie O'Hara. I am her older sister, Emma O'Hara. Sophie lives with our parents in Crosby, just up the road from us in Glen Vine. We are all in your Middle constituency."

"You said, 'us in Glen Vine'. So, you yourself are living with your fiancee presumably. You know, God does not look too kindly on that. That is why it is sometimes called 'living in sin'. What is your fiancee's name by the way?"

"It is Matthew Singh."

"I don't think God approves of mixed marriages either. But, your sister is a Manx girl, so we must help her, and other Manx people, get back if we can. I will try to get repatriation flights approved and organised. No doubt, you will find out if I have been successful. Goodbye!"

Emma put the phone down and said to Matt, "Well, I never realised, but one of our two MHKs is a heavy drinker, a racist, a patronising sexist, and a religious nut. He doesn't sound very nice at all, but he has said he will be trying to get repatriation flights approved. So, whatever your Dad thinks, I hope he succeeds, if it means we can get Sophie home."

Chapter 12, Tuesday 6 April 2027

Beryl was feeling thoroughly upset, after her telephone conversation with Emma. Lots of thoughts were running through her mind. She was terrified that Sophie would never get home. Maybe this new epidemic would kill everyone. And that was a bombshell from Emma; pregnant, in love, and getting married. She certainly wasn't pleased about any of that. Admittedly, Matthew sounded like he was doing well in his job, but he was 9 years older than Emma, and the only time Beryl had met him, she had thought he was rather opinionated and self-important. And she had heard bad things about the way Asian men treat women, and Matthew was half Asian. Beryl had waited to the age of 22 to get married, and had married Wayne, who her own parents had described as 'a nice polite local boy'. He was just 22 then, as well. Now they were both 42. She did find him a bit plodding and boring at times, but he had risen to a supervisory role in the Port Security Office at Douglas Harbour, and he was a supportive husband and father. The thought that prompted her to action was, 'Well, he is not here at the moment, and we need to help Sophie. Emma's suggestion that I should phone our MHK is sensible.' She found a number for Patrick, by looking at profiles on the Government website. She tried to ring him. She eventually got through, on her third attempt, ten minutes later.

Beryl said, "Hello is that Patrick Quinn the MHK?"

Patrick replied, "Yes it is. Who am I speaking to please?"

"I am Beryl O'Hara..."

"Are you the mother of Emma and Sophie?"

"Yes. I assume that you have been speaking to Emma then. Did you know that the Government has closed the ports and airport? Emma and her boyfriend arrived back from London today. Her boyfriend's father, Dr Singh, knew what was going to happen, and he phoned to tell them. They caught the last plane that was allowed to land. But Sophie is flying into Heathrow this afternoon, and now she won't be able to catch the Vannin Airlines flight back here this evening. I might never see her again..."

Patrick could hear sobs, but he was more interested in justifying himself than in offering sympathy. He said, "I had nothing to do with the decision to close the ports and airport. I didn't even know it was going to happen. So Dr Singh told his son, and your daughter Emma, what was going to happen?"

Beryl replied, "Yes that is what she told me. It's not right though, is it? Sophie and other Manx people who are away should also have been given the chance to get back, before the airport was closed."

"Lots of things happen, that I don't think are right. I don't think that it is right that your daughter Emma should get involved in fornication and miscegnation for example."

Beryl did not like Patrick's initial responses, but felt she had to keep going. She said, "I am not sure what those things are, but Emma is 19 years old. She has a job and has left home, and I have no control over her. But Sophie is just 17, and I am still responsible for her. I really wish I had tried harder to stop her from going to Tenerife, but she was going with her friend Olivia Cornell. God, her parents are in the same situation. Please, can't you try to persuade the Government to organise a repatriation flight urgently, in case the ultra pneumonia virus does get to Britain?"

"Yes, that is one of several things that I need to do urgently. So far, I have two names, Sophie O'Hara and, Olivia Cornell wasn't it, for a list of people needing repatriation. I will try to persuade the Government to do the right thing, and fly our people home. But I also feel that God is displeased, and, if ultra pneumonia spreads from Africa, we may need to show Him that we are sorry, and are ready to appease Him. Do you agree Mrs O'Hara?"

Beryl had not expected the references to God. She said, "I am not sure what you mean by, 'showing Him that we are sorry and ready to appease Him.' What do you think we should do?"

Patrick replied, "Well, if you and your husband and daughter come to the church where I am the minister, on Sunday, that would certainly help. He may also want us to act against those who have wronged Him. I am waiting for some Guidance about that."

"Yes I think I see. Which church is yours?"

"Well some voluntary donations helped fund the cost of converting the building, but it is God's church, and as I said, I am the minister. It is called the Isle of Man Astrological Church, and it is in Douglas. I am sure you will find it."

Beryl and Wayne normally went to another church, but Beryl felt she had to do what she could to get Sophie home.

She said, "Yes, we will be there on Sunday. But you will try to get my daughter and her friend repatriated, won't you, please?"

"Yes, count on me. We have God on our side, and on Earth we have a friend who has influence here on Mann, and in England. I am sure we will be getting those girls on a flight home."

"Thank you, oh thank you!"

Chapter 13 – Wednesday 7 April 2027

Matt drove with Emma into their offices at Sodor Information Technology Solutions (SITS) in Douglas, aiming to be there by 8.30am. He noticed a queue of traffic for petrol, at a petrol station. Matt's car was an all-electric Honda. Suddenly, he felt really glad that he had switched to an all electric car, and that he had persuaded his father to get one too. The embargo had been the main item on all the news broadcasts, and it was obvious that people were filling up with petrol because of that. He reflected to himself, "Is it rational not to panic buy, when everyone else is panic buying?" Lots of other thoughts were crossing his mind as he was driving, but, strangely, he found himself thinking about something his father had said about what things would be like. "What was it?.. Something to do with electronics.. Oh yes, that was it, 'Will the Internet servers all crash?' "

When they arrived, Emma went off to her own desk in an open plan area, and he went to his office, leaving his door open, as normal. His own role in the company could, loosely, once have been described as systems design. SITS was an expanding company that worked in a very dynamic way, with lots of exchanges of ideas, via internal media, and by face to face meetings. People could, and did chip in, with ideas that were not really their field of expertise. Emma, at the age of

19, was still an apprentice programmer, having only joined SITS six months earlier. Matt was not her boss in any way. There was no company policy against internal romantic liaisons, and they had soon started going out. Her mother had been unfriendly towards Matt, the only time he had met her parents, but she had moved in with him after about three months. In Emma's mind, that was possibly the same day that she had got pregnant. Matt had progressed to the role and title of Project Manager, and he worked directly to the Development Director, whose name was Simon Kearney. Simon was walking past his office, but did a double-take when he saw Matt. He walked into Matt's office and said, "Goodness you're here! I assumed, because you weren't here yesterday, that you were going to be stuck in England, and we might never see you and Emma again! I nearly tried your mobile but, to be honest, I wasn't sure I could have handled talking to you in that situation. You know, if you had been stuck in London, waiting for ultra pneumonia to strike possibly. You would have felt terrible, and I wouldn't have known what to say."

Matt started to reply, "It's alright I think I understand. But Emma's..."

Simon wasn't listening properly, as he closed the door behind him, and sat down. He said, "So what happened? Why did you decide not to stay on in London? When did you get back?"

Matt said, "I don't really want to go into details, but we were on the last aeroplane to be allowed to land yesterday. My Dad picked us up, and he knew all about the embargo, because he had actually spoken at a special meeting of the Council of Ministers, the previous evening. Poor old Emma is trying hard not to show it, but she is in a terrible state really. That is because her younger sister Sophie flew into London yesterday, back from her holiday in Tenerife, and now she can't get home. Oh, two more things I should probably tell you, Emma is expecting, we only had it confirmed just before we went to that conference in London, and we are going to get married. But you know, I reckon my Dad is right about the spread of ultra pneumonia. So, if we are lucky, we will survive on this island when most of the rest of the world's population has perished, and I suppose everything else seems pretty minor set against that. But that doesn't stop people on Mann worrying about their own relatives and friends, who aren't on the island."

Simon responded, "Well, that is quite a lot to take in there. Congratulations on the baby and the engagement. I don't know whether that was your plan, when she moved in with you, but she is a lovely girl, and I am sure you will both make great parents. Mind you, it could be a strange world to bring a baby into."

Matt said, "I know it might sound odd, but I have been thinking about how we, as a company, could help the island adapt and survive on its own." He looked at Simon, who looked slightly surprised by this development in the conversation.

Simon urged, "Yes, go on."

"Well, stating the obvious, our expertise is information technology. We are the biggest IT company on the island. It could be crucial for everyone living on the island to have retained as much information of all kinds as possible, and for this to be easily available. I spend a lot of my time talking to other companies because, as you know, we own servers which handle other companies' data and information processing. Again, as you know, some of those companies, we basically run their IT for them, and we offer a twenty four seven commitment to deal with any problems. We are also a Tier 3 Internet Service Provider. If the virus has the effect my Dad expects, servers across the world will start to crash, masses of data won't be accessible any more, as there won't be any Tier 1 or Tier 2 servers, or any internet as we are used to. The only information processing or sharing will be on the island, and we can be a major facilitator of that. Private individuals and businesses will still be searching the internet, but not getting any further than us at SITS, or our rivals on the island, possibly. At the same time, I can foresee that many of our current client businesses will collapse. If there is no 'rest of the world', there won't be any need for processing insurance for Chartered Union, or banking for Bangkok International Bank, or egaming for Euro Leisure. So, we will have lots of capacity. But, the island has a need to gather as much technical data as possible, to store it on the island's computers, preferably SITS' computers, and for it to be available. I haven't really thought it through further than that."

Simon had been listening intently. He had only just begun to grasp how things would be changing almost overnight. He said, "You are well ahead of me Matt, even with everything you have been doing and worrying about, in your own life. But, thinking out loud a moment, and leaving aside how this would work commercially, I could see how we, the remnants of mankind on this island if you like, could, in years to come, need expertise and knowledge that exists in the world now, but which could be lost. How to make an LPG or electric powered car, for example. Although I am guessing if an engineer on the island took one apart, he might get some ideas that way. Or how to produce steel maybe? Although maybe instead of using steel they would be trying to use wood, or rigid plastic, if we can produce that from vegetable oils or gas."

Matt commented, "I am not sure how much commercial profit will actually be a consideration. Maybe being useful will help ensure that we get fed, and we have heating for our houses, and that we are allowed fuel for petrol driven cars, or to charge our electric cars. Other opportunities for spending income will be pretty limited." He paused. "And definitely no foreign travel, except on a one way ticket perhaps!" he added with a wry grin.

"As always, you seem to have ideas Matt. Sarah Miles, our CEO, has called a meeting with all the Directors at 10am today. I imagine it is to discuss the impact of ultra pneumonia, and of the embargo on the company. I am going to ask her if you can come along. You might steal the limelight from me, but, in these dramatic times, I suppose I can regard that as an unimportant consideration!"

"Well Simon, thanks for the vote of confidence, even though it sounds like your thoughts are along similar lines to mine anyway. Yes, I am quite happy to come to the meeting. Everyone's mindset now should be on a different future from what we might have thought, only a few days ago. But I would expect it still to involve new babies being born. I certainly hope so. Anyway we are all going to have to adapt massively, including this company."

"I won't press you, but I am guessing that your father helped persuade you to come home yesterday. It is obvious that you and Emma want the baby, so you must be glad to have got back. So your father did you a double favour. He has saved life on the Isle of Man, and he made sure you were both back here to have a future. But perhaps, emotionally if not logically, Emma and you blame him for her sister not being able to get back."

"Well Emma was on the phone yesterday to our MHK Patrick Quinn. He..."

"Patrick Quinn! Oh yes I know a lot about him. He is, not only the sole member of the Manx First party in the House of Keys, but he is also the Minister for the Isle of Man Astrological Church in Douglas. They are strong believers in a Day of Reckoning. Sorry you were saying?"

"Well, she came off the phone saying he was racist, sexist and a religious nut, but she did say that he was going to try to get a repatriation flight organised, for Manx people who haven't got back. He apparently referred to my father as a 'foreign doctor from the hospital, who persuaded the ninnies on the Council of Ministers to impose the embargo.' It would be great if Sophie and her friend could get back, but suppose it is just the one repatriation flight, even then it might only take one infected person to wipe us all out on Mann."

"You obviously have mixed feelings then, as to whether this repatriation flight should happen, so you are not really sure whether you want to tell your father about the possibility? In any case, you and he had better take care with Patrick. He might have been fairly harmless up till now, but he does combine extreme and unpleasant racist and religious views, and he might try a bit of rabble rousing in these dangerous times."

Chapter 14, Thursday 8 April 2027

Vin had not been doing a lot of work for the Pathology Department that week, although he had carried out a post-mortem the day before on a man found at the bottom of cliffs near Maughold Head, which was about seven miles further north along the coast, from where he lived. The notes from the police referred to neighbours hearing him involved in an argument, not long before his body was found. Vin had found no evidence of physical assault or restraint, that was not consistent with falling a long way down a cliff, accidentally or suicidally. And, although he had taken samples of tissues and fluids from the body, he was not at all confident that it would be possible to get these fully tested. That was because they always went off to the same laboratory on the mainland, which would not happen now because of the embargo. He knew that only some simple tests could be done at the Pathology Laboratory at the hospital. Nevertheless, these could have some evidential value, such as a negative result from tests for drugs in the urine.

He put that all out of his mind, as he drove into Douglas for a meeting in the main Government offices at 9.00am. The previous few days he had been involved in a lot of phone calls. He had found himself co-opted on to the Emergency Advisory Committee which, he had been told, had been set up to deal with the numerous issues arising from the decision to impose an embargo. He thought that embargo was the right word. If anyone was being quarantined, it was the rest of the world. He assumed that the RAF had flown supplies in the previous day, and that that had now stopped. This is it; the beginning of a new era, but only if we are lucky, he thought. He knew that there were now only two ways this could go. The news about the spread of ultra pneumonia was grim. People were just beginning to die in South Africa. There were no longer any flights between Europe and South Africa, even if, so far, it seemed ultra pneumonia had not reached Europe. But he no longer nursed any faint hope that it would not, sooner or later, manifest itself in Britain and Ireland and wipe out the populations there, along with every other country. So the first possible outcome was that the attempts by Mann to quarantine off the rest of the world had failed, or would fail. In that case, they would all be dead within a few weeks. But, if the embargo had been imposed in time, and could be maintained, the second outcome was that life on the island would go on, but a lot less comfortably than before.

He went up to the second floor of the Government offices in Bucks Road, where the first meeting was being held. He was 20 minutes early, but a young woman sorted out coffee for him, and gave him a piece of paper headed "Agenda". It was quite a list, "Rationing, fuel, medicines, food, electricity supply, water supply, computer services, clothing, engineering, construction, transport, AOB."

Vin spotted Jack Coyle come into the room, and go out again. He went after him, and they spoke to each other, just outside the Gentlemen's toilets. Jack said to him, "I now think you are right about the dangers of ultra pneumonia, but I am sure that the Council of Ministers would have acted in time without your interference."

Vin said, "Well I know why you voted against the embargo. You wanted more time to get your son and your daughter in law home. You wanted time for her to give birth in England, a delay which could have been fatal to us. When you realised the closure of the airport was going to happen the next day anyway, you booked the last two seats on the 10.30am flight, causing danger, by getting a woman in full term to fly."

Jack retorted, "Don't get so high and mighty with me. Your son and his girlfiend were on that flight too, so you must have told them in advance what was happening. And it seems to me that that plane would never have landed if, luckily for everyone, my daughter in law had not gone into labour as the plane was approaching Ronaldsway. So that makes you a lucky hypocrite, Dr Singh."

A short while later the meeting was under way. Vin noted 18 people around the table, wondering if that might be too many. Everyone was asked to introduce themselves, and Vin took his chance to voice his concerns, saying, "Before we waste a lot of time following this agenda, I want to say that the absolutely key thing is ensuring the embargo is secure. Otherwise we are wasting our time, as we will all die soon anyway, if we fail to do that."

Adrian Kelly was chairing the meeting, and he gave Vin a withering look. He had drawn up the agenda himself, and was quite pleased with it. David Quayle just widened his eyes slightly, and looked at Vin with the slightest hint of a grin. Adrian said, "We can't progress by you, or anyone else, just blurting out comments. We need to do this in an orderly way, by following the agenda, and speaking through the chair. And I can tell you that we have tight control of the airport at Ronaldsway, and of the eight harbours owned by the Government, so please don't speak again, until asked to do so."

Vin said, "Look this is too important, just to delay or to dismiss. I know that there are several airstrips dotted around the island. There are quite a few coves like Port Soderick and Port Grougle where, with small boats, you could probably get people on the island without anyone knowing. In fact, around the top end of the island, at the Ayres, aren't there several miles of continous beach backed by low ground, where you could get ashore by a small boat. And we don't even normally have a continuous day time presence at all of the eight Government controlled harbours, do we? And as for night time, what happens then? If we don't secure these airstrips and the whole coastline soon, it will be too late."

Several people spoke at once, but Adrian looked furious. David said, "I know Dr Singh is not the most diplomatic person alive Minister, but he has made a vital point. This is what we would have called at university an existential crisis. In other words, if we don't get this basic point sorted out, we will cease to exist. I think that you and others around the table recognise that. Can I politely suggest we make security of the quarantine of the island first item on the agenda, and see how we go from there?"

Adrian said, "Very well. But, nevertheless we must function properly. We are not just a rabble. Let's have no more outbursts." He looked towards Peter Quinnel, who looked like a grey haired man in his early forties, wearing military uniform. "Major, I know your Reserves have been involved in maintaining the closure of Ronaldsway. What can you say about stopping planes or boats arriving elsewhere on the island?"

Peter said, "Well, I have managed to get a roster together to cover the airport all the time. I would expect all normal commerical airlines to observe our embargo, although if the situation elsewhere gets desperate, who knows? The airport obviously has radar, and we could probably trust them to advise any approaching aircraft to turn away. A light private plane could decide to land there anyway, but I think we have more or less got that covered. We also have a roving patrol most of the time in the north where, as Dr Singh has pointed out, there is a continous beach. There are two landing strips in that area. Obviously this patrol could respond to a message to head south to potential landings elsewhere. I only have 25 men and 5 women. Normally they should get 28 days notice to be formally mobilised, but they have all accepted my word that this will be treated as an emergency, and financial cover for loss of earnings will apply. But I think we urgently need more resources, and to make sure they are properly co-ordinated." He looked diagonally across the table towards one of the few women in the room, Nicola Kermode. He added, " Ms Kermode, Daniel Clague told me that you head his Ports Division. What can you say about the eight harbours controlled by your Division."

Nicola nodded and said, "Just call me Nicola. I can tell you that all the staff know that no movement of any vessels is permitted, including fishing boats. We are accompanying any boat owner claiming an urgent need to go on his or her boat. We don't allow them to remain on the boat. Dr Singh is right that, normally, our smaller harbours don't have a routine presence. But we do have staff in Douglas Port security office, most of whom, with no port traffic now, could be redeployed for a visible uniformed presence at the other seven harbours. Together with the six Harbour Keepers we could, for a few weeks anyway, keep this up for 16 hours a day, seven days a week. It would take a fair bit in overtime payments, and would not include the period 10pm to 6am every night."

Peter said, "So, basically, we have no night time cover of the ports. Perhaps we can talk about that, after we have talked about the Coastguard, which I think also comes under Nicola."

Nicola had been hoping it was someone else's turn to be put on the spot. She said, "Err, yes, the Coastguard. Well, we have five teams, who are all volunteers. They do have four wheel drive vehicles, and can get to most parts of the coast. But, their function is basically search and rescue, and coordinating rescues. That is what they joined for. I am not too sure..."

Peter interjected, "You are saying it's not their job to look out for illegal approaches and landings? But, if you think how things must have been in wartime, I am sure it was the duty then, of the Coastguard, to help defend the coast against unwanted intruders. And it seems that the situation we are in now is more grave than previous wartimes. Just one infected intruder, apparently could be the end of us all. Isn't that right, Dr Singh?"

Vin agreed, "Yes, just one."

Peter added, "So I would hope that these uniformed Coastguards would see it as their duty to help prevent that happening."

Nicola responded, "Yes I suppose you are right, but shall I tell how it works normally? Often what happens is that a

999 caller asking for 'Coastguard', or a call that is related to an incident at sea, is diverted to our continuously manned Marines Operations Centre at the Douglas Sea Terminal. The Coastguard Duty Officer then coordinates rescue efforts. This could mean getting out one of the five teams I mentioned. They have small boats, and also four wheel vehicles that can get to most parts of the coast. If necessary, the Duty Officer will alert the RNLI, and he or she can also summons helicopter assistance from the UK Coastguard. By the way, sometimes one of the Coastguard teams can get asked to assist in inland rescue off-road. They regularly train and liaise with police, the civil defence corps..."

Peter interrupted, "Oh yes, to be honest I had forgotten about the civil defence people. Like the Coastguards they have uniforms don't they?"

Tom Johnson MHK said, "Yes they do. They come under the Department I'm attached to, Home Affairs. Sometimes they get called out by Emergency Services for mountain rescue, and that sort of thing. At one time, my Department had a senior official in charge of emergency planning, who was also the Commander of the Civil Defence Corps. With the budget cuts over the last few years, this post has been axed. Anyway, now it is led by their Commandant, who is still answerable to the Department for Home Affairs. The Commandant is a volunteer, and he has five teams of volunteers, and they have their own vehicles. So, it is very similar to the Coastguards in many ways. But the Coastguards answer to the Department for Structure, and are called out by the Marine Operations Centre; whereas the Civil Defence answer to the Department for Home Affairs, and are called out by the Joint Emergency Services Control Room."

Peter said, "Sorry, I have not been fully up to speed with all our Government bodies because, well, we are the Army, and my line of command is my Colonel in St Helens, Lancashire. So, we don't really answer to anyone in the Isle of Man Government. But, let me see if I have got this right so far, about resources to enforce the embargo. There is the regular police, and presumably some special constables, there are my Manx based Army Reservists, there are Nicola's people including the Harbour Keepers and Coastguards, and there is the Civil Defence. And the UK are chipping in with Royal Navy and RAF patrols, and we could perhaps ask for some helicopter flights from their Coastguard but not for rescuing anyone. What about the RNLI? Could they patrol at all? I hope they are not still rescuing people and bringing them ashore."

Nicola said, "They last rescued someone 3 weeks ago. I don't think it is fair to ask volunteers in the RNLI, dedicated to the rescue of people in distress at sea, to act as a sort of Defence arm of our Government."

Vin felt an urgent need to butt in. He said, "In which case, have they definitely been told not to go out at all, even if someone apparently needs rescuing?"

Nicola replied, "I will make sure that the coxwains are told, and that so are our Harbour Keepers, if that is what is required?" She looked enquiringly at Adrian. Adrian felt angry that Vin, Peter, and others were making the running, but he could see people now looking expectantly at him.

Adrian concurred, "Very well, it does seem necessary."

Before Adrian could say anything else, Peter spoke again, "As I said earlier, we need to co-ordinate and organise the resources we have, to reduce the chances of any intruder getting ashore, or landing. I would hope most of the Coastguards and Civil Defence would be willing to put on their uniforms, and spend some night times on a rota watching the ports and coast, in co-operation with the police and my Army Reserves. The..."

Vin interrupted, "Major I agree that resources need co-ordinating, but what are you going to do to stop people actually landing on the airstrips, or landing in boats. I mean, if they get here alive it could be too late!"

Peter responded, "Alright Dr Singh, I think I understand what you mean. I think you are saying that we may need to use lethal force, before they get ashore, if we can? So if there are, say, five people in a boat of some kind approaching a beach, we shoot up everyone in the boat, and hopefully sink the boat?"

A bit of a murmur went around the room.

Vin said, "Yes, that's right, it is vital no-one gets here, because we don't want to take any risks with this virus spreading. It could have got into the air in the cabin of the boat, and into the air nearby. Ultra pneumonia seems to be so contagious because it can travel so far in the air, and linger for so long. So, shoot the intruders from as far away as possible, and move away quickly. But, suppose they are already standing on a beach or a quayside, having got out of a boat, or maybe standing on an airstrip, having just got out of a light plane? We might still have a chance, if they don't get near anyone."

"So, what I think you mean is, again use lethal force from as far as possible, but don't go near the bodies?" said Peter.

A louder murmur went around the room.

Vin replied, "Yes, actually move back away from the bodies, and then we would need to cordon them off for at least 800 metres distance."

A lot of talking had broken out. Vin thought that Adrian looked angry, and Jack Coyle seemed fascinated with examining his fingers, as if not wanting to be involved. But Vin could see David Quayle nodding very slightly, as if in agreement.

Adrian said, "Alright, let's have one person at a time. Nicola, what do you want to say?"

Nicola said, "I am not quite sure I can believe what I am hearing. I know Dr Singh is a pathologist, so maybe he likes dead bodies, but I thought, as a medical practitioner he was sworn to preserve human life, not to organise murder."

Vin responded, "As you say I have indeed sworn to preserve human life. But, if we want to save human life on this island, it is vital to prevent anyone coming onto the island and coming into close contact with anyone else. I think the Major and I recognise that, but frankly, if the rest of the Committee doesn't support the use of lethal force, I personally will not be wasting any of the last few days of my life sitting on this Committee."

There was more of a hubbub, but David said, "Please Minister I would like to say something which might help."

"Go on then David, what is it?" Adrian said.

David said, "It seems to me that we need to get the issue resolved of how to deal with embargo breakers, if they are confronted by any officers in the various teams. To me there seems to be no choice, but to use lethal force, in the manner described by Major Quinnel and Dr Singh. However many seem to disagree. We could proceed by voting on a recommendation to the Council of Ministers, about authorising designated personnel to use lethal force to prevent any person from breaching, or from continuing to breach, the embargo. If that is not supported, perhaps we could then discuss other options."

The room had become quieter. Adrian did not really know how the embargo could be maintained otherwise, against determined embargo breakers, but did not want to endorse killing such people. They might include friends or relatives of people he knew, desperate to get back home from England, or wherever else they had been. He thought the meeting would reject the proposed recommendation, and he decided he would quite like to see Vin voted down.

"Very well, we will have a show of hands on that proposition," said Adrian.

Hands were raised for and against, with a few people present abstaining by actually sitting on their hands. Only Vin, David, Peter, and Terry Corps the Chief Constable, actually supported making the recommendation, with six votes against. After the vote, Vin looked like he was about to walk out. David made eye contact with Vin, and mouthed quietly at him, "Wait a minute!"

"Minister, perhaps we could have a short break at this point?" asked David. Adrian agreed.

Outside the room, David got Vin away from everyone else. He said, "I had to work hard to get you on this Committee. Adrian was dead against you being included, but finally Henry Smith overruled him. He said he thought your medical background would be useful. But I reckon he thought the same as me, that you would see the issues, and speak your mind. Well you have certainly done that! Are you determined to walk out?"

Vin answered, "I am not surprised Adrian was against me. He told me how annoyed he was when he found out from the Prime Minister that I had phoned Tony Sharp. I didn't tell him that was your idea. Yes I am walking out, there is no point now, and I would like to spend my last few days or weeks alive with Martha."

David said, "Don't be so sure this embargo will be broken. The Major seems quite a strong minded chap, and I have heard the Chief Constable is very pragmatic. I think they both see the need for it to be secure. They were both in favour of lethal force, and they are in charge of people who have firearms."

Vin shrugged. David continued, "I will tell Adrian you have been called away urgently by the hospital, so you can come back to the next meeting, if you change your mind."

Vin said, "Tell him what you like, I'm not coming again."

"Okay, even though you are the very person we need most on the Committee. Before you go, there is one other thing."

"Yes?"

"Listen, I know your wife Martha a little bit, from when we were both social workers, so I also know that she is really kind and friendly. And I think, when you are not being so prickly, deep down you might be a decent chap. And I have heard you are quite a strong Scrabble player, although probably not as good as me. So, I was wondering if you and Martha would like to spend a few hours socialising with us, tomorrow evening. It might help us take our minds off things for a bit. We have a well stocked freezer for some reason, the electricity supply is still working fine, and we have a few bottles of wine tucked away, so all you need is about a litre of petrol to drive to my place in Spring Valley. My wife Amber would love some new visitors. Come over for dinner at seven, followed by a game of Scrabble. What do you say?"

"I haven't got any petrol in my car!"

"Could you come in Martha's car?"

"No we can come in my car. There is no petrol in it, because it is all electric." He gave David the ghost of a smile. He went on, "If, somehow we all survive, despite Adrian Kelly and some other idiots on this Committee, I think it will be a very fine thing indeed, having an electric motor car."

"So you're coming then. I will ask Amber to help me prepare a feast suitable for our 'internationally recognised microbiologist', and his much more pleasant wife."

"Yes that sounds fine. We will be delighted to eat your dinner and drink your wine, although it will be just one glass for me. And I will beat you at Scrabble as well. I know lots of obscure medical words."

"Well I know quite a few strange allowable Gaelic words myself, so we shall see."

Chapter 15, Thursday 8 April 2027

Around 7pm, Vin was sitting at home with Martha. He felt strangely relaxed, even though he did not want to die, and he wanted his wife and son to live. He had not invented the ultra pneumonia virus himself, and he had done what he could to save everyone on the Isle of Man. If there was a God of any kind, surely he would receive some credit for his efforts. But, he reminded himself, he did not believe in any of that religious nonsense.

The phone rang and he answered it. It was Tony Sharp.

"Hello it's Tony Sharp, you know we spoke the other day," said Tony.

Vin replied, "Hello Tony, yes of course. I just wasn't expecting to hear from you."

Tony said, "Well, I am not sure why I am ringing you. It is just you were somebody who understood what was going on, and you seemed determined to try to save a small part of humanity on that little island, that you're on."

Vin reflected on that, and felt a bit guilty about giving up so easily.

Tony went on, "Something I was worried might happen looks like it will. Our Government wants to insist on a repatriation flight to the Isle of Man. Just one flight, comprising the chosen few. I am pretty sure one of the passengers will be the Prime Minister's wife, Kathy Hardy. You know, Adrian Kelly's sister. The two youngest people I have heard about are two teenage girls, who had got back from Tenerife..."

"Yes I know about those girls. One of them is Sophie O'Hara, the younger sister of my son's pregnant fiancee, Emma. Martha and I got the news about the engagement and the pregnancy at the same time yesterday evening. So, I already knew about the younger sister being stuck in London..."

"Because of the embargo that you pushed for. So, some tensions in your family there, I imagine? But having a grandchild on the way, you must want him or her to have a chance. Anyway, there are about 120 people on the list for this repatriation flight. But I think your Government must stop this plane, if it can. The PM, and others, are saying there is time for a repatriation flight, because no cases of ultra pneumonia have reached Europe yet. I have tried to make them see that infected people have almost certainly flown from Johannesburg to London, so that really it is probably in Britain already. But politicians want to be seen as compassionate, and they also want to look after their own loved ones."

"I am not sure that I have as much influence here as you seem to think. They seem a bit half-hearted about enforcing the embargo. I, myself, half want the young girls to get back for the sake of my son and his fiancee, even though we both know how dangerous another flight from the British mainland would be. You have nothing to gain personally from stopping this flight, so I ought to appreciate your call. Hmm, I have just had an idea of an alternative to this flight."

"Tell me. I am curious."

"Put all the passengers on the repatriation flight list on a small cruise ship instead. Keep the ship well out at sea, in the middle of the Atlantic, for a minimum of three weeks."

"And if they all get the virus and die, they were going to get the virus anyway, but this way they haven't spread it around the Isle of Man, and killed off everyone there. And, if they live, they could be allowed to disembark in Douglas, eventually?"

"Well, it's an idea. Look Tony thanks for your call. I shall keep trying to do the right thing at this end. I am now going to call up David Quayle. You remember, it was he who got me to ring you on Monday. His cousin, John Quayle, is a Government Minister here. I'll find out what is going on at this end somehow. It is quite a small world here. I will do what I can to get it stopped."

"I will let you get on with that then. Well, good luck!"

Vin disconnected, and then called David Quayle who was sitting at home. Vin asked, "Have you heard anything about a repatriation flight?"

David said, "Not sure where you got that from, but I have just been on the phone to my cousin John Quayle..."

Vin interjected, "Yes he said that you were cousins at that Council meeting we were both asked to attend."

"Anyway," continued David, "John told me that the Council of Ministers had a meeting, about an hour after the Emergency Advisory Committee meeting had ended. The Ministers agreed by 5 votes to 4 to allow a repatriation flight, as proposed by the UK Government. It will be leaving RAF Northolt at 2pm tomorrow. He said that it had been a strongly worded request by the UK Government, but that he suspected

Adrian Kelly had put them up to it. Adrian was the main advocate of agreeing to the flight. John saw him talking to Patrick Quinn MHK, just before the meeting"

"Oh yes, Patrick Quinn. Emma, my son's fiancee, told me she was going to contact him about trying to get her sister Sophie repatriated. I have seen him in my village a few times. He clearly is a racist. And Matthew, my son, told me that he is a religious minister for some oddball church."

"Yes, the Astrological Church. Adrian is a regular attendee at that church, and is very matey with Patrick. Also, as you know, Adrian is the brother in law of the British Prime Minister, Keith Hardy. Keith, very nobly, would like his wife Kathy to have a chance to survive here. And then there is Jack Coyle, who would probably have been keen for his son and daughter in law to have a chance to come back, even though they have jobs and a house in Slough, or Reading, or somewhere like that."

Vin decided not to mention that he knew Oliver and Emily Coyle had arrived back, and that Emily had since given birth at Nobles Hospital. He said, "I am wondering..."

David interrupted, "I'm not really having a go at you Vin, but I had the impression, earlier today, that you did not want to be involved any more. And I don't really blame you. I might have been more optimistic about the embargo working than you were during the meeting, but,with these extra 120 people arriving several days late, the chances of the virus getting here must have shot up, don't you think? Even though, according to my cousin John, Adrian and others were saying three extra days won't make any difference, the pandemic hasn't even reached Britain yet."

Vin said, "Well, it almost certainly has reached Britain, it is just that no one has manifested symptoms and died yet. Direct flights to Britain from South Africa were stopped the same day that we stopped flights from Britain to the Isle of Man. Look, I am not an epidemiologist, as has been pointed out, but one of the criteria by which they assess a pandemic is the so called R factor. That is the number of people each infected person passes his or her infection on to. With ultra pneumonia this must be very high, because otherwise some people would have been able to avoid it and survive. I think we can guess at an average R factor of about 10 a day. That is not just 10 overall, but 10 a day, which would equate to 140 in total. If we were lucky, suppose only ten people had arrived in London with the infection by Saturday. That means that by Sunday 110 people would have it, and by Monday 1210 people would have it. On Tuesday about 13,000 people have it, and we start our embargo. If none of those 13,000 people have got on a plane or boat to the Isle of Man by then, then we are okay, so far. Meanwhile, on Wednesday in Britain about 140,000 people have it, and today about one and half million. Tomorrow, when this plane takes off, that could be 11 million people who are infected. What are the chances of none of those 11 million people being amongst those 120 passengers and 8 crew on that plane? On the figures I have used, the chances of ultra pneumonia not arriving on that plane are very small. Alright, I have no idea really what the daily R figure is, so it could be much lower. And I don't know how many cases have arrived from South Africa. But, even if the number of infections in Britain by tomorrow is only 500,000 people, rather than 11 million, that has got to be about a 70 or 80% probability of someone on that plane being infected. And suppose many fewer people have the infection, so that the probability of it being brought here on that plane is say only 10% or less, should we really be taking that risk, with the future of humanity on this island at stake?"

David was feeling glum. He said, "As I said, you sounded like you didn't want to be involved any more. And if you do want to be involved, the repatriation flight will probably finish us all anyway."

"Well I did get a bit fed up. But I have been speaking to Tony Sharp. He still wants us to survive, even though he knows he himself will perish. So, now I feel I must keep trying. I was just wondering if there is any way of preventing this flight from happening. I did mention to Tony putting these passengers on a small cruise ship, and sending it out into the Atlantic for three weeks, before allowing it to dock at Douglas. Two of the passengers on the list are only 17 years old. They are the sister of Matthew's fiancee, and her friend. Could we suggest to the Government that they provide such a ship, and cancel the flight?"

David suddenly thought to himself that, maybe, there was someone who could stop the flight. He said, "I don't think our Government will cancel the flight, or provide a ship. You know, I spoke to Major Quinnel after you went from the meeting. It is a shame that the Committee would not give him specific authority to use lethal force, but that did not seem to worry him too much. This is why. He said to me that he is a commissioned officer who has sworn an oath of loyalty to His Majesty, and that his line of command is to his Colonel, in St Helens Lancashire."

"Yes, he mentioned that in the meeting," Vin agreed.

"Well, he says that his Colonel seemed very relaxed about the Major doing whatever needed doing on the island. He thought defending the island, from intruders breaching an embargo, is very similar to defending the island against enemy forces of an alien power. He thought the use of lethal force, in such circumstances could, probably, be justified as lawful in court, if it came to it. He said that, whilst he felt the Isle of Man Government owed his soldiers a moral duty to support the use of lethal force, they had no legal right to issue military orders. So, he was going to issue a specific order to all of his soldiers, that lethal force should be used in the circumstances, such as were discussed during the meeting. I am just wondering if the Major could be persuaded to try to deter the repatriation plane from landing, with the threat of lethal force. That is given that he does not seem to feel bound, necessarily, by any requirements or orders of the Isle of Man Government. So, what I am saying to you Vin is that, maybe, we should sound out the Major."

"So, one of us needs to speak to Major Quinnel urgently. But wouldn't it be great if we could offer some of the Manx people, still in Britain, the chance that I mentioned?"

"You mean on some sort of commandeered ship to sail out into the Atlantic, and only come back here after three weeks, if they are still alive?" said David, to clarify what Vin was referring to.

"Yes. Although I don't really like the idea of anyone coming to us from anywhere at all for the foreseeable future, it would be good, if in the process of saving mankind, we also retain our humanity. I think after three weeks it should be safe, if we can be certain the ship has been at sea without any physical contact with other ships, planes or helicopters. But,

I have no idea how we would get this organised, especially as both Governments have agreed to this flight tomorrow."

"So you were serious about what could be a death cruise then. I suppose that would not be that different from dying on land. But, the key thing is stopping this flight somehow isn't it?"

"Yes that's right," agreed Vin, trying hard not to think about how Emma would feel.

"Alright let's think about your cruise later. I will phone Major Quinnel now, to see if he is willing to put his neck on the line, and if there is any sort of initiative he can come up with."

"You mean taking control of the control tower at Ronaldsway, and ordering the plane to turn away? That sort of thing?"

"Yes, I suppose that is the sort of thing that might work."

"Good luck, perhaps you could let me know what he says?"

"Okay," agreed David, "I will ring you back. Are you still coming tomorrow evening?"

"Yes we are. I have told Martha, who is looking forward to it, so there is no getting out of it now!"

"Tell her we look forward to seeing her, even if she brings you with her! See you then."

Vin said, "Yes see you then." He hung up.

Martha had heard some of what Vin had been saying during his two telephone conversations. She said to him, "Sounds to me like we are talking about some sort of armed revolt. I suppose these are desperate times with a lot at stake."

"It is desperate isn't it? David and I are now basically conspiring to interfere with what will be lawful aviation," replied Vin.

Martha said, "I don't want this going to your head Vin, but maybe I respect what you are doing." She gave him a hug. Then she said, "You were saying about cruise ships, well, I would mention something, but it would probably be a long shot."

Vin encouraged her, "Well, you are quite often spot on with the comments you make, so don't go shy on me now."

"The Lieutenant Governor, Sir Hugh Whitlock; you know, I am sure he is part of the Whitlock shipping dynasty. His family built up a cargo shipping business, and then they diversified into the cruise holiday business, with a company called Senior Sailing," Martha told him.

"I see where you are going," said Vin. "All we need is for someone, on good terms with Sir Hugh, to ask him to use his influence, to get Senior Sailing to make a cruise ship available for a three week cruise, starting somewhere in Britain tomorrow, and terminating in Douglas three weeks later, if they are lucky?"

Martha said, "Well, I did say it would be a long shot. But, would it hurt for someone to ask him? You have just said these are desperate times. I really want Matt and Emma and our grandchild to survive, so I agree about stopping the plane, if the Major is able and willing to do that. But it would be great for Emma to know we have done what we can for her sister. Cruise companies must surely have been busy cancelling cruises because of the ultra pneumonia virus, so there might be a ship available, you never know. And as for someone who knows Sir Hugh, well you do. You met him three days ago."

Vin responded, "But I wouldn't say I was on good terms with him! We have to assume, at the moment, that he knows about the flight and supports it. Even supposing he would talk to me, we can't very well ask him to organise a cruise ship for a group of people, who are supposed to be flying in tomorrow. Let's wait till we hear about Major Quinnel."

Forty minutes later the telephone rang. Vin answered it. He recognised the voice of Major Quinnel. Major Quinnel spoke, "Hello, that's Vin Singh isn't it. It's Major Peter Quinnel. You knew that David Quayle was going to be speaking to me just now, didn't you?"

Vin said, "Yes I recognised your voice, Major. But I was expecting to hear back from David."

Major Quinnel said, "Please call me Peter. I told David I wanted to speak to you myself. You know that he wants me to stop an authorised repatriation plane from landing at Ronaldsway, tomorrow afternoon?"

"Yes, he seemed to think you might be able and willing to do that."

"That depends really on what you say to me now."

"How do you mean? What do you want me to say?

Peter told him, "I love my country, which I think of as Britain. I was born in County Down in Northern Ireland. Some of the most loyal citizens of the United Kingdom live in Northern Ireland. But I am also very attached to Mann, my wife is a Manxwoman and we had a daughter born here. I am a loyal, part time, member of His Majesty's Armed Forces, which exist to defend the whole British realm, meaning the United Kingdom and the Crown Dependencies. I think I made it clear at the Emergency Committee meeting, after you left, that I would do the right thing about unauthorised people, arriving by boat or light aircraft. But, now we are talking about a normal commercial aeroplane carrying 120 people, on an approved flight."

"So you won't help stop it then?" questioned Vin.

Peter felt Vin was not being very helpful. He said, "You don't make this easy do you? I am amazed that anyone ever does what you say."

Vin exclaimed, "Well, what do you want me to say? Do you think I actually like the idea of the younger sister of my son's fiancee being forced to stay away? Do you think I have dreamed up the threat posed by this ultra pneumonia virus? Do you think I enjoy telling everyone, over and over again, what will happen if we don't enforce an embargo. Major, sorry Peter, I will just say that, if we let this plane land there is a significant risk that it will be carrying an infected person. I don't know the true probabilities. It might be as high as an 80% risk, or perhaps as low as 2%. But, even if it is only 2%, it is not a justified risk. If there is just one person on that aeroplane who has been infected, we all will die. Maybe it is here already, I don't know. Maybe, someone else will get here illegally who is infected. I just know that we need to stop this plane, and I hoped you were the man to do that."

Peter asked, "And what if we have to shoot it down over the sea?"

"If that is the only way, yes!" responded Vin.

Peter told him, "Well, I have a plan, so I don't think that will be necessary. But I need to get the plan rubberstamped by Sir Hugh Whitlock."

"But I thought you weren't going to do it?

"It depended on what you said."

"So I convinced you then?"

"Let us put it this way, Vin. You are an expert microbiologist, and I have to assume what you say about this virus is correct. I just wanted to know that you were convinced yourself that stopping the flight is the right thing to do, and despite your anguish, you clearly are convinced."

"Did you say you have to get your plan rubberstamped by the Lieutenant Governor?"

"Yes. Look, don't worry too much. I have already spoken to him on the telephone, because it is nice to get some official sanction, if possible. We know each other a little bit, because of ceremonial occasions over recent years. He has got his wife and grown up children on the island. I thought he would probably support me. He said that the Chief Minister had not seemed very happy about this flight. He even asked how you would feel about a repatriation flight breaching the embargo, you had put so much effort into getting approved. I am meeting him at 9.30 tonight."

"I would like to see him as well. I wonder if I could come along at the same time?" asked Vin.

"Why? I am not sure Sir Hugh would like you just turning up. And I think really my plan should not be disclosed to anyone, other than people with a need to know."

"It is just that I am hoping he might help come up with an alternative destination for the plane, if you manage to turn it away."

Peter commented, "Really, and then what would happen to the passengers?"

" I ought to talk about it to Sir Hugh first."

"Okay, maybe I don't need to know what you have in mind. I guess, as he knows you, and he knows that you are so committed to this embargo, he will see you. Just try not to upset him, please. We really do need his support."

"If we come up with an alternative, you will need to know, so that directions can be given to the pilot," Vin told him.

Peter said, "Right, I need to go soon. I am a bit further away than you. I have got an old Jag with 222 in the number plate. I will tell them you are with me, on the intercom outside Government House. Meet me there, and just follow me in."

Chapter 16, Thursday 8 April 2027

Peter and Vin were ushered into Sir Hugh's drawing room at 9.35pm. He said, "Hello Peter, and hello Vin, I wasn't expecting to see you again so soon."

Vin said, "Thank you for seeing me Sir Hugh. The news of the spread of the ultra pneumonia virus is terrifying. You probably know that fatalities have started in South Africa, and in my view, given that flights continued between London and Johannesburg until Tuesday, it is almost certainly on the British mainland now. It may have already got here on Mann, but allowing more people in now is folly."

Sir Hugh said, "Well, a majority of Manx ministers might not think that, but apart from the Major here and me, I can tell you of one other person who agrees with you." He looked at Peter and Vin. He thought he saw understanding in Peter's face, but Vin looked puzzled. He went on, "I am talking about His Majesty the King. He was gracious enough to talk to me for 15 minutes, when I asked to speak to him urgently, just 30 minutes ago. He is definitely of the view that the Isle of Man's embargo is the best slim chance there is, of the survival of mankind. Now, according to Bageholt, constitutionally the King's role with regard to Government is mainly advisory. But the constitution in the United Kingdom is unwritten, as it is with the Isle of Man, and is subject to development, adaptation, and interpretation, especially in times of grave emergency. Anyway, His Majesty said that a major threat to the continuation of human life, in any part of his Realm, could be regarded as a Defence issue. He said that, constitutionally, the Manx Government has no role in Defence matters, but he questioned what moral right the UK Government had to impose a major risk to the security of this small part of the Realm, the Isle of Man, when the people of the Isle of Man have no part in choosing the UK Government. Do you see? He was saying, on the one hand, the Isle of Man Government is not allowed any say in the defence of the Isle of Man, but on the other hand what right does the UK Government have to prevent the defence of the island? He concluded that, in these exceptional times, any officer with the King's Commission on the Isle of Man was entitled to look to his Sovereign for direct authority to act in the defence of the Isle of Man. And you, Major, are such an officer."

Peter said, "But the Isle of Man Government has approved this repatriation flight. So the British Government aren't really preventing us from defending the island, are they Sir Hugh?"

"They did put some pressure on," Sir Hugh responded. "They may have helped with supplies and patrols, but the PM was pretty keen for his wife to have a chance to survive. The Council of Ministers were under a lot of pressure internally as well, with friends and relatives demanding a repatriation flight. Leaving aside constitutional questions, I think the three of us can agree it was a very poor decision. When the Chief Minister phoned to inform me about a flight having been approved, he sounded pretty disgusted himself. Look, I wouldn't normally intervene, but these are exceptional times.

Peter, I can't make you carry out that plan we talked about, but I can tell you that some of us would admire you for it."

Peter replied, "I won't be doing it for admiration, but because it is the right thing to do. Is it the right thing Vin?"

Vin said, "If the plan is to stop the repatriation plane landing here tomorrow, then yes it is."

Peter looked at Sir Hugh, and said, "And you accept that if necessary, if all else has failed, we can use lethal force?"

Sir Hugh said, "Yes, use of lethal force is authorised. You have come to me for that authority. The written military order to you as a commissioned officer, that I have signed on behalf of the Crown, specifically authorises that. And I was like you, I wanted some official back up. So I have got mine from the King. It is only in the form of an attachment to an email, but I have attached a copy of it to the order which I am giving you."

"Do you want me to run through my plans with you again?" Peter enquired.

Sir Hugh said, "No, you are the soldier, not me. You just carry on, do whatever needs to be done, and I will back you and your chaps to the hilt afterwards. Will you have time to brief your chaps?"

Peter explained, "Some of the chaps are female actually, but they are all good people. We have people at the airport all of the time now, but I have warned some others for a briefing in the morning. Sir Hugh, it seems to me we have a better chance of avoiding the use of lethal force, if we can offer some alternative hope to the passengers on the plane. And I think that is why Vin wanted to see you."

Sir Hugh looked at Vin, and said, "What idea have you got in mind?"

Vin said, "Well, it seems to me that there is some small chance that no one on that plane will be infected. To be forced to return, and to remain on the British mainland, gives them no hope. However, if we could put them on a ship for 3 weeks quarantine at sea, well, if they are still alive at the end of that time, they could safely be allowed to disembark in Douglas."

"Well, yours is the most expert opinion on the island. If you think that would be safe, then it sounds all right, I suppose." responded Sir Hugh.

Vin said, "Sir Hugh, I actually think the balance of probabilities is that they won't survive, but at least the three of us in this room will be vindicated. And a ship does give them hope. We know that stopping this plane from landing is the right thing to do, but it will be hard to live with hostility from other people. To be honest, my son's fiancee has a sister who will probably be on that plane. If I can prove to her that, in the end, she did not lose her sister because of me..."

"I see what you are saying," Sir Hugh agreed. "So it is just a case of whistling up a crewed and provisioned ship at a few hours notice, ready to sail off into the Atlantic, and probably for everyone on it to die out there?"

Vin just nodded and looked at Sir Hugh.

Sir Hugh said, "Oh I see. You have heard about my family's shipping interests. Hmm... By strange coincidence, I was speaking to my brother Randolph this afternoon. He is the Chairman of the Senior Sailing company. I think he phoned me because he was interested about the embargo by the Isle of Man, or perhaps he thought that we should talk, while we still could. He thinks that Britain and most places are doomed, and he was saying how impressed he was that we had acted so quickly. Anyway, he was saying that the three ships of the

Senior Sailing line are now all being tied up because of the ultra pneumonia virus. They had learned to act quickly, from problems they had during the Coronavirus outbreak. So, let's give him a ring. I will just pop in the other room. You two help yourself to a drink from the drinks cabinet."

Peter and Vin fell silent. Then Vin suddenly said, "I am being a bit nosy, but did you say on the phone that you 'had' a daughter, rather than that you 'have' a daughter?"

"She died a few months ago. She was only 15 years old. My wife and I have struggled to get on since. I am not sure I really want to talk about it," replied Peter.

Vin decided to tell Peter about his own daughter. He said, "We lost our only daughter, Jessica, when she was a baby. It was a cot death. As a doctor, I felt I should not have allowed it to happen. We had a five years old son as well, who is now 28. His name is Matthew and his girlfriend, sorry that should be his fiancee, is expecting. So, I suppose we were lucky to still have a son, but it affected our relationship badly at the time. I probably ought to have talked about it more, but I didn't want to open up to anyone."

Peter commented, "Well, at least you still have your son. Gemma was our only child."

There was another gap in the conversation, before Vin said, "So you weren't born here then, Peter?"

Peter replied, "No, like I said to you on the phone, I was born in County Down in Northern Ireland. Part of the Loyalist community if you like. I have only got an Irish surname because there was a mixed marriage, on my paternal grandparents' side. I came to the Isle of Man with my parents, when I was 11 years old. They bought the farm which I now own, Ballabeg Farm, near Kirk Michael. They wanted to get away from the Troubles. It was before the Good Friday agreement."

Vin was a bit perplexed. He asked, "Did you say your grandparents had a mixed marriage?"

Peter replied, "Yes Catholic and Protestant. Republican and Loyalist. Basically they are two different races, the original Irish, and the plantation Anglo-Scots."

"That's amazing. I didn't know that. I have never taken much notice of Northern Ireland."

"No, most people outside Northern Ireland don't. The great thing about the Isle of Man, compared with there, is that here nobody seems to care about anyone's religion or background very much, although there does seem to have been an increase in Manx nationalism."

"I think I am of mixed descent myself. I obviously look Asian, but I was told one of my great grandfathers was white. You know, in the days of the British Raj, there was quite a bit of intermarriage."

"Presumably, you weren't born here on Mann?"

"I was born in London. I met my wife at university in England, but she is Manx. When I was looking for my first consultancy post there was a vacancy at Nobles Hospital. I got the position, and we are still here."

Sir Hugh re-emerged twenty minutes later. He said, "Some absolutely amazing luck! The Senior Serenade is tied up in Liverpool right now. It is a small passenger cruiser, but can take 300 plus passengers, as well as crew. It was due to sail on a three week cruise tomorrow, but that was cancelled yesterday. It is well provisioned, but would need more frozen supplies, assuming it won't be calling anywhere. My brother is willing to make it available, if they can get the captain, or one of his officers with a masters certificate, to sail it, and if we can get sufficient of the crew to man it. They were all due to sail tomorrow anyway, but we must expect some of the British members of the crew not to want to leave their homes and families now. As for the cost, he said the business has ample liquidity to cover it, and he thought nobody would be alive to worry about money very soon anyway. He was worried about whether the British Government would attempt to intervene, but I said I thought this was unlikely, especially if nobody tells them what is happening."

Peter said, "So, we could direct the flight to divert to John Lennon airport in Liverpool? I would expect the aeroplane to have enough fuel for that. And, presumably, some coaches would be laid on to take the passengers?"

Sir Hugh said, "Yes, they would surely have enough fuel to get to Liverpool. I forgot to mention the coaches to Randolph. I will ring him again. He will probably have worked it out himself, but I would be surprised if getting a few coaches laid on, for the transfer from the airport to the docks, will be a major problem."

Chapter 17, Friday 9 April 2027

Major Peter Quinnel arrived at the airport at 1.40pm. He was accompanied by Private Willie Moore, and followed by a bombardier and two gunners in a lorry towing a 105mm artillery gun. His Reservists had managed to keep the perimeter roads closed between 8am and 6pm on Wednesday two days earlier, when four RAF transport aeroplanes, on two return flights each, had flown in a variety of supplies. Peter had been told by his Colonel that the RAF had specialist units for delivering supplies, called the Air Mobility Force, but he was not overconcerned with such details. He just had a general faith in the British Armed Forces to respond to emergencies, and he was proud to be a part time member of the British Army. As envisaged, the planes had arrived with their own personnel and fork lift trucks, and the unloading had been done with no airport staff, or anyone else, being present at all. Daniel Clague had managed to secure storage facilities within the airport perimeter, including refrigerated units for medicines and drugs, and it had all seemed to go smoothly.

The Reservists had continued to guard the airport after the RAF flights had finished. Essential personnel had been allowed back in, and the air controllers were aware that no landings or take-offs of any kind were permitted. That was until special permission had been given for the repatriation flight, expected to arrive about an hour later at around 2.45pm on Friday 9 April 2027, three days after the airport had originally closed for traffic, and the embargo had commenced. Peter reflected that their operation on Tuesday had been in co-operation with the civil power, but, this time, what he intended could bring conflict with police and others. Not everyone would be appreciating military power overriding a government decision. So be it, he had the Lieutenant Governor's support, and also Dr Singh's, about whose views he realised he attached a lot of importance. He also thought that the most important aspect was that he and his Reservists were doing what was right.

Peter spoke to his sergeant, Sue Walker, at the vehicle entrance to the airside of the airport. "Hello Sergeant, all well?" he asked.

Sergeant Walker replied, "Hello sir, yes all things considered."

"Apart from me and the private, and the bombardier and two gunners behind us, there should be two corporals and four privates deployed by you already. Is that right?

"Yes sir that is correct. Are we still going ahead with the plan you briefed us on earlier?"

"Yes we are, although we obviously can't be completely sure how this is going to pan out. So this piece of equipment, being towed by the vehicle behind me by Bombardier Cain and Gunners Brown and Shimmin, needs to be positioned for easy access to the runway. I know the repatriation plane won't even have left Northolt yet, but people might be turning up to meet passengers on the plane, sooner or later. The terminal building is to remain closed. Can you tell the two lads and their female corporal, that I see you have patrolling there, that they are not to say too much. Tell them the line is, 'We have been instructed that the airport is closed until further notice, and that no-one is to be admitted, without prior notification of authorisation to do so.' Tell them that they have received no confirmation that a plane is due to arrive, and they can't comment on rumours. People are not allowed to linger under an Order issued under the Emergency Powers Act 1936, (but if they sit in their cars in the car park nearby we will take no notice). Sooner or later they will get an awkward customer, but your lads and corporal have got their weapons, and they are just going to have to stick with the script. I know you have a separate radio channel for your six people, but I want you to to keep your ears open for channel 2, for possibly more urgent communications with me, or with the bombardier and his two gunners on the runway."

"Sir, can I just ask, um..."

"Yes Sergeant, what is it?"

"It's just that I have heard that this flight has been authorised by our Government. Do we have authority to stop it? It's only going to carry our own Manx people, who live here anyway. Is that right sir?"

"We are members of His Majesty's Armed Forces, and we are acting under orders of His Majesty. And it is definitely our duty to follow those orders. Yet, we are also proud Manx people, and yes, these people on the plane are Manx people. Some of the people on the plane are probably friends or relatives of some of our group. But, you know this ultra pneumonia virus is the worst enemy anyone has ever faced. So, Sergeant it is simple really, the arrival of these passengers could be the end of life on this island, and possibly anywhere in the world. I think you understand that. I need to count on you Sergeant. Sue, tell me I can count on you. We really are not doing this for fun."

"Yes sir. I do understand really. I just needed some reassurance. You can count on me, but you need to be able to count on the Gunners too."

"We all like reassurance. As for the Bombardier and the Gunners, they just love playing with their big toy, so I think we will be alright there."

"Yes they do, but they haven't had any practice for over six months. Let's hope they remember how to do it, sir."

"Well, I hope we won't need to find out. With any luck, they won't need to fire it."

Peter parked his vehicle, as the Gunners behind drove towards the airside of the terminal building. The Major and Private Moore walked towards the control tower. Peter said to Private Moore, "Your weapon is loaded isn't it, Private?"

"Yes sir, but I won't have to use it, will I?" replied Private Moore.

Peter stopped walking, and looked at Private Moore. He could not remember, exactly, how old his records said Willie Moore was. He was sure he must be his youngest member. He looked like he was about 19 years old, and he thought that Private Willie Moore still lived with his Mum, in a flat in Douglas. Peter said to him, "I know you heard your conversation with Sergeant Walker, so you know how important this is. It may be that not everyone in the Control tower will understand the need to turn this plane away, but I need them to realise that they have no choice. So, I need you to look like you would have no hesitation in shooting someone, if I were to give you that order. Look me in the eye, and imagine that I am repeatedly punching your mother!"

Private Moore looked into his Major's eyes, and imagined his mother being punched by him. He felt his eyes narrow, and his mouth tighten.

Peter exclaimed, "That's it! You've got it! Keep a serious face anyway, and keep your weapon ready in both hands at waist height, pointing sideways. And, if anyone does start getting argumentative, remember that mental image."

They went up to the door of the Control tower, which was a separate building from the passenger terminal. Major Quinnel was not surprised to find a keypad control and intercom. He decided to try the intercom. A male voice answered, "Yes who is it?"

Peter replied, "Hello, it's Major Peter Quinnel of the Army Reserve. We have taken over security of the airport since Tuesday's embargo..."

The male voice said, "Yes I heard. Do you want to come up? Most VIPs who come here like to have a look from the tower. I will buzz you in. There is no one in the ground floor level radar tracking room, so just get in the lift, and I will meet you up here."

They went up in the lift about 15 metres to the Control room, with its clear lines of vision along the runway running on an axis of about 265 and 85 degrees, or on a line running from just slightly south of westwards, to just slightly north of eastwards, towards the Irish Sea. The eastern end of the runway ended at a low cliff, just above the sea. Peter saw two men sitting at panels, below two massive windows facing that direction. The older looking one stood up. He said to Peter, " I am wondering why you are here, apart from to enjoy the view? Has the Government changed its mind again? On Tuesday I was here, when the Chief Constable gave us an order requiring the airport to close. Then on Wednesday, it was okay for the RAF to fly in and out, without anyone in the Control room, or on the airport at all. And this morning, we were told to come in, and get ready for a one-off repatriation flight, from RAF Northolt, with call sign VARF. A police sergeant brought the order in, just so there could be no doubt. After all ..."

Peter interrupted, "I will explain. As I said on the intercom, my Army Reserve has been supervising this airport continuously since the embargo. You would have had to get past some of my lads and lasses to get in this morning. By the way, I mentioned my name, Major Peter Quinnel, so can I ask yours?"

The man replied, "I am Sam White the senior controller, and this is Harry Blake, who is the only other controller on duty. I knew you Army Reservists were watching the airport, but this is the first time you guys have been in the Control tower, isn't it?" He looked briefly at Private Moore touting his weapon. "Wait a minute is this some sort of coup? Why do you need the armed escort?"

Peter said, "As I said, I will explain. The Government took a decision under some pressure internally, but also under duress from the British Government, to allow a repatriation flight. This was contrary to expert opinion by the British Government's Chief Medical Officer, and by our own renowned microbiologist Dr Vihan Singh, that further admissions of people to Mann would present a very serious risk. The risk being that the ultra pneumonia virus would be introduced, and thereby result in human life on the island being eliminated. The decision to allow this flight has not been formally overturned, but I have received what I consider to be a lawful order from the Lieutenant Governor, endorsed by His Majesty the King. The order is to make whatever interventions I consider necessary, to protect that part of His Majesty's Realm known as the Isle of Man from mortal danger, in particular from the ultra pneumonia virus. I can show you that order, if you wish, but, on the basis of that order, I am now demanding your co-operation, in getting this flight turned away. And no, we are not overthrowing the Government, even if I might think some of them are a bit useless!"

Sam responded, "Well Major, I don't think I am going to worry whether you have got a lawful order, or an unlawful one, or maybe just acting on a whim. You have a man with a weapon standing there, and we are going to do whatever you say. Off the record, I personally wasn't happy anyway about Mann being exposed to another 120 people, any of whom could be carrying this virus. But, if questioned about this later, I will have to say that Harry and I were acting under duress."

Just then Harry Blake spoke up, "Bloody hell Major, that looks like an Army lorry on the runway, towing an artillery piece along behind it. Are you planning to shoot the plane down?"

Peter looked out towards the east. He could see the full length of the runway, with the Gunners' lorry about a quarter of the way along it. He said to both men, "Well, the idea is we persuade the captain to turn around before they get close enough for that. That 105mm gun has a range of less than 15 kilometres at ground level, much less than that, if the target is at say 20,000 feet height. So, if we make radio contact with them, and they co-operate, let's hope it won't be necessary! Oh, by the way, we have managed to lay on a 300-berth cruise ship, with a crew and supplies. This will be an option only meant for the passengers on the plane. It will sail from Liverpool. There will even be four coaches waiting to transfer them from John Lennon Airport to Liverpool Docks, and then to board the Senior Serenade ship tied up there."

"So, will it just have to anchor offshore for a bit?" asked Sam.

"Dr Singh thinks a 3 week quarantine period well away from any land is required, so it will have to go out into the Atlantic. Now, can you tell me what the normal procedure is, for establishing contact with a plane coming into Ronaldsway?"

"Well, for a flight from anywhere in London, it is under air traffic control from NATS at Swanwick, most of the way. The airspace in the Irish Sea around the Isle of Man, however, comes under NATS at Prestwick in Scotland. So, roughly speaking, when it reaches the Lancashire coast, it would be handed over to Prestwick. But, at more or less the same time, it would be given a lower flight path by Prestwick, and Prestwick would ask us to establish contact with the plane, and take over control."

"So, for how long in advance of a plane landing here would you be in contact with it?"

"It varies a bit according to the flight path, the speed of the aircraft, and at what point Prestwick contact us, but generally speaking ten to twelve minutes."

"Here's what I want you to do. Don't indicate to anyone, Swanwick, Prestwick, or anyone else, there is any problem with the flight landing at Ronaldsway. That is, not until you have radio contact with the plane, and responsibility for air control of it. We are not seeking any unnecessary confrontation with anyone, which might happen if the plane has too much warning. Once you have established contact, you are to say to the captain of the plane that Ronaldsway is now under military control, the aircraft is refused permission to land, and that I, Major Peter Quinnel, will speak directly to him or her. So please show me where I can sit, and what I need to do to do to talk to the pilot myself."

"Okay! Will you be telling the captain to fly to John Lennon airport, and will you explain about the ship?"

"Yes, although we could not risk warning John Lennon airport, in advance. There should be some coaches laid on by Senior Sailing, sitting there waiting. And I have a telephone number for the airport to use, to contact the ship's master, if they want to confirm the onward travel arrangements for the passengers, if I can put it that way. It will all be fine."

Harry stood up, and intervened in a loud voice, "This diversion has not been approved by our Government, or by the UK Government has it? It sounds illegal to me, and very cavalier for your Army Reserve to be driving down our runway with a piece of artillery which, for all I know, you intend to use. I think you should all leave, before this goes too far."

Peter responded, "The cavalier behaviour is that of the two Governments agreeing to this flight, three days after the embargo started, potentially bringing extinction to this island." He noticed that Private Moore had moved closer to Harry Blake, that the barrel of his SA80 weapon was three inches higher than before, and that he was giving Harry the same look that the Major had got from him earlier. "Good lad," thought Peter.

Peter turned to Sam saying, "Right, I can't really trust Harry. We don't want to have to shoot anyone, but I require both you and Harry to remain in your seats all the time, until this flight has been dealt with. Give me the keys for this room please."

Sam indicated to them, on a hook nearby. Peter took them, and went and locked the door. He came back and said, "If anyone needs the loo, ask before getting up. You will have to take this bin over to the corner, and use that."

Peter then looked out of the enormous windows again, and saw that the artillery lorry had got to the eastern end of the runway. He decided to call his Gunners up on his radio. He said to Bombardier Cain, "I can see where you are, from the control tower. I thought you were just going to pull over somewhere, with easy access to the runway."

Bombardier Cain answered, "Well, there was nowhere obvious to wait, so we ended up driving onto the runway and... Well, I thought it would make sense to drive right to the end, and check it out so to speak. We'll move straight back now, if that's your order, but sir, it seems to me that this would be a good position. The plane's pilot, if it hasn't turned around, he will see us, as soon as he sees the airport. Our line of fire will be the same as his approach. We would be able to fire off those warning shots you talked about."

Peter thought to himself that the positioning made sense. He said, "Okay make the gun ready where you are. Remind me, how many shells do you have?"

"Just four sir."

"Okay! Get ready, and await further orders."

"Yes sir!"

Peter wondered if Bombardier Cain sounded a bit too enthusiastic. He thought, "Not much I can do about that now. Chances are that the plane will turn away anyway, when I speak to the Captain. If not, I will make sure that Bombardier Cain remembers that he is not aiming to shoot the plane down, without a specific direct order from me."

Peter asked Sam, "So, you agree that this planeload of people represents a serious hazard to our survival on this island?"

"Yes I do, but having not been given any authority to turn the flight away, I just need to re-iterate, I am co-operating because there is an armed soldier in the Control room, and I have no real choice," replied Sam.

"Actually, there are two armed soldiers, because I also have my Glock pistol. So, just to confirm, you will do as I say?"

"Yes that's right."

"We are expecting this plane to arrive at about 2.45pm, correct?"

"Yes, but we should have direct verbal contact with the flight crew about ten minutes before that, as we said earlier."

" Okay, let's just go over it again. No saying to anyone that there is any problem about the airport, or the flight landing. Okay?"

"Yes, fine."

"Only when you have been given air traffic control of the plane, do you say about the airport being under military control, the airport being closed, and handing over to me Major Peter Quinnel."

"Yes, got that."

"And, once I have persuaded the plane to divert to John Lennon Airport, you and Harry can contact whoever necessary, about air traffic control for the flight path to John Lennon, and about landing there. I will obviously be willing to talk if necessary, but that is the arrangement that gives these passengers some hope of a future, so it would be useful if you could be persuasive about this as well."

Things went fairly quiet in the Control Room, for a while. Then Sergeant Walker called Peter up on the radio. She said, "Sir, I have got a uniformed police sergeant with me. He is demanding admission to the airport. And our lads round the front of the terminal building have been reporting some hostility from people, presumably relatives and friends of the passengers. Word must have got out about our intervention. Anyone on the coastal path, between the runway and the sea, can see our 105mm gun, 20 metres away."

Peter replied, "Okay Sergeant, it sounds like you are being kept busy. Let the police officer speak to me on your radio."

A male voice came through on Peter's radio, "Hello Major. I am Police Sergeant John Christian. We have had ministers and MHKs on to us, saying they think you are going to stop a repatriation flight landing, despite it having lawful authority. And I have been told you have a piece of artillery at the end of the runway. Is this true? And where are you?"

Peter replied, "Well Sergeant Christian, as part of a combined effort, involving my people, your people, and others like the Coastguard and the Civil Defence, we are trying to stop anyone from breaking the embargo, and entering the island. I seem to have been given particular responsibility to safeguard the airport. As for authority to stop this particular plane, I have a general duty to defend the King's Realm against mortal threat, and this plane, most definitely, is a mortal threat. Also, I have specific authority from the Lieutenant Governor acting on behalf of His Majesty King, which has been specifically endorsed by His Majesty. The Isle of Man Government has no authority over the Army Reserve. I am hoping this ends without bloodshed. We do have artillery. It's a 105mm gun, but it is not my intention for the plane to be shot down, and I am also very keen to avoid any sort of shoot out with armed police. Listen Sergeant, I am not meaning to be rude, but whereas I am the most senior Army person on the island, you are not the most senior police officer. I doubt if authorisation, for armed police to take on the Army, would be given any lower down the chain than the Chief Constable himself, Terry Corps. Before Terry does that, he might want to speak to me. Hold on a moment."

Peter turned to Sam, to ask, "Do we have a phone that can be dialled directly from outside?"

Sam replied, "Yes this one, the number is on its stand."

Peter spoke again to Police Sergeant Christian, "The direct number is 202167. I prefer land lines, don't you? It is the Control tower, which is where I am, to answer your last question. The call needs to be soon, because I might be a bit preoccupied in 15 minutes time. Oh, in the meantime, please can you move 400 metres away from the entrance. Thank you."

At 2.30pm the telphone rang. Peter asked Sam to put it on "hands free".

Peter said, "Hello Major Quinnel here. Presumably that is Terry Corps?"

Terry replied, "Hello Peter. Do you know, I had some idea you might do this? You personally are in the Control tower at Ronaldsway, and your men are on the runway, with a piece of artillery, which is pointing out to sea in the direction of any approaching aircraft. Is that right?"

"That's right. Very succinctly put. Listen Terry, we don't have long to chat. I am going to be busy soon."

"Look Peter, whatever you and I think about the wisdom of a repatriation flight, what you are doing is illegal. Please order your men to tow their gun away immediately, and you come out of the Control tower, and let the controllers get on with their job."

"You know we are not going to do that, and I think you would be disappointed if we did, because I believe that you know we are doing the right thing. I do have the authority of the Crown, and I would put up a damn good fight in court to say that I was acting lawfully. And it is not a military coup. I will be too busy to govern the island, as I have got a farm to run. But lawfulness isn't really relevant. I know some university types would call this an existential crisis, but it is more than life or death. Looking at the news, and listening to Dr Singh, even if he does get very agitated, it could be a question of the survival of the human race. So, to repeat, we are not leaving just yet."

"I need to resolve this somehow, and I have to weigh up the immediate and short term risk to human life, putting concern about the virus to one side. Two things, are the controllers free to leave and under no threat, and can you guarantee not to fire your shells at the aircraft?" asked Terry.

Harry Blake had been listening to this on the phone speaker, and he had not been physically restrained. He stood up and shouted out, "The door is locked. We can't even go to the toilet, and there is an unfriendly looking soldier, holding a bloody great weapon, as well as the Major, who has got a gun as well."

Private Moore said, "Hold this please sir," and he gave the Major his weapon. He pushed Harry hard back into his chair and said loudly, "Don't move again, unless we say so. Got it?"

Terry called out, "What's going on Peter, are the controllers alright?"

Peter replied, "You can speak to one now if you like," and he indicated for Sam to talk.

Sam said, "Hello, I'm Sam White, senior controller, and the other voice you heard was Harry Blake, also a controller. We're fine really. They haven't hurt either of us. Yes, the door is locked, but I think the Major will let us out soon."

Peter spoke again, "So, we are not going to hurt anyone. And the 105mm gun won't be used to shoot down the plane." He did not voice the 'if we can help it,' that he thought. He looked at his watch, and spoke to Terry again, "Terry, I have got to cut you off soon, and concentrate on speaking to the incoming plane. I don't think a shoot out between police and Army Reservists this afternoon is what you want, and probably it won't help you get this plane landed here. If it makes things any easier for you, I promise to co-operate fully in any enquiry, or investigation, into what we have been doing here today."

Terry replied, "Very well, I am going to have to trust you, and hope you don't drag me down with you. Let the controllers go within the hour, and make yourself available for a formal interview at our HQ building in Douglas, tomorrow morning at 9.30."

Peter said, "Very well," and then he disconnected.

He gave Private Moore his weapon back. The SA80 weapon was quite an impressive looking piece of kit, but he thought to himself that, if Private Moore could have had his own Glock instead, it might have been less 'over the top'. He said to Private Moore, "Take our friend Harry to sit right over in the corner there, and if he gets up, or says, or does anything, without your say so, I will leave it to you to decide how to deal with him, as I expect to be busy. Are you okay with that Private?"

"Yes sir, no problem at all," replied Private Moore, whilst looking intently at Harry.

Harry had heard this, and he was feeling and looking much more timid. He quietly went over to a corner with Private Moore, and sat where he was told.

Peter said to Sam, "It is a shame your colleague couldn't have just accepted the situation, like you did. We really don't want any rough stuff."

"Yes, he does get a bit excitable sometimes. Not really a good quality to have, for an air traffic controller," responded Sam.

Peter started saying, "I want..." He stopped when he heard a male voice through the speakers saying, "Ronaldsway Approach, are you receiving?"

Sam answered, "Caller, this is Ronaldsway Approach. Please identify yourself."

The male voice said, "This is flight VARF, at altitude 18,500, approaching from 155 degrees approximately 35 kilometres distance, current speed 310kph. Requesting..."

Sam had been looking at Peter, looking at him. Sam said to the aircraft, "I have to advise that the Isle of Man Airport is under military control, and that it is closed to all traffic. I am now handing you over to Major Peter Quinnel."

Peter said, "Hello flight VARF, this is Major Peter Quinnel. Please confirm that you understand that this airport is closed, and that you must divert. I have information about your new destination, and alternative plans for your passengers, when you are ready."

The male voice responded disbelievingly, "What is this? Is this some sort of illegal stunt? If you are not really Ronaldsway Approach Control, I suggest you get off the radio now. You are jeopardising the safety of an aeroplane carrying 120 passengers and 8 crew."

Major Quinnel said, "This is completely serious, and I need you to confirm that you will turn away, as soon as you are given a new course. I am Major Quinnel, as you were told. I have orders that this airport is to remain closed to all traffic. Please confirm that you understand, that you are denied permission to land at this airport."

The speakers went quiet for about thirty seconds. Peter felt even more anxious than before. He said to Sam, "If I call them, they will hear won't they?"

Sam confirmed, "Yes the channel is definitely open."

Peter said, "Flight VARF, please confirm that you have understood. The airport is closed. You are denied permission to land. I have alternative arrangements for your passengers."

The same male voice was heard again, "My first officer James Quirk knows you. You are a sheep farmer, near Kirk Michael on the west coast aren't you? Must be a long drive for you, in to Douglas, for drill on a Wednesday evening, mustn't it? Because you are just a part time pretend soldier, aren't

Philip Kelly

you? A bit like that Captain in that old TV programme, except that you say that you are a Major..."

Peter, "You mean Captain Mainwaring, but we don't have time for insults..."

From the speakers again, "Listen Major. This is a Vannin Airlines aircraft and crew. We were due to fly home on Tuesday evening three days ago, having flown out that morning, without any warning that the whole island was about to be closed off. We have every right to come home. Our passengers are all Manx people, trying to get home from business or holiday trips. I have flown in and out of Ronaldsway about 150 times. The weather is good. I don't need your permission or help to land there. I can manage fine without any help, and we are coming in to land."

Peter responded, "You will leave me no choice. I have artillery..."

Sam interrupted, "He has closed down that channel. Let me try to call him back up. But you are not going to fire your artillery at him are you?"

Harry, at that point, felt an urge to go over to them, but he looked at Private Moore, looking at him, and thought better of it.

Peter ignored Sam, and called Sergeant Walker and the Gunners on a shared channel on his own radio, "Major Quinnel here to Sergeant Walker, and Bombardier Cain. Bombardier, get your gun ready to fire one warning shot, as soon as you get sight of the plane approaching. Its final approach will be from 85 degrees, if my map reading has been correct..."

Bombardier Cain "Sir..."

Peter went on, "Just listen please Bombardier. I want you to aim slightly left of it, probably about 80 degrees. Get close enough for the pilot to know that a shell has gone past his cockpit. We have lost contact with the aircraft. I did not have the opportunity to warn him about our 105mm gun. I fully expect him to deviate away from the runway, once he realises that he has been fired at. However, if necessary, will you be able to able to adjust your gun so that it faces due east, 90 degrees, for a second warning shot?"

Bombardier Cain replied, "Yes, but it might take 60 seconds to do that sir. I think the onboard traverse mechanism might take longer than just pushing the gun round on its wheels."

Peter was thinking. "Hold on a moment," he said to Bombardier Cain.

He turned to Sam, and asked, "When would we first have visual contact?"

Sam replied, "From the tower, usually about 4 minutes before landing. Your gunners are further forward, but not so high up."

Major Quinnel spoke on his radio again, "Right Bombardier, I will be looking out for the plane, and will let you know if I see it before you. But don't wait for any further orders for those two shots. As soon as you see the plane, and it is in range, fire your first shot. Immediately adjust your gun ready for a second shot, and then fire it straight away, if the plane has not deviated away. Understood so far?"

"Yes sir."

"After the second shot adjust your gun, so that it is in exact alignment with the runway and the incoming flight path, about 85 degrees. Await further orders for a third or fourth shot. Understood?"

"Yes sir."

"Right, repeat those orders back to me please, Bombardier."

"We are to look out for the plane. You will let us know if you see it first. When it is in range fire off a warning shot, to the left, 80 degrees. Move the gun round. If the plane is stiil coming, fire off a second warning shot, to the right, 90 degrees. Move the gun round to the flight path and runway direction, 85 degrees, and await further orders. Sir."

"Excellent. I can see your lorry. Please can you park it so it is facing inland with the wheels of the gun just behind it. I might want you to move, with, or possibly without, your gun, very quickly."

"Yes sir," confirmed Bombardier Cain.

Peter then asked, "Are you still there, Sergeant Walker?"

She replied, "Yes sir, I thought that..."

"Things have not gone to plan, as you probably realise. I didn't even get a chance to tell the captain of the plane about our 105mm gun. There are you and three others at the vehicle gate, aren't there? Leave your corporal at the gate, and you and the two others get in your patrol vehicles, and drive down into the middle of the main runway. There, you will find it is intersected by another slightly shorter runway, aligned approximately 25 to 205 degrees. Wait there."

Sergeant Walker started saying, "But sir..."

Peter did not want a debate. He said, "Do it now please Sergeant, straight away."

Sergeant Walker replied, "Yes sir!"

Sam said to Peter, "There is still no radio channel open to the plane at the moment, but I will keep trying. The Captain said that the first officer, James Quirk, knows you."

Peter told him, "Yes this island is a fairly small community really, isn't it? His parents are older than me, and they own the neighbouring farm. Luckily they have a younger son, who looks like he is going to take over running it, sooner or later."

"Just as well then, as they might not be seeing James again," commented Sam.

Bombardier Cain came over on Peter's radio, saying, "Sir, We have just seen the plane, I estimate 8 kilometres, my bearing 85 degrees, approximately 4000 feet altitude."

Just then, Peter and Sam heard through the speaker, "Ronaldsway Approach, this is Captain Smith on flight VARF on final approach, heading 265 degrees, 7 kilometres out, 3600 feet. Please accept responsibility for keeping airspace and runway clear...What the hell! My radar just picked up an incoming missile that has come and gone, and there was a definite wind vibration to my starboard side. Are you trying to shoot me down? Are you insane?"

Peter said loudly, "Please divert immediately, and your aeroplane will be safe. We have alternative arrangements for your passengers. Do not continue your approach, as you will be shot down if you do. Please divert northwest, bearing 315 degrees, immediately."

There was no immediate reply. Sam and the Major could overhear heated discussion. Then they heard, "We are diverting south west bearing..."

"No you must turn to starboard..." replied Peter with urgency.

Captain Smith spoke again, "You are still shooting. That was another missile and it was even closer. It went across the front of the cockpit. If I had started turning 5 seconds earlier, it would have hit the plane. Please stop firing. We have changed course to 180 degrees."

"We have stopped firing. Please confirm that you will make no further attempts to land, and then we will advise alternative flight path, and destination."

Captain Smith said, "Just a moment. It is pandemonium in the cabin. I need to help get everyone calmed down."

The radio channel went dead again.

Peter spoke to Bombardier Cain on his radio, "Okay Bombardier, you followed your orders exactly. Now I..."

Bombardier Cain interrupted, " Sorry sir, we nearly hit it with our second shell."

"Not your fault. I should have realised it might turn left and south, away from the hills, and it turned just at you fired. I don't trust him not to have another go at landing, possibly onto the shorter runway, from over Castletown Bay. Can you attach your gun and drive quickly round the southern perimeter, until you get to where that runway crosses it."

"We are on our way, sir," confirmed Bombardier Cain.

Peter then called up his sergeant, "Sergeant Walker?"

"Sir?" she replied.

"I can see you from the tower. Your two patrol cars are right where I want you to be, at the intersection of the two runways. I want you to be ready to move the two vehicles about 60 metres away from where they are, in opposite directions, so that they are 120 metres apart on the same runway. This will probably be the shorter runway, that runs 25 to 205 degrees. I will let you know. If we need to do this, you should then leave the patrol cars, and move away from the runway on foot, as far as you can."

"Yes sir, I get the picture, just let me know when and where, sir."

Peter thought to himself, "I'm definitely feeling the strain, but my lads and lasses are doing well." And then he thought, "We have only got two shells left. Can we afford another warning shot?"

"Sam, is the radio channel to the aircraft open?" he asked.

Sam replied, "No but I will try again. But we can see on this screen that the plane has circled back. It now appears to be heading towards the shorter runway from a bearing of 205 degrees. Wait, the radio channel is open again."

Peter called the aircraft, "Flight VARF, please turn away east from the airport immediately. We have artillery ready to shoot you down, and vehicles parked on the runways."

Captain Smith retorted, "Go to hell Major. You weren't aiming to hit us before, and your gun is in the wrong place now. We are coming in."

Peter and Sam could see, on the display, that the plane was keeping its course. They could also hear arguments going on inside the cockpit... "Are you crazy? Change course"... "No we all need to get home"... Then they heard a voice shouting, "Jimmy, come and give us a hand."

Bombardier Cain's voice came through on Peter's radio, "Sir the plane's a lot closer than last time, but we have the 105mm gun right in line."

Peter ordered, "Fire one shot to go over the plane. Do it now."

"Yes sir," was the Bombardier's immediate reply.

Peter ordered, "Sergeant Walker, two vehicles, 120 metres apart on the short runway, now."

"Yes sir," she replied.

All four people inside the tower could hear, on the Major's radio, the 105 mm gun being fired. Harry shouted, "You are all mad!" Private Moore stared at him, twitched his weapon slightly, and said, "Just keep quiet, I won't be so gentle next time I lay my hands on you." Harry calmed down again.

Bombardier Cain came through again, "Sir, we have one round left. I estimate the plane is 4 kilometres away. Do you want us to shoot?"

Just then a voice was heard from the aircraft. "Major Quinnel, this is First Officer Quirk. I am just taking over from Captain Smith. He is being pulled from his seat now."

Peter could hear scuffling noises, and the Captain's voice, "Let go of me Jimmy, don't you want to go home?"

First Officer Quirk said to Peter, "Give me a chance. I will alter course as soon as I have full control."

Peter started saying, "I can give..."

Bombardier Cain was speaking at the same time, "Sir, do you want me to shoot? I reckon it will be too late, in about 70 seconds"

Peter replied, "Wait 40 seconds, and then shoot to hit it, if it hasn't deviated."

Peter told the aircraft, "You have a maximum of 30 seconds to deviate. Deviate by 25 degrees right, heading 50 degrees, and climb immediately." He could still hear raised voices from the aircraft.

Eventually, he heard Pilot Officer Quirk saying, "Okay deviating course and climbing now."

Peter looked at his watch. He made it 39 seconds since he spoke to Bombardier Cain. He radioed him, "Bombardier Cain, cancel, cancel!" He noticed the plane start to rise and bank to the right, just before a shell was fired into the path it had been on one second earlier. It was much closer to the aircraft than any of the previous three shells.

Bombardier Cain came through, "I am sorry sir, I had just given the gunners the shoot order, when I heard your call. By the time I tried to cancel, the lads had fired. So just as well that we missed."

Peter and Sam could hear background noises of screams, and then a door closing. Peter said to the aircraft, "Can I take it you won't be making any further attempts to land at Ronaldsway?"

First Officer Quirk replied, "That is absolutely correct. But I have a planeful of terrified and angry passengers and crew. What am I supposed to tell them? And where are we supposed to go? We have insufficient fuel to fly to London."

"We didn't want to shoot at your plane at all, but your Captain Smith really left us no choice. Look James, we know each other. Do you think I wanted to stop you getting here? But the ultra pneumonia pandemic is coming. There are almost certainly infected people in London now. And it is killing everyone 2 weeks after they get it. So, you know why we had to stop you."

"Don't call me James. We might know each other Major, but we are definitely not friends. You might think it is your duty to shoot at civilian aircraft, but my duty is to the crew and passengers on this plane. What do I tell them?"

Peter said, "Fly to John Lennon Airport in Liverpool. We need to get you back under NATS control as soon as possible, and we will get John Lennon Airport advised to expect you. There will be coaches there, waiting to take all your passengers to Liverpool Docks, where a cruise ship, the Senior Serenade, will take everyone on a cruise for 3 weeks. It won't be able to call anywhere, but I am told it is a comfortable ship. After 3 weeks or so, if all is well, the ship will dock in Douglas, and everyone will disembark."

"What about the crew of this plane?" asked First Officer Quirk.

Peter replied, "As you are a Vannin Airlines plane, crewed by Manx people, I would hope they will take you on the ship as well. The ship can take 350 passengers."

Sam spoke to First Officer Quirk next, "I have contacted NATS in Prestwick. They know your flight code, and your destination. You should hear from them now."

Peter said to Sam, "Maybe I should be doing it, but I feel a bit drained. Could you advise NATS that Ronaldsway remains under military control, and is closed to all traffic. Any flights across the Irish Sea should be routed well clear of the Isle of Man. Thanks. Also, Sam, I would add that you have been sensible and helpful in what we needed to do today, and I appreciate it. From now on, I think we will have a continuous Army Reserve presence in this tower. I am not sure whether Daniel Clague, or anyone else, has decided that the tower should continue to be manned, but the presence of the Army Reserve, in the tower, will re-inforce that nothing should be landing or taking off."

Sam replied, "Yes I understand."

Peter thought about speaking to First Officer James Quirk again, but decided that there was nothing he could say to him, to make the grim situation any better. It would be better to say nothing. He decided, instead, to speak on the radio to his men and women on duty, at the airport. He said into his radio, "Thanks everyone, for doing your duty, and for following my orders. You all did well. It got a bit fraught at times, but we achieved our objective, of preventing a flight landing today. Not everyone on the island may know or appreciate it, but your actions have probably allowed the continuation of human life on this island. I am saying well done, and thank you, on behalf of all the people of this island."

Chapter 18, Friday 9 April 2027

Vin and Martha arrived at David's house, at around 7.10pm. Vin was not thinking about people dying, for a change. He was congratulating himself on listening to Matthew, and buying himself an all-electric Honda car. He had had a special charging socket for it put in at his house, and the electricity tariff for it was still at a reduced rate, from Manx Utilities. He wondered if that would last, given that the electricity supply could be reduced, eventually, to relying largely on the one power station using gas, from the pipeline from the Irish Sea.

Martha and David knew each other from when David had originally been another social worker, although they had been on separate teams. It was soon obvious to Vin that they were pretty relaxed with each other, even if David was the Chief Executive of her Department. Vin wasn't surprised by this, as he knew Martha to be a hard and conscientious worker, and he had come to see David as a very reasonable and friendly type. Vin and Amber had never met before, but he took an instant liking to her, when she made some derogatory remark about Adrian Kelly, and she laughed when Vin also made some negative comment in reply. The conversation was pretty light over dinner, as all four tried hard to keep it that way. When desert had been eaten, Amber got out her Trivial Pursuit, and she and Martha wandered into the lounge. David produced a Scrabble set with a turning board, and he and Vin stayed at the table in the dining room.

"Right Vin, don't expect to win, just because you know a few obscure medical words. I am pretty good at this, even if I say so myself," boasted David.

Vin replied, "We'll see. We're using Collins Scrabble Words Dictionary 2023, I presume? I've got a word checker based on that on my smart phone."

David asked to have a look. Then he said, "Yes, that is the same app as mine. At least it is not an online app, so it should keep working, for as long as the smart phone keeps going."

The game took over an hour and a half, with them taking their time deciding what words to form, whilst they also discussed events. David said, "Did you hear about the plane this afternoon? It sounds like the captain was determined to land?"

Vin put down the first word, and said, "Yes, Peter rang me afterwards. We had had a bit of a chat in Government House yesterday evening, and he said he would let me know how things went. We were really lucky there, getting Sir Hugh to get the cruise ship for the passengers. I hope they survive, and the ship can tie up in Douglas in three weeks, but that no one decides to let the ship come here before then. I have to admire Peter for his determination in getting the plane to turn away. It must have been terrifying for the passengers, with artillery rounds being fired near the plane, but that was the Captain's fault really."

David said, "I can sort of understand the Captain though. He is a Manxman flying local people home, on an Isle of Man based aeroplane. I was told that plane and its crew should have flown in on Tuesday evening. Looking at it from his point of view, turning the aeroplane away wasn't going to improve his own prospects of survival. I don't even know if they got to Liverpool, and onto the boat alright?"

"Well I have heard from my son. Did I tell you one of the people on the aeroplane was the younger sister of Matthew's fiancee? Anyway, they have heard from her that she and her friend, and most of the rest of the passengers and crew, are on the ship. They were expecting it to leave early this evening. Matthew says they sound frightened."

"With this virus now killing everybody in South Africa, everyone is entitled to be frightened, if not actually terrified. But Vin I must tell you something. I admire you greatly, and also the Major, for putting your necks on the line. But when I say people are terrified, I am including people living on this island. And some of them are angry as well. It is probably not rational, but they are looking for people to blame for the ultra pneumonia virus, and messengers often do get the blame for the message. People who were expecting their friends and relatives back this afternoon must be feeling angry, and the Major and you are the clear targets for that anger. I need to tell you that Adrian Kelly was in the office today, seething with rage at me, as if I have any influence over you. He said that he had promised his sister Kathy that she would be safe, he had promised constituents of his own that their relatives were coming home, and that he had promised his church minister and fellow MHK Patrick Quinn, that the repatriation flight was going ahead. But instead, now he was being told that Major Quinnel had been talked into commandeering the control tower at Ronaldsway, and taking an artillery gun on to the runway. He also had a minor rant about the Chief Constable being either weak or in on it, because he wouldn't authorise intervention by armed police. In normal times, having Adrian Kelly and Patrick Quinn as enemies would not matter too much, if you don't have to work with them. But these are not normal times. Patrick could well use his pulpit for a bit of rabble rousing. His church is the Isle of Man Astrological Church, and one of their quirks is a belief in a day of reckoning. This virus could be presented as the day of reckoning, but he could well twist it, so that you and others are part of the problem that has to be dealt with, before everyone can be redeemed."

"Well, thanks for the friendly warning about those two. I already knew that Patrick Quinn represents his Manx First Party as an MHK. I have recently been told by Matthew about Quinn's church. I must tell you this though. Before I knew anything about Patrick Quinn, I had an unpleasant encounter with him, soon after I moved to Baldrine. You know where that is, don't you? It is on the coast north from Douglas, before you get to Laxey. Anyway, he lives there too. Leaving aside the religious stuff, he seems to me to be an outright racist. The first time we saw each other, in the local store, he said to me 'You're a long way from home aren't you?' to which I said, 'I don't know what you mean, but I have lived and worked on Mann for over 20 years, although I have only moved to Baldrine this week.' He then said something like, 'Bloody hell, they're getting everywhere these days.'"

"I am sorry that anyone should think it right to say that sort of thing to you. But that game of Scrabble we just had, I don't think I have seen the word INFARCT before. Is that something to do with an infarction?"

"Yes, its the name of the lesion you get, when you have had an infarction. But where did you get the word QUAICH from?"

"It is a Celtic bowl of some kind. Anyway, I won fair and square."

"Mainly because you had both the blanks. Assuming I am not lynched or something in the meantime, would you and Amber like to come to us next time, say two weeks today? Amber and Martha seem to have got on well, and I need to get my revenge at Scrabble."

"With such a gracious invitation, how can we refuse?"

Chapter 19, Saturday 10 April 2027

Vin was not very surprised to see Peter Quinnel in the waiting area of the Headquarters Building of the Isle of Man Police, at 9.25 that morning. Peter was wearing civilian clothes, which Vin thought made him look more like a typical farmer. Peter had told him on the phone early the previous evening that, during his airport intervention, he had promised to submit to a formal interview with the police, the next morning. Major Quinnel had already reported his presence to the public counter clerk.

Peter said, "Hello Vin. I am wondering why you are here. Presumably, they have asked you to come in in connection with diverting the repatriation plane, as well?"

Vin replied, "No I got a phone call at 8 o'clock this morning telling me there had been reports that I had breached the Official Secrets Act, by telling my son in advance about the commencement of the embargo, and thereby endangering national security. They were hoping for my co-operation. 'Would I please attend Police HQ in Douglas, at 9.30 this morning.' "

"That's a bit rich considering, not only were you the main person trying to defend 'national security' as far as I can make out, but the idiot Government then caused far greater danger, by authorising that repatriation flight yesterday."

"Maybe they are right though. I invented a serious car accident to Matthew's mother, to persuade Matthew and Emma to come back urgently, on Tuesday morning. And I am glad I did. But what if just he or Emma, from that last flight in, have contracted the ultra pneumonia virus? The extinction of life on Mann would then be my fault."

"Huh! If we survive on this island it will be thanks to you, and despite the stupid decisions of others. You didn't actually breach the Act, because you didn't actually tell your son the information did you? And anyone else would have done the same. I am sure that any Ministers, in the same situation as you, would have told their son or daughter outright."

"Yes, I know one, who I am fairly sure did just that. I saw his son and daughter in law..."

At that moment Jack Coyle walked into the waiting area. He had not been expecting to see either Vin or the Major. He said to them, "Well this is a bit of a surprise. I suppose you are both here because of that escapade with the repatriation flight, yesterday. If it wasn't so serious, I could see the funny side of Adrian Kelly not managing to rescue his sister after all. Vin, I know we haven't exactly become mates, but did you have to go telling the police about my son and daughter in law arriving back on Tuesday? That's why I am here, an alleged breach of the Official Secrets Act."

Vin replied, "No it wasn't me. And that's why I am here too. Like you said, if your daughter in law had not gone into labour, that plane, with my son on as well, would not have landed. But your daughter in law, presumably, gave birth at Nobles Hospital. Their arrival back won't have been a secret. Everyone on the plane knew she was in labour, so everyone on that plane would have explained to several other people how it was that the plane nearly got diverted, but didn't. It's a small world here, but it wasn't me who told the police."

Jack told Vin, "Okay I believe you. Her name is Emily by the way, and my lad is Oliver. Anyway, the police can't prove anything. I phoned Oliver's landline in Slough from a pay-as-you-go mobile phone, that I have now seem to have lost. And Oliver and Emily made their own airline booking."

Jack looked at Peter, and said, "I know I called it 'an escapade' at the airport, but seriously you did well. I admit supporting the flight, but that was foolish of me. You should be getting a medal, not a police interview."

Terry Corps appeared. He said, "Gentlemen thank you all for coming in. Come along to my office please."

They followed him into his office. He said, "You are all here as suspects of offences. Normally you would have had to be formally arrested, but these are exceptional times, and, anyway, none of you will be leaving the island. I have taken the view, therefore, that none of you need to be arrested, if you agree to a formal interview under caution. Of course, if you want legal representation you are entitled to it, but that would cause delay."

Peter told him, "I don't want a solicitor. Let's just get on with it."

"I think I know what I am doing, without one," was Jack's answer.

Vin said, "I am just going to tell the truth. What you do about it is up to you. If I wanted a lawyer, I would probably phone my cousin in Ilford."

Terry spoke just to Vin, "We could try to brief your cousin by phone, and then he could advise you, before we start the interview. But, we couldn't really keep interrupting the interview. So if you want one during the interview, it would be best to find someone locally."

Vin repeated, "No, as I said I am going to tell you the truth, and what you do then is up to you."

Terry Corps said, "Right then, no one wants a solicitor. We can get on. You might think that, because these are exceptional times, and because you are playing critical roles, that we should not be worrying you about events that are now in the past. But I am determined that, whatever the future has in store, I will do my best to uphold the law. That is a basic requirement, if we are to remain a civilised society. There are a lot of anxious and angry people out there, and we don't want anyone taking the law into their own hands. The police have to be seen to be doing the right thing, when allegations are made against leading members of the community. You will be interviewed by uniformed inspectors, two of whom I have dragged in on unpaid overtime. They will caution you, tell you what offence is being investigated, tell you what information and evidence they have, and then question you. You will be given ample opportunity to give answers and explanations, to show your innocence if you can."

Within a few minutes the three men had been taken to separate interview rooms.

Jack Coyle was with Inspector Corkish who ran through the formalities, and then said, "Mr Coyle, it is basically a matter of record that you were at a Council of Ministers meeting last Monday evening. At that meeting, it was decided to approve an embargo to stop anyone entering the island. This embargo came into force on Tuesday afternoon, at 2 o'clock. Two tickets were booked online very late on the

Monday evening, for your son Oliver Coyle and his wife Emily Coyle, on what was to be the last flight into Ronaldsway. It left Heathrow last Tuesday lunchtime. Airline regulations prohibit women more than seven months pregnant from flying. Emily gave birth at Nobles Hospital on Tuesday evening. They are calling the baby Jacqueline, I believe."

Jack allowed himself a smile. He knew why they had decided on that name.

Inspector Corkish continued, "So, it is pretty obvious that someone told your son to get back to the island straightaway, imminent birth of child notwithstanding! And that person has to be you."

Jack replied, "You know Inspector, your Chief Constable was right, when he implied some of us have got better things to do. For the record, I did not phone my son after that meeting, and there is no computer or phone record which will show otherwise; I did not make the airline booking, and no computer or phone record will show otherwise; and I did not even know they were coming, so I was not at the airport to meet them. You have missed the obvious answer, as to who decided that Oliver and Emily ought to come home at such short notice, and that is that they did. They are bright people, actually brighter than me. Stupidly I voted against the embargo, but Oliver and Emily obviously realised how ultra pneumonia could spread, given that there were flights from Madagascar to Johannesburg, and from Johannesburg to London, and from London to here. They decided to give themselves a chance, whilst they could. Inspector, has anyone actually said that I told them, that I told Oliver and Emily what to do, and why?"

"In an interview it is normally the police officer who asks the questions, but I can tell you that no-one is saying you have made any admissions about this."

"So, there is nothing else to discuss really. You may or may not believe me, but you don't have any evidence that would secure a conviction, do you?"

"You are not the only one who doesn't like wasting time, which extending this interview would be. This doesn't look like we will be taking it any further, but we would have the right to re-open the matter, if new evidence comes to light."

Inspector Cornish formally concluded the interview, and Jack then left the building.

Vin was being interviewed at the same time by Inspector Murphy. Inspector Murphy ran through the formalities, and then he asked Vin, "So, Dr Singh, were you at the Council of Ministers meeting on Monday evening, when they decided to impose an embargo of people coming to Mann?"

Vin replied, "Yes, I helped talk them into it, and then I went with the Chief Minister to Government House to talk about it. Sir Hugh signed the Emergency Proclamation in front of us."

"So, did you know it wasn't to be disclosed, before it came into effect?"

"Yes, that's why I had to make up a reason for my son Matthew and his girlfriend Emma, or fiancee rather, to come home urgently."

"Sorry, but are you admitting that you phoned Matthew because of the Proclamation, which you knew you shouldn't disclose?"

"Yes."

"But, you didn't actually tell him about what was going to happen?

"Well no, but in the end he didn't believe my story."

"So, you told him then?"

"No not really. He worked it out, when I met him and Emma at the airport."

"Can you just run through each conversation you had with him please?"

"Well I phoned him at his hotel on Tuesday morning fairly early, once I realised he hadn't got back the previous day..."

"So you helped organise a closure of all our ports indefinitely, not checking first whether your own son was going to be on the island when they closed?"

"That doesn't sound like a loving father does it? I guess I was preoccupied with the bigger picture, and Martha, that's my wife, had said he was coming back on the Monday evening."

"So, then you found out he was still away on Tuesday morning, and you phoned him at his hotel in London?"

"Yes, in London. I said his Mum had been in a serious road accident. My next call was whilst he and Emma were on the way to Heathrow by taxi, to tell him about the seats on the plane, and the booking reference. Then, he rang me from Heathrow to say that he had worked out that she hadn't been in an accident. I felt absolutely terrible, but he said he trusted me, when I said he just had to get home straightaway, and I would explain then." Vin felt a couple of tiny tears in his eyes, and dabbed them behind his glasses.

Inspector Murphy was looking at Dr Singh and felt some sympathy, but wasn't sure why he felt that way. He said, "So that was your last conversation with him, before his plane landed down at Ronaldsway?"

Vin replied, "Yes, they nearly didn't make it. It was only because of..." He stopped, having thought that there was no point in bringing Jack Coyle into it.

Inspector Murphy said, "But the plane did land, and Matthew and Emma are back on the island, unlike some others."

Vin started saying, "Are you are talking about the repatriation flight..." The interview was being taped, but there was no visual recording. Vin saw the Inspector shaking his head, and holding one finger vertically in front of his mouth. Vin stopped talking.

Inspector Murphy hastily said, "You probably know that we are talking to Major Quinnel about what happened yesterday. Now, turning back to Tuesday, if what you are saying is true, you haven't actually disclosed a secret, so there is no offence. But we had heard, from a third party, that Emma had said that you had told them about the embargo, which is why they had flown back."

"If it is a third party, maybe the message has got distorted. I definitely rang them with the motivation of getting them home, but never disclosed what was happening until they were standing in Arrivals at Ronaldsway, about 20 minutes after the Proclamation had come into effect. I am sure Matthew would remember, but I would rather you didn't get him involved."

Inspector Murphy assured Vin, "I don't think that will be necessary. Technically it seems there has been no offence, and we won't be taking this any further, unless contrary evidence comes to light."

The interview was formally terminated. Inspector Murphy surprised himself by then telling Vin "Dr Singh, can I tell you something in confidence, you seem like a man of integrity to me, even if you did lie to your son."

Vin replied, "I suppose so, so long as it doesn't cause any trouble."

"Well, it is a warning about trouble I suppose. The Chief Constable and most of the senior police officers don't really want you, the Major, or Jack Coyle to be charged with, or convicted of anything. You and Jack only did what anyone would do to get loved ones home. And the Council of Ministers approving that repatriation flight, three days after the embargo had started, was crazy. I am guessing you had a hand in stopping that, but please don't tell me. Anyway, what I want to say is that the atmosphere is getting unpleasant. Everyone is very fearful of what is happening, and some are angry about their relatives or friends on that repatriation flight. People, irrationally, are looking for someone to blame and to punish. They look for some sort of meaning to what is happening, and they all want to live, or at least get salvation. These are dangerous times, and you could be a prime target in some way."

"Everyone seems to be talking about dangerous times, and that I could be a target of some kind. Perhaps because I am Asian, even if I was born in England like, maybe, 20% of the population here?

"Well I am of Irish stock from Liverpool, a combination that doesn't always get a good press, but we have both done okay, here on Mann, haven't we?"

"So, will I be getting police protection at home, and at work, if I am under threat?"

"As you know, we are a bit stretched at the moment with the embargo needing to be enforced, but, if there were to be specific threats targeted at you, we would have to consider that I suppose."

Vin shrugged and said, "Can I go now?"

Inspector Murphy replied, "Yes, of course, I'll see you out."

Peter's interview was with Inspector Crellin. Inspector Crellin cautioned the Major and went on. "There are are a number of possible offences to consider all linked in with your actions yesterday. Let's just mention two, the unlawful detention of the two controllers, and endangering the safety of an aircraft. But the caution applies to all offences relating to yesterday's episode at the airport. Would you be willing to tell us what happened yesterday?"

Peter obliged, "In a nutshell we took control of the control tower. The two controllers in there were detained. My private and I were both armed. One controller was co-operative, the other less so, but the absolute minimum of force was used against him, a bit of a shove and verbal encouragement to comply. He was a bit excitable, but understandably not very brave. You are probably more interested in the artillery, a single 105mm gun. This was placed at the eastern end of the main runway, and two shots to miss were fired at the aircraft as it approached. It did veer away to the south but we guessed it might try again, using the other runway from the south over Castletown Bay. We managed to get the gun relocated to face it as it came in. We only had two shells left and the plane was getting very close. I ordered an immediate shot over the top of the aircraft, and this seemed to cause the first officer to try to seize control from the captain. But the plane was still closing on the runway, and I was determined to prevent it from landing. I told the first officer he had thirty seconds to comply with my requirement that he diverts aways. Forty seconds after that we shot at it again, but it had just veered to the northeast so we missed."

Inspector Crellin asked, "So you were actually trying to shoot it down with that last shot?"

Peter replied, "Yes absolutely. I hated being in that position, but our Government, by its stupid decision to allow a repatriation flight 3 days after the embargo had started, gave me no choice. If we hadn't stopped this flight we would have an extra 128 people on the island now. Any one of them might have been exposed to the ultra pneumonia virus in those 3 days."

"Well, we don't know for sure the virus hasn't already arrived before last Tuesday, and equally, we don't know that anyone on the repatriation flight actually was infected."

"Yes, both things are possible, but it was ridiculous taking the additional risk. I would add that I knew that there was a ship they could board for a quarantine period, although the captain of the plane didn't give me much chance to tell him that."

"So, you thought you would take it on yourself to try to shoot down a lawfully authorised flight, and kill 128 people?"

"Yes, to give the other 84,000 people on this island a chance. It seems to be fairly likely that that planeload was going to wipe us all out. But, if we are lucky, we will find out in a few weeks time."

"I think you are saying, never mind the legal position, never mind you trying to kill 128 people, you have moral superiority, you know better that the Government."

"I think a few people do know better that the Government, whose lawful authority to jeopardise the security of the island can be disputed anyway."

"Are you making reference to the Manx Government's position with regard to Defence? And are you saying that you as a part-time Major in the Army Reserve have the authority to decide that it is a Defence matter, and that you are entitled to do what you did?"

"As it happens, I did have authority signed by the Lieutenant Governor, on behalf of His Majesty. It specifically covers the use of lethal force." Peter then produced the papers, and showed them to the Inspector. He went on, "I told your Sergeant Christian about that yesterday."

Inspector Crellin had not done her homework properly. She said, "Oh, that seems to have been overlooked. Still, let me think about this."

Peter volunteered, "Shall I do some thinking for you Inspector? Lots of tricky hurdles to overcome. Did His Majesty act unlawfully? Did the Lieutenant Governor act unlawfully? Would you want to bring him into this? Even if the order was unlawful, did I reasonably believe that I had lawful authority? Would any offence be a matter for a criminal court or a military court, and how would you convene a military court, if everyone in Britain is dead? Would it look good to be prosecuting me, if news is received of everyone on the Senior Serenade ship dying? Would my prosecution really be in the public interest, in any event? You would need to consult the Attorney General in London anyway, on this sort of case, under the terms of the 2018 memorandum of agreement about prosecutions, but again, the Attorney General will be dead soon. And on top of all that, isn't the most important thing to do is to drop the whole thing, so that I can concentrate on enforcing the embargo? My Army Reserve lads and lasses are damned fine people, but they do need me around to give them direction. Not to mention my farm workers."

Inspector Crellin responded, "It might help if I do a recap. Your account of what happened yesterday agrees pretty much with the information and evidence we have. With your admissions, normally we would have sufficient grounds now for you to be charged with serious offences. But, if you were charged, your defence would be that you were acting under orders you considered to be lawful. The issues of lawfulness and public interest are matters that need to be referred for others to consider. So, at this stage I have no further questions, but I cannot confirm whether or not any further action will be taken. Do you have anything else you wish to say?"

"No, just do whatever you have to do. If you are saying I am still under threat of prosecution, I am beginning not to care," said Peter.

Inspector Crellin said, "I will terminate the interview at 10.03am." She sorted out the tapes and then said, "You know everyone is living in fear, and the relatives of the people on that plane are angry. You and Dr Singh might actually be saving the island between you, but some regard you as villains not heroes. Just watch out for anyone carrying out any acts of revenge that's all."

Peter was feeling misused. He said, "Well thanks very much! Our idiot Government forces me to nearly shoot down an aircraft with 120 passengers, the police won't say whether I am being prosecuted or not, and apparently members of the public might be out to attack me in some way. My Army Reserve people deserve better, but if this is the level of support I am getting from everyone else, then maybe they will have to manage without me. So I am off now, back to my farm, where there is a lot to do."

Inspector Crellin told him, "I understand, but the Chief Constable did ask me to ask you, if you could possibly go to his office for a chat about re-inforcing the embargo, before you go. Please, will you just give him a chance to talk to you before you go anywhere?"

Peter sighed, "Alright, take me to his office then."

"Sorry Major, but would you mind waiting just a few minutes, whilst I update him about our interview?" requested the Inspector.

Peter sighed again, shrugged, and relaxed back into his chair. Inspector Crellin disappeared. She returned ten minutes later to take Peter back to the Chief Constable's office.

Terry offered Peter a comfortable seat, and enquired, "Are you alright Peter? You look a bit weary."

Peter replied, "Well, yesterday was a very tense day. And now I have been interviewed by police, oh, and warned about the risk of angry people taking some sort of revenge on me. And you know what? I feel frightened and sad about what is happening, like everyone else, but I am also wondering why I am bothering."

"Yes Peter, I can see you have been under a lot of strain, and you were doing what you thought was the right thing. Probably it was the right thing, but given the atmosphere on the island now, surely you understand that we had to show that we would investigate what happened yesterday? I have decided that the papers must go to the Prosecution Division, undoubtedly to be reviewed by the Director of Prosecutions herself, Claire Wilson. She will be made fully aware of the existence of the order you were given, and your belief that it was lawful. There will certainly not be any recommendation by police that you are prosecuted. But I can't just drop it myself. Probably, by the time a few weeks have gone by, it will be obviously against the public interest to prosecute. So Peter, shall we review where we are on keeping the embargo secure? I mean really, after your efforts yesterday, it would be terrible if some infected people managed to get on the island some other way, don't you think?"

"My trouble is that I have a sense of duty. Most people my age might feel it towards their children or grandchildren even, but we only had one child. She died from leukaemia, six months ago. But I feel it towards people who rely on me, my farm workers, my Army Reservists, and my long suffering wife Amanda. And, if the embargo is breached, they will all die. So very well, let's talk about securing the borders."

They talked for a while about the harbours, the coves, the beaches and the airstrips. The Chief Constable pointed out that a helicopter could land almost anywhere. He said, "Peter, what I think we need is an appeal to the general public to look out for boats, light planes and helicopters, and ask them to report immediately any suspected intrusion. I think then, that we use our mobility to arrive at the scene, as rapidly as possible. The trouble is that, whilst we have mobile coastguards and civil defence volunteers, they are not armed. I have 12 trained firearms officers, and I am certainly willing to use them on overtime to cover what we need as far as possible, but how many of your Reservists are trained and equipped for using firearms?"

Peter replied, "Well, all of them are trained in the use of personal firearms. We only have twelve SA80 weapons, but they can be shared, so that anyone who is on duty has got one. Realistically, taking account of nights and weekends, only six to eight of them can be armed and on duty at the same time. But, are we agreeing that lethal force will be used to prevent people coming ashore or landing their planes, if we can?"

"Let's put it simply, yes we are."

"We had to fudge round that a bit at the meeting of the Emergency Advisory Committee though, didn't we?"

"Some people still haven't quite grasped how just one infected person on the island is the death warrant for everyone else. But that Dr Singh certainly didn't hide his feelings did he? Shame he's off the Committee. Anyway, you and I have command of the only armed personnel on the island, the absolute imperative is that we keep intruders out, and if that requires lethal force then we must approve it; no in fact we must give clear orders to that effect. As you now realise yourself, this might result in questions being asked afterwards. Well so be it."

"We need to make sure, that we can get an armed Reservist or armed police officer to where they are needed, as quickly as possible. That means, I think, that our patrols should be mixed up. For example, we could have four mobile units out in different parts of the island at the same time. We might have a Civil Defence vehicle and driver, and, say, two of my armed Reservists with him. Another vehicle could be a Coastguard vehicle and Coastguard volunteer driving it, with say just one of my armed Reservists, and an armed police officer. So, we would endeavour to have four vehicles, each able to get quickly to an incident, and each vehicle would have three people, two of whom would be armed."

"Yes, those are the lines I was thinking along. Let me just clear this mixed teams business at Ministerial level first. I think the two involved, Peter Corlett for the Civil Defence, and Daniel Claque for the Coastguard, were two of the four Ministers against the repatriation flight, which is a good sign. If I can get the Ministers on board, the Commandant of the Civil Defence and the Rescue Team Manager of the Coastguard will feel obliged to co-operate." Terry paused to think, and then added, "You know that artillery gun you have at the airport, is it the only one?"

Peter replied, "Yes, and I thought we had run out of ammunition for it, but my lads have told me they have found another caseful, so we actually have another 12 shells now. I think I know what you are thinking. It is the only weapon we have that might be able to take out an aircraft. Preferably that would be over the sea, but the same could be said about taking out decent sized boats. But whatever we want to aim it at, we can't expect a very fast response hitching it up, and towing it along to where we want it."

Terry said, "So, perhaps you should keep it at the airport, and if it is needed somewhere else, hope there is time to move it. We can only do our best with what we have."

Peter finally came out the police HQ building at 11.40am. He walked to his car which was in the car park at the front.

He found his beloved Jaguar car had been sprayed with white paint across its windscreen. It said "Army scum." He thought to himself "This is a criminal offence, committed outside a police building," and thought about reporting it. Then he shook his head slightly, and said to himself, "No, what a waste of time that would be. I have spent enough time here today. I can see well enough to drive, so I am going home."

Chapter 20, Sunday 11 April 2027

Emma O'Hara was sitting in her living room with Matthew at 10.20am, when they heard a beep from outside. Emma said, "So you are definitely not coming then, Mattie? To pray for Sophie? We could go together in your car or mine, instead."

Matthew replied, "I really hope Sophie gets back here, that her ship is free of the virus, that Mann is free of it, and that life can go on. But, you know I don't do religion. And you don't, normally. And Patrick Quinn said our relationship was 'miscegnation'. I think that's what you said, that your Mum said, that he said. And, he and your parents blame my father for Sophie not getting back. They probably think this virus is his fault as well. So, no thanks my darling. Oh, don't forget we are expected at my parents by 1pm, for lunch. Despite all the bad news, I think they are pleased we are engaged, and that they will be getting a grandchild. They are looking forward to seeing us both."

"It is a shame my parents can't be nicer to you. I had better go, they are waiting," Emma told him. She kissed Matthew goodbye, and stepped outside. She got in the back seat of her parents' car, and her father drove into Douglas. All kerb spaces near the Astrological Church were already occupied, and they had to park a 10 minutes walk away. They went inside the building, which was a 1920s built warehouse, converted to a church in 2021. Although it could hold 300 people, Emma and her parents Beryl and Wayne were only able to get seats in the back third of the church. By the time the service started all the seats were full, and about twenty people were standing at the back.

After a hymn and a prayer, Patrick Quinn stood at a lectern, which had a microphone connecting to loudspeakers, and began his sermon. He said, "My fellow Manx people, it is clear that the time is near. We know, because it is written in the Scriptures, that the current world will end. This pestilence, the ultra pneumonia virus as it is known, is clearly God's work. We can assume He began it in Madagascar, because that is where He felt the greatest anger. He was angry with the kind of people who dig up dead ancestors, and venerate them rather than Him, their true Lord. We cannot be sure whether we on Mann have definitely been chosen to survive into the new righteous world that will exist, when all evildoers have perished. We know that He looks kindly on those that pray to Him in humility, and on those who strive honestly to do what is right. So, we should pray for the salvation of our fellow Manx people who are not with us now, and He will look more kindly upon us for that. So, shortly I will ask you to pray with me for those passengers on the Senior Serenity ship, who who were so cruelly denied the chance to return here. But, He also wants us to purge evildoers from our midst. We must do this by demonstrating and protesting, that such people should be cast adrift, in the same way that befell our fellows now on the Senior Serenity ship. These evildoers should be placed on a small ship in Douglas Harbour, with provisions and fuel, and told never to return. They may survive elsewhere, if God in His infinite wisdom wishes it. This way, Mann will redeem itself in His eyes. These evildoers include Dr Singh, who bullied others into creating the embargo, before all our decent fellow Manx men and women could return. The evildoers include Major Peter Quinnel, who gave the cowardly order to his soldiers to shoot at the unarmed aeroplane bringing them home. And, it includes all alien residents, who generally don't demonstrate their loyalty to Manx customs and traditions, including the regular worship of God in Christian churches. This is how we must redeem ourselves. Will you campaign and demonstrate with me? Will you do this?"

Emma had listened to Patrick Quinn with horror as he denouced her fiancee's father, the grandfather of her unborn child. Now, she could hear a loud ripple of assent to Patrick's mad proposals. She had no idea how many people generally would support him. She obeyed an overwhelming urge to get up. She said to her mother and father, "I can't listen to any more. I will get Mattie to pick me up."

Wayne started to rise saying, "Wait a moment Emma, I will..."

He was interrupted by Beryl saying, "No let her go, but we must stay and show Him our support."

He thought Beryl was talking about support for Patrick, as it was far from obvious to Wayne what God really wanted. He also thought that they were supposed to be there to pray for Sophie's safe return. He stopped talking and sat down, deferring to his wife as usual.

Beryl was thinking, whilst Patrick started the prayers. She thought that Patrick was basically right. It was all Dr Singh and the Army Major's fault that Sophie was at sea in the Atlantic somewhere, rather that safely at home with her and

Wayne. The thought that Dr Singh would be the grandfather of Emma's child was unfortunate in several ways, but she felt that she and Wayne would make up for his disappearance by being good grandparents themselves. Emma's child would probably look fine really, as Matthew wasn't that dark. And they would definitely encourage Emma to bring the baby up as a good church going Manx child.

Emma called Matt on her mobile from outside the church, and he came to pick her up within 15 minutes. He found her sitting on a low wall at the front of the church. It was still only 11.30. He could see she looked a bit upset, and had perhaps shed a tear or two. He said, "Are you alright baby?" as she stood up, and he gave her a hug.

She asked, "Is there time to go home? I can compose myself a bit, and change into a less churchy outfit."

Matt replied, "There's plenty of time. I was doing some hoovering would you believe, and..."

Emma was taken by surprise, and said, "Hoovering? You never do the hoovering. Well not since I moved in."

Matt agreed, "Yes true, but I thought I would get in practice at doing a bit more at home, other than making omelettes and coffee whenever her ladyship feels the need. Because you might have to take it a bit easier soon for a while, you know?"

Emma smiled at him, thinking to herself, "For a male chauvinist he is okay really isn't he. He's kind, funny, makes great omelettes, nice body and good in bed, and being well paid isn't a bad thing either. And for some reason I really do care about him."

After they got home, Matthew made her a cup of coffee. He looked at her looking worried, and said, "Please don't say how awful it is, or I will have to stop making you coffee."

She was a bit puzzled, and then realised she was being teased. She said, "Matt you idiot. Why do I ever listen to you? Well don't worry too much, because coffee will soon be considered a luxury item, and we will be drinking potato juice or something instead instead. But I am very worried about things in general, and about you, and your Dad, would you believe?"

Matthew replied, "I am guessing you might be thinking about what that strange Patrick Quinn was saying, in that so called church of his. Do you want to tell me about it now?"

Emma, "He really seems to think that ultra pneumonia is God's doing, and for the Isle Of Man to survive it must get rid of evildoers. And then he listed, in particular, your father and the Army Major who stopped the repatriation plane from landing. Then he went on to include alien residents who don't follow Manx cultures and values or something, and who don't go to Christian churches regularly. That sounds like he might be including you, even if you were born here and your mother is Manx. He wants people to protest and demonstrate, until these evildoers are put on a ship in Douglas, and forced to sail away never to return."

She started crying, "It is going to be bad enough, but I couldn't bear to lose you!"

Matthew held her and said, "Yes, it is definitely my coffee that gets you going. But listen sweetness, I'm not going anywhere. I'm going to stick around, make an honest woman of you, and be a proud dad. And a lot more hands on than my dad ever was. And I've got things to do. You know we've been talking at work about how everything will change. Well I've been leading it really. Our company will be massively important but..." He tailed off and then spoke again, "Sure Patrick is mad and evil as well, and I know some people are scared and angry, but I really can't see our Government sanctioning such an evil plan, nor that the police are going to allow mob rule."

"Mattie, you weren't in that church less than an hour ago. That congregation sounded to me like they wanted some sort of revenge. It sounded crazy to me, but you could tell others were going along with it. My mother, she is normally a kind woman, but she had a strange look in her eyes, as Patrick started talking about evildoers being cast out. And people were shouting, 'Yes send them away.' I'm not sure you're safe."

"At the moment no one is safe, because we don't know that no one has brought the virus on to the island. Even us possibly. But, I can't believe this would happen." Then, what he thought was an amusing image came into his mind. He went on, " Perhaps what we need to do is organise some sort of counter movement. Maybe even a bit of direct action. Patrick Quinn mentioned that Army Major, with a similar surname to his. Maybe he could lead it. And he has an artillery gun he likes to fire, doesn't he? We could march on Patrick's house, fire a couple of shells through his front door, and put him in chains on display at Tynwald Hill, with a sign round his neck saying, 'This is the real evildoer on this island'. What do you think?"

Emma said, "I was thinking earlier that I like your sense of humour." She gave him a weak smile.

"But, maybe that wasn't my best effort?"

"Maybe not."

Chapter 21, Sunday 11 April 2027

Emma and Matthew arrived at his parents house just after 1pm. Not counting the pick up from the airport five days earlier, Emma had only met Vin and Martha a couple of times, because Matt mainly went to see them on his own, whilst Emma was seeing her parents without him. He had only met her parents once in fact, although Sophie had come to see Emma and him a number of times.

Vin and Martha both came to the front door. Martha said, "Hello Matt," and reached up to put a kiss on his cheek. She turned to Emma, "And its lovely to see you again Emma, with your two exciting pieces of news." She glanced at Emma's left hand, and was pleased to see that she was wearing an engagement ring. She glanced at Emma's abdomen under her jacket, but it was too early for the baby to show.

Vin and Matthew said hello to each other. Vin looked at Emma, and remembered sadly again about her telling him, that her sister Sophie was still away. He thought, when she looked at him, she was looking pensive, but they said hello to each other and air kissed each other's cheeks.

Emma exclaimed, "What a lovely display of daffodils you have at the front. I think everything is a bit late this year isn't it? Who planted those?"

Martha told her, "I planted them over the last three years, and they pretty much look after themselves. Vin cuts the grass, and I plant flowers. But, we will be growing stuff to eat in the greenhouse and outdoors this year, because... you know! Anyway, do come through. I will just go and check the oven. Come with me into the kitchen, and you'll be able to see some tulips in the back garden."

Matthew and Vin talked in the living room. Matthew had been taken aback by the hug his father had given him at the airport 5 days earlier, and now he looked at his father and thought he looked strained. He felt concern, but decided that he needed to tell him about Emma's visit to Patrick Quinn's church. He said, "Dad, Emma was at Patrick's church this morning. Her parents wanted her to go with them, to pray for Sophie's safe return. I hope you understand. She got upset by what Patrick was saying, and I had to go and pick her up."

Vin asked, "What did he say that made her upset? Did she tell you?"

"You know, I had already told you a bit about his church. Well, it as bad as we had thought. Emma told me that he was saying that ultra pneumonia is part of God's plan. The only way the Isle of Man will be spared is if all evildoers have been cast out. Then he named you and the Army Major in particular, but also said all alien residents, who don't follow Manx ways and attend church regularly, or something like that. And, being cast out means being put on a ship in Douglas Harbour, to sail off and never be seen again. He was trying to stir the congregation up to support him."

Vin sat still, feeling a bit shaken. Matthew thought some humour was called for. He said, "Some fool thinks it is a good idea to put unwanted people on a ship, and now somebody else wants to do it. See what you've started?"

"Yes, but this is not funny, is it?" Vin said.

Matthew reasoned, "Okay Dad, let's be serious. These are desperate times, and Patrick is a trouble maker, and some people might be convinced by him. But, that doesn't mean that his plan to get rid of us is at all likely to happen. Poor Emma was worried for me, even though I didn't get a specific mention by Patrick, like you did. I told her I had no intention of going anywhere. By the way I was wondering if ..."

At that moment Martha and Emma walked in the room. Emma said, "Vin, I was saying to Martha what lovely gardens you have. It must have been dark when I came before."

"Well, my son probably thought he would only risk you getting two fleeting glimpses of his parents, before today. Otherwise, we might have put you off him. Well, it looks like you are committed to him now. You can see his Mum is very nice, but you want to watch out for me, as I am officially an evildoer, apparently," Vin told Emma. He smiled to show that he felt no malice towards Emma.

Matthew saw his mother frown slightly. He said hastily, "It's alright Mum, it is just that Dad has been caught out chopping up live bodies for a change, and their relatives told him that he was evil. Really though Dad, I am sure Emma is fine is with both of you."

At that point Emma decided to do her own bit of jesting. She shook her head, made her eyes wide, and said in a mock shriek in Matthew's direction, "No they are horrible, take me home!"

Everyone laughed. Martha asked, "Well won't you at least stay for a bit of roast pork with vegetables, and gooseberry crumble to follow, before you go?"

Matthew answered, "That sounds good to me."

Emma pretended reluctance, saying, "Oh alright then, I will stay. It's a long walk home from here, if Mattie is staying." But she gave Martha a big smile.

Emma enjoyed having lunch with Matt's parents. They talked about how Vin and Martha had met at university in Norwich, where Vin had been a hard working medical student, but he had still found time to get to know Martha. Martha's version was that she was a hard working modern languages student, who had still found time to take Vin under her wing. They had met at a party, but had both joined the university rambling group. Vin recounted that Martha would say that the Norfolk countryside was not as good as the Isle of Man, and Vin would say she was lucky, because the Norfolk countryside was much better than any countryside anywhere near Forest Gate in East London, where he was from. The story after that was that they moved in together and never separated, getting married somewhere along the way. It had been a financial struggle at first, with them both trying to establish careers in London. She became a qualified social worker; and he set his sights on micro-biology and pathology, which involved long hours of study, as well as gruelling shifts in hospital. He qualified for appointment as a Consultant Pathologist at the age 31, and started looking for a suitable post. One of the first vacancies he saw was on the Isle of Man. He had been there on a few visits over the years with Martha, and he was keen to apply for it. Martha warned him it might be considered a professional backwater, and she worried that

Vin might feel the distance from his relatives and the frequent family gatherings. In truth, she also worried that she herself might feel it to be a bit parochial, having lived away for so many years. And there were no vacancies for social workers at that time. But she decided that the Isle of Man would be a great place to bring up a new baby, as by then Matthew was on the way. So Vin applied for the post and got it. They bought a house in Onchan, brought up Matthew, she got back into social work, Vin got one promotion when the post of Senior Consultant was created, and a few years ago they moved to this house in Baldrin.

It seemed to Matthew that Emma had listened to this potted history with interest, and he thought that was nice. They went on to talk a bit about Matthew's childhood, and some old photos were produced, which made Emma smile. But there was a slight underlying tension, because no mention was made of the baby girl, 5 years younger than Matthew. Matthew could remember her hazily. He knew she was called Jessica, and she had died, when only six months old, in her cot one night. He had the feeling that his father became less demonstrative of his affection for him, and for his mother, at that time.

After dinner Martha said to Emma, "Would you like to have a potter round the garden with me, and I can tell you about all the plants that aren't in flower yet, as it is way too early this far north. Have you ever been in southern England in Spring time? I lived in Norfolk, and then South London for over ten years altogether. Everything there is always two or three weeks ahead of here. Only the very late daffodils will still be in flower there." She went quiet, thinking how things would become there, when ultra pneumonia took hold.

Emma broke into her thoughts, saying, "Yes, I would love a look round your garden. You told me earlier about Matthew playing in the garden, but that would have been in Onchan wouldn't it?"

Martha said, "Yes that's right," as they went out into the garden.

Matthew found himself in the living room with his father. He wondered how to break the silence, now it was just the two of them together again. Matthew knew that his father was keen on Scrabble, but that game left Matthew cold.

Matthew suggested, "Do you fancy a game of chess Dad? I am sure we used to play each other occasionally, before I went off to university."

Vin agreed, "Alright Matthew, that would make a change."

They found a chess set and started playing. Matthew said, "I might not usually mention this Dad, but I just wanted to say that I do care about you. It's not nice to hear about you being denounced by that Patrick Quinn."

"I know I haven't always been the most affectionate father, but these are desperate times, so I am going to say this, possibly for the first and last time. I love you, I am glad you made it back, and if turns out that you have brought ultra pneumonia back with you, well I am still glad. That's because I have decided that you and your Mum are much more important to me than the rest of the people on this island."

"Thanks Dad, but what if it is Emma?"

"She's a lovely girl. I am not sure you deserve her, but she seems very fond of you. And I can tell you are fond of her, so that means I care about her too."

"Good, although that wasn't quite what I meant. But Dad, I think you are being a bit harsh on everyone else, even if I don't really blame you. Hasn't that Major Quinnel put himself on the line? Isn't Mum's Director, David Quayle, now a friend of yours? Aren't the doctors at the hospital appreciative of your advice?"

"Yes, maybe you are right. I like to think that I have served the community here well over the years. There has been the odd unfriendly remark which has been aimed at my race; you have probably had a bit of that yourself. But I suppose, overall, the people here deserve to survive, like they do everywhere really."

"So you have been pro-active in trying to bring about survival where you can, which is here. And if you have succeeded, that is brilliant. But, I have been thinking a bit about the future, if it turns out be Mann alone. I have quite a creative role at my company SITS and..."

"You are doing quite well there, aren't you Matthew? I think your mother said that you had been promoted to be a project manager, a while back."

"Yes, that's true. One or two ideas I have come up with have been quite useful to clients, and have helped our company get new business, and to grow. So, they think quite well of me, if I say so myself. Anyway, we were talking on Wednesday on how everything would change, and I thought about how this would affect my company in particular. All of our big overseas clients will not exist anymore, but there is a clear need for some sort of continuity of an internet or database available to all people and businesses on the island, including the Government. Both my boss Simon, and the CEO Sarah, think that SITS, as the biggest IT company on the island, should be represented on the Emergency Advisory Committee, and they think that representative should be me.

I think that I could really be helpful, not just about IT but, you know, imaginative and clear thinking about all the issues. And Dad, you were on the Committee weren't you, and now you know David Quayle and a couple of the Ministers?

"Yes, but I am not sure that my recommending that you be on the Committee would help you. It is not just Patrick Quinn who has a negative opinion of me. Adrian Kelly, the Minister who is chairing the Committee, seems to dislike me strongly. The man is a fool anyway. In fact, with him running this Committee, I think we will all be back in the Stone Age very quickly."

Matthew felt a bit deflated by this. He said quietly, "Oh I see."

Vin went on, "I don't mean that you should not be on it. I am sure you would add a lot of positive, useful energy to it. Look, I will give David Quayle a ring anyway. David is on the Committee, and sometimes manages to steer Adrian Kelly in the right direction for a while."

They continued with their game of chess, as Martha and Emma joined them again. Vin noted how often his wife seemed able to strike up a friendly relationship upon meeting someone, much more easily than he could himself. But, he thought to himself, that was why her profession suited her, whereas he liked to think that he was a determined investigator and evaluator of the evidence he found, before reaching solid reliable conclusions, and not given to emotional factors of any kind. And, then he reflected on the events of the last week, and decided that the evidence pointed to a solid reliable conclusion that he could, in fact, easily be swayed by emotion.

The next piece of solid evidence to confront Vin was that Matthew had him in checkmate, even though Matthew was playing with the black pieces and had gone second. And Matthew's play had been imaginative, luring Vin to take Matthew's last bishop, thereby opening himself up to being checkmated in three more moves, with the queen and a rook.

The four of them talked about wedding plans. Emma said, smiling, "I don't really fancy a church wedding, whatever some people might think. But I like the idea of a June date, as this will make an honest woman of me, well before baby is born." She thought to herself, "I didn't quite mean it like that, but I do want our baby to feel as secure as it will be possible to be."

Matthew and Emma eventually made their way home, after tea and cakes, at around 7pm. On their way Emma said, "Your parents are nice, aren't they?"

Matthew replied, "If you say so. Yes my Mum is great. My dad always felt a bit cold to me, even if he could get worked up about work, or the news, or something. Today is the first time he has ever told me he loves me."

Emma responded, "Wow! With me it is the other way round. My mum is the stand-offish one. Poor old Dad is pretty much under the thumb, but he is kind and supportive with me and Sophie." She suddenly felt sad again, because of what ultra pneumonia was doing, because of Sophie, because of Patrick's horrible sermon, and because her mum just would not accept Matthew.

Chapter 22, Monday 12 April 2027

A meeting of the Council of Ministers started at 9.30am. Henry Smith said, "Well everyone, we were introduced to reality about the ultra pneumonia virus a week ago by Dr Singh, but I don't think we have handled things well since. The Emergency Advisory Committee doesn't sound like it is actually dealing with the issues properly, or making useful recommendations. I have the impression that the key issue of keeping the embargo secure was not resolved, although fortunately I know that the Chief Constable and the Army Major are working well together about this."

Adrian Kelly was muttering, and trying to interject. Henry Smith added, "We will come back to that later. I think we need to deal with the repatriation flight first. This was very nearly a tragedy in its own right, which it need not have been if we had kept calm, and thought for ourselves of the solution, that others found for us."

There was more muttering from Adrian.

Henry Smith continued, "We will hear from you Adrian, but that will be when I am ready. We should never have approved the repatriation flight. It is pretty clear that it would have greatly increased the risk of ultra pneumonia getting to us. South Africa is literally dying as I speak. There must be people in London who have got off flights from Johannesburg and other South African cities, when they were still running, and who are carrying this virus. We must fervently hope or pray that anyone, who arrived on the Isle of Man before we closed the borders on Tuesday, has not been infected. If we do survive, it may well turn out to be thanks to the initiative and determination shown by Peter Quinnel and his Army Reservists."

Adrian Kelly interrupted, "I don't think it was just his mad idea. I reckon that that Dr Singh was putting him up to it. And it was crazy, they very nearly shot that aircraft down."

Henry did not agree. He said,"Well good for him, if Dr Singh was involved. He wants to save us, and yet social media is full of messages saying he and Peter Quinnel are evil, and should be cast away, so that we can be saved. It beggars belief really. And Adrian, you still don't get it do you? There is the most vicious, lethal pandemic ever known, about to sweep through the rest of the world from Africa, and the only real option we have is for us to keep the rest of the world securely quarantined from the Isle Of Man, and hope we have acted in time. And yet you support new flights arriving, and you attack people who bravely prevent this from happening. Well, we need to get a grip and start doing things properly, and I must admit my own failings in not acting earlier. First of all, I want a show of hands that we will entertain no more attempts at repatriation or re-opening the border at all."

Jack Coyle spoke, "Sorry Chief Minister, I would just like to make one comment."

Henry acceded, "Go on then."

Jack said, "I have reflected on my own circumstances and behaviour. I greatly regret supporting the repatriation flight.

The most important thing now is to give ourselves a chance, by keeping out everyone not here already, as best we can."

Peter Corlett spoke, "I don't think we have much choice now, but we need to recognise lots of people are frightened, and some are angry. Many are looking for some sort of Divine explanation as to why there is this pandemic, and how they might survive. Regretably perhaps, Patrick Quinn and his Astrological Church seem to have hit some sort of a chord with many. In a nutshell, they say it is the end of the current world. The new world will only be populated by the righteous. They are saying that God started with Madagascar, because He was angry with their venerating false idols or dead ancestors rather than Him, but Mann will only be spared if all evildoers are cast out. And he has cited Dr Singh and the Major as evildoers. We need to be careful not to align ourselves too closely with those two."

Henry said, "Hmm, I hear what you say, although I don't like it much. Now, let's just get it clear about no more returnees at all."

Adrian asked, "When you say 'no more returnees at all' presumably we are going to let the Senior Serenity come here and disembark in three weeks, if they are well."

Henry said,"I am guessing your sister opted to board that ship when the plane got to Liverpool."

Adrian said sadly, "I don't know. I haven't heard from her."

Henry stated, "Well, I think allowing that ship to come here, and to disembark, should be done only on the advice of our Senior Consultant in Pathology, Dr Singh. Now, that show of hands."

All of the Ministers followed Henry's lead, to confirm that no more repatriations would be allowed.

Henry addressed them all again, saying, "Now I want to move on to the Emergency Advisory Committee. I am sorry Adrian, but it needs a lot more drive, and I think you have allowed yourself to get distracted by various personal concerns."

Adrian responded, "I think that is unfair. Dr Singh was a very disruptive influence on Thursday, but now he has gone..."

Jack interrupted, "Dr Singh was at least trying to get the Committee to deal with the most important point first, the security of the embargo. There is still a lot that that Committee needs to get going on. Food for example. You may, or may not, remember that we as a Government did have recently a policy of encouraging gradual import substitution. Well, now complete substitution is going to have to happen overnight, except that for many things that will be impossible, for example tea, coffee, wine, bananas..."

Henry said, "Thank you Jack. Food obviously is a vital subject, but just now we need to focus on getting this Committee working properly. Jack, I think you would recognise that the whole economy is being completely shaken up, not just the food sector?"

Jack agreed, "Well that's right of course. A lot of businesses will lose 99% of their income, for example finance and insurance. But we will need more people producing food I think. I am sure that quite a few people are figuring these things out. I think we will need to run basically a command economy at the beginning anyway, a bit like Britain was way back in the Second World War, even though the main party in power the Conservatives was ideologically pro free enterprise. We will still need money as a means of exchange even though the Bank of England will be no more, and presumably all the banks other than Manx Bank will also not exist."

Henry stopped him by saying, "And, if you were chairing the Committee, how would you feel about getting some technically minded and innovative people involved to help you?"

Jack had not expected to be asked that. He said, "Sorry Henry, that has taken me a bit by surprise. Are you really are thinking about asking me?"

"Well, we need someone who has some grasp of the realities, and determination to get things done, and that describes you. I just think you will need lots of help coming up with answers. That's why I mentioned other people being involved."

"I am never shy about stealing other people's ideas, unless I think they are wrong of course. So yes, make me chairman, and I will definitely have bright young people on the Committee, and we would be seeking input from outside Government generally."

"Very well, that's settled. Jack will be taking over chairmanship of the Emergency Advisory Committee forthwith. Of course the Council of Ministers will still be meeting regularly, and hearing what the Committee have been doing."

John Quayle intervened, "Chief Minister, do you mind if I just mention one bright young person who I think Jack could use on the Committee. Matthew Singh, who works for SITS, that's Sodor Information Technology Solutions."

Adrian Kelly chipped in, "He must be Dr Singh's son, I am guessing."

John nodded.

Adrian added, "Well this is ridiculous. Dr Singh has upset half the population, and he is a very loose cannon. I really can't believe his son will be suited for..."

John challenged Adrian, "Why won't he be suited? Is it because he doesn't have a Manx or British surname, or that he has an Asian father?"

Peter Corlett joined in, "Well, actually Adrian does have a point. These are very alarming times, and a lot of the population are not thinking rationally. Many seem to be taking heed of the rubbish Patrick Quinn has been saying, which is that evildoers need casting out, and this includes alien residents not following Manx customs and Christian worship. Maybe it would be best not to antagonise the population, if this rubbish becomes a popular sentiment. We will need them on our side, to accept the changes and hardships that are probably inevitable, rather than that they decide to foster insurrections of some kind."

John could not accept that. He said, "Did you know that Matthew Singh was born here? His mother is a Manx woman who is a social worker, helping our less well functioning members of society, his father has been a pathologist on the island for nearly 30 years, and he oversees a pathology department giving invaluable advice to other doctors, and Matthew himself is a very highly thought of senior employee, within our most dynamic IT company on the island. So Peter, lets not worry about the kind of mumbo jumbo that Adrian listens to, when he goes to that church run by his nutty mate Patric Quinn."

Gemma Cain decided to make a contribution, "I am not that interested in the mumbo jumbo, or the family history. But, I have contacts with quite a few businesses, and I am sure

Matthew's name has been mentioned several times as being someone who has helped them sort out IT, and more general organisational problems. It sounds to me like he is someone who could help."

Henry started to speak, "So perhaps...Wait a minute, is that chanting from outside?" He walked over to the window and looked down on the street below. He could see a procession of about 100 people, mainly aggressive looking young men, accompanied by four police officers. Some were carrying banners saying, "Cast out unbelievers," and, "Cast out evil doers," but the chants were "Singh out! Major out!" Henry observed that the onlookers were more varied in appearance than the marchers, but that quite a few were clapping them. Henry thought to himself, "Maybe we do need to handle the situation very carefully."

Henry said, "As I have said Jack, I want you to take over the Emergency Advisory Committee. At the current time it might be a good idea not to include Matthew Singh in any official capacity, if you understand?"

Jack replied, "Yes, I understand."

When the meeting broke up an hour later, Jack had a three way conversation with Gemma and John in his office. He said, "Can you two tell me a bit more about Matthew Singh. Not that it should make any difference about Matthew, but I must admit I have changed my views about Dr Singh. Realistically, we would definitely be doomed without the embargo, and all credit to him for haranguing us into that. And that Major Quinnel may have saved the day as well. Anyway, Gemma what do you know?"

Gemma answered, "Just what I said earlier really. Until ultra pneumonia came along, this island was becoming increasingly prosperous through offering a low tax, but sensibly regulated, regime for businesses to operate within. All credit to this and previous Governments for that. But, it has also required well educated and trained employees to run and operate these businesses. And, in the IT sector, one of these key people is definitely Matthew Singh."

They turned to John. He told them, "I will be honest with you, I didn't know about Matthew, until I got a call from my cousin David. He just said that he heard, I presume from Matthew's father, that Matthew wanted to help the Government adapt to the situation, and that he had ideas he thought would be helpful. I decided to speak to two people at SITS where he works this morning, and they were full of his praises, and were very keen that he should be involved with the Government. Of course, they might be hoping that it helps their company as well. I have got Matthew's mobile phone number if you want it, bearing in mind what Henry said."

Jack replied, "Well yes please, as I am intrigued to speak to him. Sure I will keep it unofficial, but I don't see why, however bad the situation is, we should descend to mob rule, pursuing some depraved racist or religious agenda."

Chapter 23, Tuesday 13 April 2027

Vin was feeling like eating some breakfast, having been up for twenty minutes. But they were practically out of milk and cereal, so he decided to wander along to the local store, on the main road through Baldrine, to see if he could get some. He had heard that food rationing would soon be introduced, but, in the meantime, he knew that many shops were restricting sales to their usual customers only. Vin walked out of the shop with a 1 litre carton of milk and a box of shreddies. He noticed Patrick Quayle's car, a white Audi, pulled up on the other side of the road facing the wrong way. As a white transit van drove fast towards it, the Audi passenger door started to open. The van had already started to pass it. The road was fairly narrow and a blue van going the other way, which had right of way, had kept going. The two vans just avoided a collision with each other, but the white van hit the open passenger door of Patrick's car with a loud bang. There was also a scream, and Vin saw that it was Patrick's wife, Theresa, in the passenger seat. Vin rushed over, and saw that Theresa's left leg was broken below the knee, with blood spurting from the break. Patrick had already got out of the driver's side onto the pavement. He was calling out, "Help, someone please, call an ambulance."

Vin said to him, "We've got to stop that bleeding straight away, it's obviously a main artery. Give me your tie." Patrick was shaking as he pulled at the tie, without success. Vin said, "Is it okay if I take it?" Patrick nodded his head, and Vin pulled the tie loose at the knot.

Theresa was still screaming, and Vin said to her, "We will deal with the pain soon, but we have got to stop the bleeding." He put the tie around her leg, just above the knee, and pulled it tight. Vin said out loud, "I need to make it tighter with a stick, or something, to twist round the tie."

A female voice said to him, "I thought you would, so I have just grabbed this out of the store." Vin looked up and recognised the young woman, Molly Smith. Molly handed him a plastic, but sturdy looking, long handled cooking spoon. Vin placed it above the knot he had made, tied the loose ends around the spoon, and twisted it several times. Theresa passed out, but Vin could tell that she was still breathing. The blood was no longer spurting out of the wound.

"Has anyone called an ambulance?" Vin asked Molly. She told him, "I have just tried, but I can't get a signal. It's not usually a problem here."

Another voice spoke. It was Maggie the shop keeper. She said, "I have rung on the landline, from the shop. They are on their way."

Vin was thinking to himself, "I hope they get here soon. This tourniquet is extremely crude, and the leg below still needs a blood supply to prevent serious tissue damage, or even the loss of the lower leg."

Patrick was feeling very unnerved. He demanded of Vin, " In the name of Christ is she going to be okay?"

Vin told him, "I don't think Christ will have much to do with it. But I do know that the paramedics on the island are brilliant, and they should be here soon. Also, we have a fantastic orthopaedic surgeon, who has got people walking again after some quite nasty breaks. Only thing is, he is an Asian like me. His name is Ayeez Karachi. I am sure he will do a great job, if he is not forced off the island on a ship to nowhere." Patrick looked scared. Vin had no idea what Patrick thought about his last comment.

The ambulance arrived ten minutes later.

One of the paramedics said to Vin, "I think I have seen you at the hospital. You are a doctor aren't you? In fact, you are the supposedly evil Dr Singh according to ..." And then she noticed Patrick Quinn standing there, and the paramedic shook her head in amazement.

"That's right, I am Dr Singh, and I have my faults, but I don't think I am evil. I am actually the Senior Consultant in Pathology, which some people thinks means I only know how to deal with dead people. Anyway, this is definitely right outside my usual comfort zone, of dealing with people after they have died," Vin replied.

"Well, she is still breathing, and it looks like you have stopped her from bleeding to death, so well done. But you probably realise that your tourniquet is far from ideal. We really need to replace it with our standard tourniquet, which can be regulated to the right pressure for each patient. The main problem is that there would be further blood loss, whilst we replace your tourniquet with ours. We should give her a drip anyway."

"I would say we probably got the bleeding under control within about 3 minutes. But, it was spurting before that, so she must have lost quite a bit. As you can see, she is unconscious, which might be partly the pain, but it can't be a good sign."

"Well my colleague has got the drip in now. We will radio A and E to stand by for an urgent trauma case. The police still aren't here. Could you go round to the driver's side, and help from there to ease her out onto our trolley?"

They managed to get Theresa out of the car, onto the trolley, and into the back of the ambulance. It set off just as a police car arrived. Vin, Patrick and other witnesses were spoken to by the two police officers. One of the officers took some photographs of the scene. A second police car arrived, and after a few minutes, it took Patrick off to the hospital. Eventually, Vin was able to wander off home, in a bit of a daze, with the cereal and milk he had gone out for in the first place, about an hour earlier.

Chapter 24, Wednesday 14 April 2027

The day after the incident with Patrick's wife, Vin was at the hospital, trying to catch up with his work again. He knew that his Consultant colleague, Philip Patterson, and the rest of the staff were dealing with as much as possible, but they still needed him to review and direct their work. He still felt a bit shaken by the incident. He reflected that in Southern Africa people were dying in their millions, so he should regard the road accident as nothing by comparison. Apart from his conversations with Matthew on Sunday, he was aware, from social media, that some people were becoming very unbalanced by the news of the relentless spread of ultra pneumonia through Southern Africa. They were afraid, and Patrick's irrational ideas as to how to win God's approval were gaining support. Vin was in his office talking to Philip, when Patrick opened his door and walked in. Patrick had a wild look in his eyes, and Vin felt slightly alarmed.

Patrick said to him in a strange voice, "It has been revealed that you are not an embodiment of evil, but that you are the second Saviour. My wife's injury was obviously a demonstration to me, by God, that you are a great and benevolent Saviour, here on the Isle of Man trying to save us all. Theresa is still alive thanks to you, and it looks like her leg will mend well. I know that you have been behind the decision stopping all our people from coming home, and I now accept that this is the Will of God. That it is also his Will, that you should lead us to salvation. It is not for me to question why you have been chosen, but I will be doing all I can, from now, to get others to recognise you as the second Saviour, and not to thwart God's Will by opposing you, or by trying to cause you harm. When I meet you, or speak about you, I will refer to you as the Lord."

Vin thought to himself, "This bloke is completely bonkers, even if that is not a recognised psychiatric term. Whilst I am more clued up than a lot of people, I am certainly not a divine choice of some kind. But we can use Patrick to influence people in the right way, and to accept the tough measures that will be needed."

Vin asked Philip to leave him for 10 minutes. He then found himself saying to Patrick, "You are right, I have been chosen, and I am a Saviour. The accident was clearly meant to demonstrate my benevolent power to you. It is best that you don't refer to me as the second Saviour, because it is God's Will that this has only been revealed to you, as the Minister in the Astrological Church. Please don't refer to me as your Lord either. Refer to me as Dr Singh, and call me Dr Singh if we happen to meet. I can tell you that God has caused this plague, because He is angry with man's inhumanity to other men. Your church is correct that the old world had to end. He does not intend anyone outside of Mann to survive, but it is His Will that a good and kind society is now created here on this island, embracing all human beings who were here when the embargo began. He wants all those within this sanctuary to be treated equally. He wants Major Quinnel, and me and my Earthly family, to be treated with respect. It would make

Him angry, if you foster any more hatred against anyone at all. He wants you to preach tolerance and forgiveness. He has chosen the Isle of Man as a last sanctuary for mankind, because of the name of the island. That is His design. I have been chosen to help this happen. What He wants you to do, as your first task, is to explain to all those who you influence that it is God's Will, that no one should be persuaded or compelled to leave Mann. I know you have a lot of influence, Patrick. Use it in accordance with God's Will. Can I count on you Patrick?"

Patrick looked and sounded a lot calmer, as if he was glad to have it confirmed that there was indeed a Saviour on the island. He said, "Yes my Lord... I mean, yes of course Dr Singh. I will use my influence to get the deportation idea dropped. What shall we do about Adrian Kelly? He was particularly keen on you and others being cast away."

Vin felt tempted to suggest something unpleasant for Adrian Kelly but instead said, "Tolerance and forgiveness are what God wants, and this is to be shown to everyone including Adrian Kelly. But you yourself have attacked me, and Major Quinnel and non Manx people, so He is looking for you to make amends for that. Please go on social media, and describe all who you attacked as being God's children. Say that people not born on Mann are people who have brought special skills and talents, that will be needed in this new world."

Patrick was feeling eager to please. He replied, "Yes Dr Singh, I will."

Vin added, "And, when you have done that, you will prepare a sermon that you will give in your church next

Sunday, making it clear that God's design is that no one is cast out, and that we are all to work together."

Patrick readily agreed, "Yes Dr Singh, I will do that. And thank you for saving my wife. We never had children, but she means so much to me. Theresa would like to thank you herself, but in view of everything, I would quite understand if you don't want this to happen."

Vin said, "No it is fine. I will go along to her ward later today".

Patrick left, and Philip came back in the office almost straight away. Philip said, "So you are the Saviour now are you? Should I bow, or kiss your hand?"

Vin jested, "If you don't watch out, you will have to kiss my posterior, not just my hand. The key thing is I have persuaded Patrick to reverse his position about deporting me, the Major, and my fellow ethnic minorities. He has a lot of influence, so I am confident that won't happen now."

Philip jested back, "Thank goodness for that. There may still be a chance of getting a decent curry occasionally then." He smiled, and punched Vin lightly on the shoulder.

Vin commented, "Opinions about me seem to vary wildly then. Some people think I am divine, and others think that I am a curry cook. Although I suppose I could be divine at making curries."

Philip said, "Well you certainly are not a divine character, going by how crotchety and sharp tongued you can be. But you did invite me round for a curry once, a few years back. Do you remember? Anyway, putting curries to one side, I do know you are a good man trying very hard to get the right things done, so I am glad it looks like you will be sticking around."

Chapter 25 Wednesday 14 April 2027

Peter was at his farm. He had about two hours, before he was due to go off to his weekly drill meeting. Although his Reservists were now effectively working full time as Army soldiers, Peter had decided to keep Wednesday evening meetings going, as an opportunity for him to see many of them face to face. That way he stood a better chance of finding out about any problems. The telephone rang and he answered it.

It was Vin saying, "Hello Peter, it's Vin here."

Peter replied, "Hello Vin. We only spoke a few days ago at police HQ. Presumably you're not ringing just for a chat?"

"No. If I didn't mention it then, you did a brilliant job diverting that plane. But, you and I, in trying to save Mann, we have been making ourselves some enemies."

"I realised that when I came out of police HQ on Saturday, to find 'Army scum' sprayed on my car. And I have seen social media attacks on both you and me, and non Manx people for some reason, and there was even a demonstration in Douglas I heard mentioned on Manx Radio."

"That's why I am ringing really. Certainly there is a lot of fear around. It is understandable, and looking for scapegoats is nothing new. But the chief rabble rouser has undoubtedly been Patrick Quinn, probably only second generation Manx himself, but leader of the extremist Manx First party, with some influence inside the Government. And he is a minister in a church believing in the end of the current world."

"Yes, I have heard of Patrick Quinn."

"Well, by amazing co-incidence, I was on the spot when his wife was seriously injured in a car accident, and I kept her alive till the paramedics arrived." And Vin went on to explain about Patrick now believing that he, Dr Singh, is a second Saviour, and that he will be reversing his campaign, so that he would show support for Dr Singh and the Major.

Vin added, "But don't tell anyone else about the Saviour thing, or it might backfire. Anyway, everyone is probably looking for positive signs, and I think we could both take this as a positive sign, don't you?"

Peter queried, "So you are pretty convinced that most of the trouble making will stop now?"

"Yes I am. What little psychology I have done tells me that Patrick is not a true leader. There are lots of people who are good cheerleaders for others, when they see someone who shows stronger leadership than they do, and whose aims suit themselves. They often then give fairly unquestioning loyalty to that leader. The German people and the Nazis were like that with Hitler."

"So, are you thinking of emulating Hitler?"

"No, it is just that we need to manipulate Patrick to be a good influence, not a malign one, and I am confident that I have done that."

"I didn't really see you as a mad dictator. Great. I will tell Amanda. She has been even more down than normal since Saturday. She saw the graffiti on the car, before I could wash it off."

Peter hung up and swivelled in his chair, as he had done a few days earlier after speaking to David Quayle. And again, Amanda was standing there. She asked, "What are you going to tell me?"

He explained to her what Vin had told him, and that Patrick Quinn would now reverse his campaign.

Amanda checked, "So you definitely won't be put on a boat, and cast away?"

"It was unlikely anyway, but no, I am definitely not being put on a boat," confirmed Peter.

Amanda had started gently sobbing. Peter looked at her, and felt surprised and moved. When Gemma had died, they had been unable to comfort each other. They began sleeping in separate rooms. He stood up, and put his arms around her. She said, "I couldn't bear to lose you as well."

He said, "No, we have still got each other." He kissed her on her neck, and she responded. Suddenly, he had dragged her into the bedroom that they used to share, and they made their marriage a physical union for the first time in six months.

They cuddled together afterwards. "You are still only 38, and I am only 44. We could have another child you know," Peter told her.

She said, "I wouldn't want anyone to replace Gemma. She was a perfect daughter."

He responded, "Well not quite perfect, as she could be quite wilful. Do you remember that time she hid the newspaper, and said she wouldn't tell me where it was, until I had read her the next chapter of 'The Big Friendly Giant'?"

Amanda laughed. He said, "So we will always remember her." But he thought to himself, "But perhaps the Isle Of Man, struggling on its own, will not be such a great world to bring another child into."

Chapter 26, Thursday 15 April 2027

Jack Coyle spoke to Matthew Singh outside the conference room, before his first meeting as chairman of the Emergency Advisory Committee began.

Jack held out his hand, saying, "Hello I'm Jack Coyle. You must be Matthew Singh. I know we spoke on the phone last night, but we've never met before, have we?"

Matthew smiled confidently, "So how do you know that I'm Matthew Singh?"

Jack smiled back, "Maybe you look a bit like your father, although you are taller and younger."

When everyone was in the room Jack addressed everyone, "Thank you all for coming. It would be an understatement to say that these are challenging times, but we are going to do the best we can. There will be all sorts of problems. I thought the most useful approach would be to have a bit of a brainstorming session on each subject, to start with. That can sometimes be useful in innovating solutions to problems. And, if any urgent actions are identified as necessary, we can agree those. But, before that, the most important subject has to be the security of the embargo. Without that, we are probably all doomed anyway. Although it is of prime importance, I am hoping it won't take long. At the last meeting we got a bit bogged down, but, would I be right in saying to Major Quinnel and Chief Constable Corps, that you have agreed basic working arrangements to secure the embargo within the limits of the resources available to you?"

Terry Corps nodded. Peter said, "The arrangements between us and the Coastguard and the Civil Defence seem to be working well enough, but there is perhaps what could be a serious resource issue, in that we don't have really significant firepower against a seriously armed boat for example."

Terry added a comment, "Except for that 105mm artillery gun of yours."

There were a few smiles and a couple of frowns at that remark.

Jack said, "Until the British military collapses, along with the rest of the UK generally, we are benefitting from their assistance. After that, we just have to hope that you will be able to deal with whatever arises, using that artillery piece if it helps. I think I am not alone in having gained a lot of confidence in you recently. Major."

That remark induced a couple of quiet "Here, heres!" around the meeting, which Peter found quite uplifting.

Jack went on, "And just to be absolutely clear this meeting will record," and he looked at the secretary who was taking the minutes, (even though the meeting was also being audio-recorded), "that it absolutely supports the use of lethal force as necesssary by uniformed officers serving Mann, in defending the security of the island from any breach of the embargo."

Jack looked around to see if any dissent needed to be discusssed. He saw Nicola Kermode was frowning, and he caught her eye. He raised his eyebrows, as if to say, "Do you disagree?" and Nicola shook her head.

Jack went on, looking at Peter and Terry, "Good, that seems to be security covered. Obviously, if any concerns arise that you feel my input, or discussion by this Committee, would be useful, do come back to us."

He talked to the wider meeting, "Now, as I said I would like to start each subject with a brainstorming session, to see if it throws up ideas that are useful. You don't have to stick to your own field, but obviously it helps it we don't all chip in at the same time. We are going to start with internet and banking issues. You might not think these issues are vital, but you may think otherwise once you have heard from young Matthew Singh here. He works at SITS, the fastest growing, and now the biggest IT company on the island. He's been brought in because he has a glowing reputation in the commercial sector, partly as an IT whiz, but more generally as an innovator, who comes up with practical solutions to business problems."

Matthew felt his confidence sag slightly. He was more used to winning people round more gradually. He said, "Hello everyone. In case you had any doubt, my father is indeed Dr Singh, the pathologist. He is great at finding out what is wrong with dead people, although I sometimes wonder if that is leaving it a bit too late."

This drew a few chuckles, and Matthew relaxed slightly. He went on, "So brainstorming eh! Well, I think I can see more problems than solutions. But, in the spheres Jack has just mentioned, I have some ideas. So what are the problems? Take the internet and files in the so called Cloud. Once this virus starts marching across America and Europe, the internet is going to fall over pretty rapidly, and people might find data they thought they had securely on file is lost. A related problem I can see is money and banking. Only the Manx Bank is based on the island. They might survive, but will the other banks, which are essentially just branches of banks with HQ s in London or China? And we don't have a Central Bank." Matthew stopped speaking, and looked at Jack.

Jack asked, "Didn't you say you had ideas, Matthew?"

Matthew replied, "Yes, but this is a brainstorming session, and people often are more supportive if they have been involved. So has anyone else any ideas, before I tell you mine?"

A couple of people were muttering. Suddenly Nicola said, "Do we need different banks? Wouldn't one do? The Government could take over Manx Bank. It could have its own accounts with that bank, and everyone else could have accounts with it too. I would have thought paying or receiving money would be simple."

Peter Quinnel chipped in, "The internet is jolly useful. I think the data people most usually access is stored or retrieved through big servers. Couldn't we get as much as possible transferred to main frames here, which could presumably act as servers for internet users on the island."

Terry commented, "A lot of data is bound to be lost. We do need to think about safeguarding key data. Perhaps each business or organisation needs to come up with a plan of its own to save its data."

Jack added, "But, then they turn to experts to help them achieve that?"

Peter said, "About money again. What if your company has, say, £500 million in overseas bank accounts? Would it be able to transfer that back to the Isle of Man? Would that create inflation? What about if you own assets abroad instead, say property or businesses, you will lose it all."

Jack commented, "Could we all start from scratch again, maybe? Everything already owned on the island stays with the current owner, and if the Government needs to take it over, compensation is paid. But, say, everyone else is decreed a fair starting balance in a Manx Bank account, that bank being taken over or controlled by the Government."

Nicola objected, "That could be very unfair. Someone might have been saving for years to buy a house, whilst someone has debts built up through extravagance."

Terry said, "Given the circumstances, it might still be useful to start afresh, but say with upper and lower limits for individual accounts."

There was a bit of a pause, as if people were waiting for Matthew to make some sense of things. He said, "It is interesting what you have been saying about Manx Bank. I am pretty sure their records are basically Cloud based. They don't own mainframes, and I don't think they have much in the way of inhouse IT knowledge. They have a contract with a USA located datacentre, which includes service level agreements, but that won't do them much good if everything disappears in the USA, like we think it will everywhere. Look, some of our major service based businesses are going to crash anyway, because their customers won't exist anymore. So, there is no point in worrying about them. But, with Manx Bank and other businesses that we need to survive, we need to move quickly, to ensure that their data is safe, and that they will be able to process it. My company SITS does have its own

Datacentre on the island, with features such as redundant power and spare capacity. We can definitely help."

Shirley Down spoke for the first time, "I'm not wearing a uniform, so I will have to tell you that I am the Chief Financial Officer. The Treasury has already been thinking through issues around banking, assuming the collapse of overseas banks and the disappearance of the Bank of England. Some interesting comments have been made about banking and IT. We do need to act quickly, before these things start falling over. Perhaps I could chat with Matthew after the meeting, and let us take it from there?"

Jack agreed, "Okay do that. Let's talk about food and drink next. Perhaps I should have ideas, but I am going to copy Matthew and ask you all to chip in now."

Peter responded, "When I am not wearing this uniform, which Shirley sounds jealous off," smiling at her as he said it, "I own and run a dairy and sheep farm near Kirk Michael. I have got four thoughts, just off the top of my head. 1. Thank God we still have an abattoir on the island. 2. I won't be able to export livestock, but on the other hand we won't be competing with imported meat. 3. What about feedstuffs? If I can't get feed for my cattle I will have to reduce my dairy herd, so there would be less milk output. 4. Maybe milk or dairy output would have to go down, with nowhere to export to."

Matthew said with a rueful smile, "The thought off the top of my head is that, soon I won't be getting my fixes of coffee by day, and wine at the weekend."

There were a few light laughs. Matthew went on, "Well it is okay to laugh, but seriously, amongst the many things we won't be importing any more, will be lots of items of food and drink we did take for granted."

Peter commented, "Most farmers will try growing different things, if they think it will make a profit. If I keep fewer cows, or none at all, I could use the spare pasture as arable land."

Terry drew on his experience, "I have seen cannabis grown in a few unlikely places. I bet you could grow coffee in a greenhouse. Maybe it would need heat, and I would guess that heating fuel will be less plentiful, as you can infer by the queues at the petrol stations."

Matthew wondered, "So coffee could still be available, but at a much higher price."

Jack said, "Maybe farmers would have to be directed to produce more staple items, just so no-one starves."

Peter was not convinced, "State control of agriculture didn't work too well in Communist Russia, did it?"

Jack responded, "Well, perhaps collaborative discussions would be held, between my department and farmers' representatives, such as the Manx NFU."

Matthew asked, "What about wine? Could farmers grow grapes?"

Nicola asked, "What about bananas, or sugar, or fresh tomatoes in February?"

Peter told them, "In southern England, there are quite a few vineyards. But the climate here just isn't warm enough for grapes outdoors. In a greenhouse yes, but at a high cost. Matthew, I think you would probably develop a taste for beer or cider or perry, or some other fruit based alcohol, instead. And Nicola, I think some things we will not see ever again, like bananas; and other things might become seasonal, like tomatoes. But maybe someone could grow sugar beet, if we could refine it."

Jack wanted to add some direction, so he said, "Several themes seem to be emerging. Cost and availability of fuel. Let's put that to one side as a subject in its own right. Some food produced now for export, what happens to the farmland used for that. Substitution, can farmers replace any of the imports not obtainable such as sugar. And will consumers, such as Matthew, be willing or forced to switch from wine to perry, say? But, I feel the overriding concern must be that we make sure that everyone has enough to eat, full stop."

Peter remembered the RAF supplies, and said, "I checked out some of the supplies flown in by the RAF. There are sacks and sacks of flour and sugar. Some very large bottles of cooking oil. Masses of toilet rolls, which isn't food I know, and boxes of tinned vegetables and fruit. Large tins of coffee. It seems more geared up for feeding an army, than supplying individuals and families. Presumably Shoprite and the other supermarkets have got some supplies still to put out on shelves, or in their own warehouses. Talking of supermarkets, I was pleased to note my local Shoprite was restricting customers from taking more than one of some items."

Jack commented, "Some things like coffee will be gone forever, sooner or later, anyway, but it's nice to hear we definitely have some coffee in reserve. Even if it is in big tins, at the moment. But, I think we need a proper system of rationing."

They talked about food for another 25 minutes, and then moved on to fuel and energy. Jack said, "We are lucky that just one year ago we started piping gas from our own waters in the North Sea. Whoever persuaded the UK Government to give us control of territorial waters around Mann is a hero in my book."

Peter asked, "Yes, but some of our electricity is still being produced by diesel isn't it?"

Jack answered, "Yes, and we also get some wind powered electricity, and some hydro-electricity. They are now about 5% of our supply. So diesel is only about 20% now, I think."

Peter commented, "I don't know what the stocks are, but we have a finite amount of petrol and diesel to use. Only about 30% of cars are all electric, and they will need recharging from a reduced electricity supply. My farm tractors use diesel."

Nicola contributed, "Well, some of you car owners may not have realised, but two years ago Vannin Buses started buying Mercedes Citaro all electric buses on a big scale. Electric buses now comprise about 70% of the fleet. So, I would have thought it should be possible to continue to run a reasonable service between Douglas and all the other centres of population."

Matthew said, "Someone was telling me that we don't use all the gas we produce, some of it gets exported to Ireland. Could we use that in place of oil at all? Don't some cars run on a kind of gas, Liquid Petroleum Gas."

Shirley knew something about that. She said, "You may be surprised, but I know something about LPG, as my husband thought having an LPG conversion in his car might save money. Basically he didn't do it because it is not that cheap to convert, you have to have an extra fuel tank in your boot, and there was only one outlet for it, in Castletown I think. But it works on any petrol engine, apparently. It is basically a byproduct of oil or natural gas. We should have some continuing supply of LPG with the natural gas. So, any cars already capable of using LPG should be alright."

Peter added, "To do an adaptation you would need tanks and pipes and possibly valves, by the sound of it. They probably need kits in other words. Maybe our engineering firms could produce the kits, if they don't run out of supplies of steel or whatever they need."

Matthew commented, "If you have a farm or house that relies on oil for heating, you might want to convert to LPG, if we have the technology to do that. Most places using heating oil aren't near a gas pipeline, are they? Maybe Manx Utilities could extend their pipelines, but I don't suppose we have many pipelines lying around unused on the island. I have just remembered my parents actually use wood chips for their heating."

Jack was cheered by Matthew's last comment. He said, "The continued supply of wood chips or timber generally should not be a problem. There is a sawmill at St Johns which is supplied more or less 100% from island forestry."

They continued freeflow discussion about fuel for another 15 minutes, and then Jack summed up, "Well it is perhaps not as bad as we might have thought, assuming nothing goes badly wrong, like the gas supply from the Irish Sea failing. It seems likely that the electricity supply will be a bit reduced but with increased demand, and that we have a dwindling finite supply of petrol and diesel oil, which we will need to husband carefully. I know that most economists tend to sing the virtues of a free market economy, but I think, to avoid civil unrest, a system of rationing for petrol and diesel fuel is necessary."

The meeting went on for several more hours. David Quayle was still on the Committee. He had listened with interest, although he had not felt the need to contribute very much. He reflected that there was still a lot to resolve, but he was beginning to feel more confident that, under Jack's leadership, urgent matters would get dealt with, and sensible decisions would be made.

Chapter 27, Friday 23 April 2027

As they had arranged, Vin and Martha were hosting a meal for David and Amber, in return for their hospitality two weeks earlier. Vin heard a car pull up, and went outside to see David and Amber getting out of an electric taxi.

Vin said, "So you came by an electric taxi then. I suppose that will save your petrol." He shook David's hand, and did an air kiss near Amber's left cheek.

Vin told them, "Well come on in, and David, don't think you are going to win at Scrabble against me again tonight. This time I have home advantage, and I think it's my turn to get those bonus friendly blank tiles."

David replied, "Yes, a warm greeting to you too. The taxi was mainly so we can drink all the wine you have stashed away. Now, where is the nice person who lives at this address?"

Ah, there you are, Martha," David said to her, as he wandered into the kitchen. "You look good, and something smells good. I could not get any flowers, for the same reason you can't get a lot of things now. I did manage to get this box of Milk Tray, and also I hope you can make use of these runner bean seeds. Just get the old man to make himself useful, by digging a bean trench soon."

Vin had followed David into the kitchen. Vin said, "To make the beans palatable, we need a variety of herbs. I have already started off some chillies and tomatoes, in the greenhouse. I just need to get hold of some growbags, or, if not I suppose there must be stables with old manure I could get, and mix it with soil from the garden," said Vin.

David commented, "I have just noticed your boiler. It runs on wood chips is that right? Matthew mentioned it in a Committee meeting."

"Yes, we sometimes burn the wood chips in the fireplace in the lounge as well. I have lit a fire in there just before you came, so it will be cosy later on."

"So you have an electric powered car and a secure source of fuel. Did you know, years ago, we would be cutting ourselves off from oil supplies?"

"I did have bad dreams about a terrible pandemic. But Matthew is the one who persuaded me to get the electric car."

A couple of hours later after dinner, the two men were sitting near a coffee table in the lounge playing Scrabble on a proper board, whilst their wives, as before, preferred Trivial Pursuit in the dining room. David said, "I am glad we seemed to keep the conversation over dinner fairly light hearted, despite your ridiculous insistence that West Ham are a better football team than Manchester United, but I heard from Tony Sharp today. I am sure he said he was going to ring you too."

"Yes he did."

"So you know, then, that the first cases have started in London. The ones that have been admitted to hospital have died within a few hours. It is absolutely unbelievable. So they have a period between getting infected and showing symptoms of about 2 weeks, I think you say, and then people die within a few hours."

"Yes, they have gradually increasing breathlessness until they literally can't breathe even with oxygen. During those 2 weeks without symptoms, they will have infected lots of people directly, and those people that they have infected will have further infected lots more people, and so on. So we can expect, spreading from London probably, everyone on the mainland to be dead within 2 to 3 weeks of the first cases. But, because it has only recently started, there must be a very good chance that we are clear on Mann. Possibly on the ship the Senior Serenade as well. It seems to have got to London and Britain later than I thought it would."

"Well, the main thing is that you persuaded us to act in time. Have you mention the deaths in London to Martha?"

"No, she's an intelligent adult, so I should have done. It's just that she had seemed so cheerful, during the last couple of weeks. Not sure why. Tony was saying they thought about trying to keep it out of the news, but that there would be no point, as it would spread rapidly through social media."

David decided to follow two lines of conversation. He said, "Perhaps its the thought of a grandchild that is making her cheerful. Tony said to me that the Government are hoping there won't be any riots or looting."

Vin responded to both lines. He said, "I suppose a grandchild will be nice. So they just want people to die quietly without causing a fuss. None of it will make any difference within a few weeks anyway. Did you tell Amber?"

"Yes, I did mention that you and Martha will be becoming grandparents. But no, not the situation in England. I am surprised that she doesn't seem to have seen anything on social media. Unless, she is trying to hide it from me of course," David said. A thought crossed his mind. He went on "How long have Matthew and Emma been back now?"

Vin told him, "Seventeen days. I am now very optimistic that they are okay, and that we will all survive. You know I would still have been glad they got back, even if they had been infected. That sounds selfish and ridiculous I know, but I don't really care. We seem to have all become closer Martha, Matthew, and me, and even Emma, who is a lovely bright girl. By the way, did you know that Jack Coyle's son and daughter in law came in on the same plane as Matthew and Emma?"

"No, I didn't. So, presumably Jack tipped them off. He kept that very quiet."

"Not that quiet. His daughter in law gave birth to a baby girl, now named Jacqueline, at Nobles Hospital, after getting an ambulance straight from the airport. Jack and I were both interviewed by police on the Saturday before last, for possible breach of the Official Secrets Act. We both got off the hook, Jack lied about it and they had no proof, whereas I admitted telling Matthew and Emma to get back straightaway, but I got off because I hadn't actually divulged why to them. And poor old Peter Quinnel, instead of getting a medal for diverting the repatriation plane 3 days later, got a grilling by the police as well. Oh, I forgot to mention, after I heard from Tony, I used my position to make enquiries about the latest deaths at Nobles, and about acute respiratory admissions. There is nothing that matches ultra pneumonia, so as I say, I am now very optimistic we are in the clear. We just need to keep the embargo watertight."

"Well, Peter Quinnel and Terry Corps seem to be doing their best."

Vin went on, "Those repatriation passengers on the boat too, including Emma's sister; well I now think there is a decent chance that they are in the clear. We said it would be another week from now, before the boat could disembark in Douglas. We will need to confirm they had no contacts with any boats, or helicopters, or gone into port anywhere. I certainly don't think we should make any exceptions to the embargo for any other boats... Wait, what is this? We shouldn't make any exceptions to the English language for Scrabble either. What is this word 'COMEOVER' you have just played? That is no good is it? Just because you couldn't fit 'OVERCOME' on the board."

David told him, "Check it out. It is a word we Manx sometimes use to describe people who live here, who weren't born here." He smiled at Vin, "I am surprised you haven't heard it."

Vin looked at his word checker app on his smartphone. "Yes, it seems to be valid. I have heard worse insults, usually "effing Paki" which is a bit much, considering my parents were Sikhs from Mumbai. Oh, have I told you about why Patrick has reversed his whole campaign?"

David answered, "I have had the gist of it from Matthew at the Emergency Advisory Committee meetings. So, secretly you are the second Saviour, eh? Well I suppose it is plausible, if we consider that you might actually have saved human life on Mann. It is just the rest of your character doesn't seem to fit with words like, you know, saintly or angelic. Talking of words, what is this one you have just played 'MITOSIS' ? Is that some kind of problem to do with cells?"

Vin told him, "Just normal cell duplication. Anyway I am out of letters and the score is 423 to me, and 411 to you, so I have won and I have my rightful revenge. Hooray!"

"Yes 'thank you very much for a close game' is what you really mean I am sure. I think I will have another glass of your port, so I can celebrate with you."

Vin topped up David's glass. Vin said, "Well, when this bottle is gone, I expect never to drink port again. It seems to have gone from the supermarket shelves, and I would be amazed to be told that the RAF had delivered a huge stash of port."

"I suppose a shortage of port will be well down the list of our worries. We haven't really talked about the millions, billions, of people dying in Africa, now in Britain, and soon the rest of the world as well. Do you know if people will suffer very much?"

"The main suffering will be psychological, waiting to get the symptoms yourself, whilst some people around you have already died. I think I said earlier that people seem to die very quickly. It starts with slight breathlessness, which increases in severity, until they lose consciousness and die. Oxygen masks only prolong it slightly, and with breathing apparatus really you are just ventilating a corpse. Besides, the nurses and doctors are all dying as well. It is not painful, but it is not pleasant either. If someone breaches the embargo and we do get it here, I would say, when you first get the breathlessness, just go to bed with a bottle of whisky, if you've got one. Did you know I've got relatives in London?"

David replied, "No, sorry, I should have thought about that. I'm guessing your parents are probably dead?"

"Yes that's right. I did have a much older brother and sister – yes I was a little afterthought – but they have both gone as well. I have nephews and nieces and cousins, but I have been very bad at keeping in touch with them. I am trying, now, not to think about them in particular. In fact, with Matthew and Emma having a child on the way, it's good to have something positive to think about. It would be great if the baby's aunt-to-be could survive as well, but we shall see about that."

"If man does survive on Mann, do you think there will be others elsewhere?"

"If it is a larger population on another island say, they are more likely to have had contact with ultra pneumonia. If it is a much smaller island, maybe they would not get the disease, but would lack the resources to survive. Yes, I think there will be remnants of humanity elsewhere, but David you probably know better than I do, this island has a lot going for it. It is used to running its own affairs, dealing with problems, and so on. It is not over densely populated. If you think sufficiency of food and fuel are the main factors, then we are probably reasonably well placed. Where else, this small, could survive better than us? We have a gas pipeline supplying our own power station. We have forests, we have fishing boats, we have agricultural land that can support different crops, fruit, livestock, dairy cows. We have engineering and manu-facturing companies. They might run out of supplies, but they have technical know-how, and I hope they can come up with imaginative solutions to problems."

David's own feelings, about the long term future, often veered to pessimism. Sometimes, in his recent work in his Department, and on the Committee, problems could feel overwhelming. He felt lifted, hearing this intelligent and optimistic personal assessment by Dr Singh.

Chapter 28, Monday 26 April 2027

Peter Quinnel was dreaming about Gemma's 8th birthday. He was looking at her smiling, as he showed her her new pony. Then he could hear the noise of church bells ringing. He woke up, and realised it was his phone's call tone. He squinted at the time on it, 4.10am. He was pleased to recall that he was sharing the marital bed with Amanda again, as she stirred next to him. He picked up the phone and said, "Just a minute" into it. He got out of bed, dragged on his dressing gown and walked out of the bedroom.

He spoke on the phone again,"Yes who is that please?"

"Is that Major Quinnel?" enquired a female voice.

"Yes, who is calling me at 4 o'clock in the morning?"

"It's the Marine Control Centre. I am calling you first, but I will pass this on to the Emergency Call Room as well, in case the police need to know. We have had a call from Holyhead Coastguard Operations Centre..."

Peter was surprised. He asked, "So they are still operating?"

"I heard rumours Dublin and Liverpool have started going down," the female voice told him. She continued, "It is amazing that, at Holyhead, they are still willing to go in to work. Anyway, apparently it was mutually agreed by the Irish and British Governments on Saturday morning, no traffic of any kind would be permitted indefinitely, anywhere in the Irish Sea, right the way from St George's Channel up to North Channel. I wonder if that was mainly to help us. So, what I need to tell you is that there is a report of a yacht, belonging to a Russian millionaire, having sailed from Rosslare at around midnight, or about four hours ago. It sailed north up the Irish Sea. This report says it had reached same latitude as Holyhead, but about 30 kilometres west of Holyhead, and it is now on a bearing of 25 degrees. In other words, it is heading towards the Isle of Man."

"Do we actually know, for definite, its intended destination is the Isle of Man?"

"No, but I know what I think."

"What about the Royal Navy? Can't they intercept it?"

"It's not really my role to tell you what to do Major, but given the pandemic is now killing everyone in Britain, how much help can we expect?"

"So you want to rely on the Army Reserve here, with our 105mm gun?"

"Some of us thought what you did, turning the repatriation plane away was brilliant, so I personally was hoping we could rely on you. Maybe I was wrong."

"Of course we will do what we can to stop it berthing on the island. Tell me... sorry what is your name?"

"Its Amelia. Amelia Callister."

Peter said to her, "Amelia, you are better acquainted with maritime affairs than me, I would think. Do you have you any idea where it might dock, or what they might do?"

Amelia thought she knew. She told him, "Maybe I have watched too many spy and thriller movies. But, I reckon some of these Russian oligarchs are pretty arrogant. He probably thinks, by now nothing much is going to stop him, and his well armed henchmen, berthing right here in Douglas marina, with all its facilities, for as long as he likes."

"Did you say 'well armed henchmen'?" asked Peter, feeling some concern.

Amelia merely said, "I am only guessing Major."

Peter reflected and said, "Hmm. Maybe you are right about the henchmen, and maybe it won't make any difference to how we deal with it. Okay, leave it with me. Goodbye, Amelia."

Amelia signed off, "Thank you Major, and good luck!"

By this stage Amanda had got up. She said to Peter, "I'll make you a cup of coffee while you sort out your gunners."

"How do you know I will need them?" he asked.

Amanda pressed herself against him, and said, "Isn't that how you like to deal with problems. Get the big gun out?" and she just gently ran her hand down the inside of his dressing gown.

He decided to call up the three gunners who had manned the 105mm gun on Friday 9 April. He was assured by Bombardier Cain that a lorry and a case of shells were still at the airport, although the Reservists guarding the airport wouldn't know how to load, aim and fire the gun. Peter had been promised he would get a decent petrol ration as a key person, but he had to promise to divert to Onchan to pick up Bombardier Cain. The other two would be met at the airport. He allowed forty minutes to get to Onchan.

Amanda said to him, "It won't take you more than 25 minutes to get to Onchan." And she moved her eyes around his body.

Peter remembered how much he liked the way she used to want him, as much as he wanted her. Her desire seems to have returned, he thought. He said, "It really will have to be a quickie."

She agreed, "Alright, that will at least leave me with something to remember you by, for a while."

A short while later he was saying goodbye to her in the bedroom, saying there was no need for her to get back up. She said, "Please take care," and he brushed her lips with his, and he was gone.

Chapter 29, Monday 26 April 2027

Bombardier Cain was waiting outside his house in Onchan, when Peter arrived in his old Jaguar at 5.18am. That was eight minutes later than he had said he would. Bombardier Cain got in. Peter could tell he was itching for more information.

Peter told him, "In a nutshell we are going to shoot at and sink a Russian yacht belonging to some oligarch, and I don't even know his name. The idea is to kill everyone on the yacht. We don't want any survivors coming ashore."

Bombardier Cain responded, "Wow! So we are just aiming to sink it as quickly as possible, no warnings, or warning shots sir?"

"Yes that is right. It looks like we have kept Mann clear of this ultra pneumonia virus so far. It would be a pity to spoil that now. I know that I am asking you to deliberately take human life, but the yacht owner has given us no choice. We only know that he was in Rosslare in Ireland up till last night. They may well have the virus on the yacht. The Irish Sea has been closed off by the Irish and British Governments, since Saturday. He has absolutely no right to be in the Irish Sea at all, never mind coming to the Isle of Man. If we don't stop him, it is very likely that all 84,000 of us on this island will die. I repeat we have no choice. Can I count on you, Bombardier?"

"Absolutely sir. I don't think we let you down last time. And we will definitely let the bastards have it. It sounds like they deserve it. Sir!"

"Thanks Bombardier. Now I would like to discuss my plan with you, so that you can let me know, if you think I have got anything wrong or missed something. It is thought it will make for Douglas marina. If we tow the gun up to Langness, you know the bit of headland between Castletown Bay and Derby Haven..."

"Sorry to interrupt, sir, but, if time is critical, I need to say something now, please."

"Time could be important. I am not sure how fast this yacht can go, but we might only have 45 minutes or less, from now."

"We need to get the gun to Douglas Head. Can we get the Gunners Brown and Shimmin to tow the gun there now, and we can meet them there, sir?"

"Are you sure?"

Bombardier Cain responded by nodding emphatically and saying, "Yes sir, I am positive. I've got the Gunners' numbers in my phone."

Peter consented, "Okay do it, and then explain to me why."

Bombardier Cain rang Gunner Brown and talked to him. Then he said to Major Quinnel, "We were in luck, sir. They were by the gun already, with it hitched up to the lorry. They should be on St Ann's Road, just above Douglas Head, in twenty minutes."

Peter said, "So far so good Bombardier, but I really would like an explanation now."

"Yes, of course sir. I know the coast well. Langness and Dreswick Point might look good on a map, but the target we would be shooting at could be 8 miles, sorry 12 K, or even further away, if it is trying to sweep wide before approaching Douglas. Boats tend to keep well clear of the coast down there, because of the currents, anyway. We might not even see it, if it is as murky at daybreak, as it was yesterday evening. At Douglas Head we will be concealed behind a building, and in a slight dip, so they won't know what's hit them, when they come into view. There's a big sort of turning area, so we will have plenty of solid tarmac to set up the gun. We will have plenty of elevation. Accuracy should be much better because of that, and we will be able to hit the target at 5K easily, assuming its course by then is something like 270 to 300 degrees. It will be coming almost straight towards us. If we stop it with the first shell, we should be able to hit it again with a second and third shell, just to make sure it sinks with all on board if possible.

"Oh yes, I think I know where you mean. You seem to have given this a bit of thought, since I phoned you. And your thinking sounds about right to me. Everything suggests they will keep well clear at first, and then as they approach they will abandon any attempt of not being seen, or pretending they are merely sailing by. So if, as you say, they alter course to come in on a heading of 270 to 300 degrees, this might be at speed, possibly ready to shoot at anyone trying to interfere. But, it will be at a much slower speed than that plane was, so it should be no problem for you and the gunners, should it?"

"I would hope not, sir."

"There are things that could go wrong. It might choose to berth in Port Erin, for example."

"I reckon we will find out soon, sir."

Peter drove to the exact spot at Douglas Head that the Bombardier had suggested. It had started getting light. Peter said, "Well we are very close to our base here. Shall we give these Ruskies a warm welcome?"

"Yes, I think we should sir."

Peter had a look around. He said, "Yes it has good sight lines over boats approaching Douglas, except for anything hugging the coast from the south west despite the currents. Well done, Bombardier." He thought to himself "Yes, it is a good compromise. We won't be seen by the yacht until they have turned in towards Douglas. We can take turns looking out for the yacht, from the south side of this building. Ideally, we would like to sink them as far away as possible, but it will probably still be 5 kilometres or more, and their course will be almost towards us, making them easier to hit, and making it harder for them to get away quickly, if we miss with the first shell. It's a shame that I hadn't spent time Googling the coastline." And then he smiled, as he recalled how he had used some of his time instead.

About 15 minutes later, Gunners Brown and Shimmin turned up in a lorry, pulling the 105mm gun. They set up the gun facing 80 degrees over the approaches to Douglas Bay, with the lorry and gun both completely concealed from view from the sea from the south and southwest. They set the range for 6 kilometres, allowing for the elevated position of the gun above the sea.

Peter said to Bombardier Cain, "It is great they won't be able to see us until too late, we hope, but we need to know when they are coming. Can you get your two gunners to take 30 minutes shifts at going the other side of this building to look out for it. They can have my binoculars, and tell them to take their hats off, and put on this civvy jacket I have got out of my boot. If the yacht sees the lookout, they might just assume it's a birdwatcher."

After 25 minutes of waiting, Gunner Brown ran back to the others from his look out position on the south side of the building. He was agitated. He said, "Sir, they are coming. We have about two minutes, before they will come into view this side. I don't know whether they saw me or not. I can't believe it. There are three of them on the top deck, behind the bridge. One is holding what looks like an RPG launcher, and the other two were crouching over what must be a mortar gun. They might struggle to hit us with an RPG, but mortars have improved a lot, haven't they sir? Jesus, I didn't go to bed last night expecting to be shelled before breakfast."

Peter said firmly, "That's enough Gunner. You signed up to the Army, and our duty now is clear. You and Gunner Shimmin will man this 105mm gun and, under Bombardier Cain's direction, keep firing until the yacht is completely sunk. Do you understand?"

Gunner Brown replied, "Yes sir, I'll do my best."

Peter moved away, apparently in thought, but actually hoping that Bombardier Cain would have a reassuring word with Gunner Brown. Bombardier Cain quietly said to Gunner Brown, "Look Bob, those guys are lurching about on a boat with peashooters, compared with our 105mm gun. We are going to blast them out the water, and be bought drinks for a fortnight on the strength of this." Gunner Brown seemed to perk up a bit, and Peter thought to himself, "Well done Bombardier."

Peter said to Bombardier Cain, "When you consider that you are ready, I want you to commence shooting and continue shooting, adjusting your range and aim as necessary, until this yacht is completely sunk. You don't have to await any further orders from me. Alright Bombardier?"

Bombardier Cain replied, "Yes sir."

Peter said to the two gunners, "Okay gunners. Follow directions from your Bombardier. I have every faith you are going to send this yacht to the bottom of the sea, where it deserves to be. Carry on!"

Major Quinnel walked to the corner of the building, closest to the sea. He peered around the corner and saw the yacht, about 6 kilometres out, turning in towards Douglas. He withdrew his head from their sight, guessing that they would come into view of the gunners, in about 20 seconds. He actually made it 21 seconds on his watch, when the yacht came into plain view. He heard the bang and felt the whoosh as the 105mm gun fired. He saw it had hit the bow of the yacht. Three seconds later, he saw the mortar gun discharge from the yacht. Suddenly, the wall to his right was hit with with an almighty bang, bits of masonry flew everywhere, he felt a blow to the right side of his forehead, and he passed out.

Chapter 30, Wednesday 28 April 2027

Vin said, "Things are pretty bad you know. I was told you were coming round. That's why I popped in."

Peter Quinnel was feeling very strange, a bit light headed, and his vision was a bit blurry. He asked, "Is that Vin, my doctor friend?"

"Yes, it's me. We're in a surgical ward at Nobles Hospital."

"You said things are bad. What do you mean? Did those Russians get into the marina? Were my gunners killed? Or have we got the virus here?"

"No, it's none of those things. It looks like we are staying clear of the virus. The Russians did not get in, and your gunners seemed fine on Manx Radio. Okay, I will tell you what they said happened. You were injured by an incoming mortar shell, apparently after your artillery gun had hit the yacht, without causing too much damage. Your gunners were a bit further away from where the mortar shell hit, and were unharmed. They said their first shell had seemed to stop the boat moving. So they figured that another shell, on exactly the same trajectory and direction as the first, would hit the yacht around midship. They said the second shell did hit the yacht, and must have ruptured fuel lines, because it caught fire, and within about 20 seconds it exploded and then sank. Oh incidentally, whilst they were loading their second shell, there was a second incoming mortar shell, but that fell well short on ground below them."

"So, are we sure none of the Russians survived?"

"Apparently they didn't see any survivors, but, after sinking the boat, I think they must have decided it was more important to check you out."

"Wrong priority, but we all make bad decisions sometimes. So we are not sure then?"

"No, everyone seems sure. Quite a few of your armed Reservists and several armed police were on Douglas promenade, and along Marine Drive, for hours, ready to shoot anyone with a Russian accent having a swim."

"Vin, I feel a bit light headed. So, what is pretty bad?"

"You are. I mean you are stable, and my colleagues are very optimistic you will recover fully. But you have had bleeding under your skull, which they have had to drain twice. The internal bleeding seems to have stopped now, but you want to be careful to avoid any knocks or stress. In fact, plenty of rest is the best thing. And what is also bad, is the amount of medical supplies we have used up, looking after you." He smiled at Peter, but Peter had nodded off.

A nurse came up to the bed. He said to Vin, "I've got his wife Amanda on the phone. I told her that her husband had regained consciousness, but it looks like he has drifted off again."

Vin told him, "Let me speak to her. I know Peter, and I understand his condition and treatment."

Vin followed the nurse to the ward office, which was not off-limits to him, as a Senior Consultant. He picked up the phone, and said, "Hello is that Amanda. I am Dr Singh. I have just been speaking to Peter, but he has drifted off again."

Amanda was not feeling calm, but she recognised the name. She said, "Hello, aren't you Vin Singh? Peter has mentioned you a few times. Please how is he? Are you one of the doctors dealing with him?"

"I can tell you how he is, although he is not my patient. He is stable. In fact, he seems to be improving. He was awake briefly, and we talked for a few minutes. But you know that he had quite a blow to the head, so that he suffered a subdural haematoma, or bleeding inside the skull."

"Yes, I was told that he had burr hole surgery to drain the fluid on Monday, and that more fluid was drained yesterday."

"Yes that's right, but they think the bleeding has stopped now."

"I want to come to see him."

"Yes, of course."

"This sounds so feeble. I have probably got enough petrol in my car, but it won't start. Peter's car is still at Douglas Head. The four hands are all busy, and Peter wouldn't want me to divert them from their work. I have tried getting a taxi, but you would think Kirk Michael was on the moon. They all say they haven't got time to get here, between other bookings."

Vin thought that it really isn't good enough, that the wife of a hero, who nearly dies saving 84,000 people, isn't being looked after. He asked her, "Would you like me to fetch you?"

"Well yes please, if you can spare the time. I really want to see him," said Amanda. She could not quite suppress a couple of sobs.

Vin checked, "Let me see, if I have remembered this right. It's Ballabeg Farm, near Kirk Michael?"

Amanda gave him directions, "Yes, if you follow the B road through to Baldwin, past the reservoir, keep going straight, following signs to Kirk Michael. Go through Kirk Michael, following the coast road north, signposted to Ramsey, and we are a signposted turning on the right, about a mile and a half after Kirk Michael. If you get as far as Ballaugh you have missed the turning."

Vin told her, "I am not too bad with finding my way. Unless you have invented this farm, I will get to you in about 30 minutes from now."

Chapter 31, Wednesday 28 April 2027

Vin pulled up outside the farmhouse, and Amanda came out straightaway. She was carrying a bag she had packed with things for Peter. She looked younger than Vin had imagined, although he knew that she was a few years younger than Peter. She thought Vin looked how she would imagine a senior Asian male doctor in his 60s would look. Amanda got in, and Vin started driving back to the hospital. There was a slightly strained silence. Vin felt guilty somehow, because of Peter's injury. He felt he should try to show some sympathy. He said to her, "Peter and his men have probably saved us all, you know?"

Amanda felt an urge to talk about Peter. She replied, "Yes, he had to put himself on the line, didn't he? He is an Ulsterman by birth, and is very loyal to the British crown. His family came to the Isle of Man when he was 11, and at 18 he went to university in England, where he joined a university reserve regiment. A lot of people here don't feel any special loyalty to Britain, but he does, as well as to the Isle of Man. I remember we talked about it once, and he said, 'Go up Snaefell, and on a clear day you can easily see Northern Ireland, Scotland, England, and sometimes Wales all in different directions, all part of a United Kingdom. Manxmen fought world wars for the British, we trade with them, our boats and planes connect with them, we go to university there, and lots of people have migrated between Mann and Britain in both directions.' And now he's got a serious injury, and life is petering out in Britain."

Vin said, "He probably cares more about you, than about Mann or Britain. Certainly he put himself in harm's way, but I suspect mainly he wanted to keep you safe in particular."

Amanda suddenly felt an urge to confide in Vin emotions she hadn't shared with anyone else. She told him, "I love Peter dearly you know. We went through a hard time when we lost our only child last year. It didn't seem right to hold him, when I couldn't hold Gemma any more. I know he loved her as much as I did. I was just too wrapped up in my own pain to comfort him. But, we seem to have come together again. When there was that horrible campaign against him on the social media...you were targeted too... I realised how much he meant to me."

Vin found himself talking about himself, "My wife Martha and I lost our baby girl when she was only 6 months. It was strange, a cot death. Being a doctor made it worse, somehow. I felt sure I should have prevented it. I didn't want to talk about it. I just worked as hard as I could, and read up medical papers in the evenings. I was no use to Martha at all, and I struggled to show any affection to our son. But Martha was great. She carried on being a loving mother to our son, and she was loyal and supportive to me. We are a bit closer now. I think this pandemic is drawing some couples and families closer together. In fact, recently I have given my son a hug, and I have told him I love him."

He decided not to mention the grandchild on its way. They fell silent again for rest of the drive. When they got to the hospital Amanda said, "I have just thought, no disrespect to you Vin, or other doctors here, but does the Isle of Man have neurosurgeons of its own? I have heard that sometimes surgeons come over from Liverpool, or that neurosurgery patients are flown over to hospitals in Liverpool."

Vin looked at her. She looked vulnerable, but he decided that honesty was the only real way forward with health care, even if he was sometimes criticised for a lack of diplomacy. He said, "You are right, in that we don't have resident neurosurgeons on the island. But the surgeons who did the operations are good chaps, with lots of experience of dealing with all sorts of injuries. This procedure would have been within their capabilities, and the evidence is that there is no more bleeding, and no pressure on the brain." He stopped talking and looked a bit hesitant.

Amanda asked, "But there is a but, isn't there Vin?"

Vin admitted, "My colleagues would not have been able to identify or deal with any internal damage. So they, or we, can't be sure how fully he will recover. In the majority of cases there is full, or nearly full, recovery without further interventions."

Amanda asked again, "But what sort of problems might there be?"

Vin replied, "Sometimes there is a stroke or strokes, which can cause varying levels of disability. Also, very cruelly, sometimes there can be a serious change of character. But don't be too pessimistic. The main thing, at the moment, is that he gets physical and mental rest, which will reduce the risk of a further bleed."

Vin carried her bag to Peter's ward. Peter was awake again. Vin said, "I will leave you two to it then," and he walked away.

Amanda lent forward, and gently brushed her lips against Peter's. She reached her hand out, and gently stroked around and over the bandages, over the burr hole surgery. She felt a couple of tears run down her face. She said, "Thank you for saving us again, my warrior husband."

Peter took her hand, and looked hazily into her eyes. He said, "Hey, it's going to be fine. I'll get better soon, and be running the farm again."

He stopped and tried to think about the farm. Everything felt a bit vague. She said, "Well take it easy now, but yes, I do need you home eventually. Then, maybe you can think about looking after the farm, and me, and your next child."

Peter looked at her with a puzzled expression, and said, "Next child? Yes that would be great to have another child, if we can."

"Well, we are having another child," she told him.

"How do you know? We haven't been - you know - until when was it?" he asked.

Amanda replied, "It's Wednesday now. It was two weeks ago. And you definitely didn't use any protection!"

Peter did not understand. He asked, "But it is too early to know isn't it?"

"I am so regular, you can set a clock by my periods. I am two days late. I have no doubt at all that I am pregnant, that we are expecting another child, and that I love you, and need you. So please get better, my darling!" pleaded Amanda.

Chapter 32 Wednesday 28 April 2027

Emma and Matthew were in their house together. It was just before 8pm. They were hosting an online Zoom meeting with Sophie, on her ship the Senior Serenade, and with Beryl and Wayne, just up the road. Sophie already knew about her sister's pregnancy and engagement, from previous calls. Matthew thought to himself that most of the satellites being used for any sort of communication would probably keep going, on their orbits, for years after there was no-one left to send any messages to. But the servers in the USA and elsewhere, where Zoom or other messages were routed to, could be expected to crash soon.

Beryl and Wayne came into view first on Emma's PC. Emma exchanged greetings with her Mum and Dad. Then Matthew said, "Good evening Wayne, and good evening Beryl."

Wayne said, "Hello Matthew, how are you doing? I think you have been busy with that Emergency Advisory Committee haven't you? The petrol rationing system sounds like it should work okay, don't you think?"

Emma wondered if she was the only one to notice that her mother had not acknowledged Matthew, and she decided she would have to confront her about it. So she intervened. She said, "Yes Dad, Matt is very busy, and I know he was involved in working out a good system for petrol rationing. Mum!"

Beryl replied meekly, "Yes Emma?"

Emma asked, "It's great that Matthew is helping us all adjust to this situation, isn't it?"

"Maybe, but his father caused the situation in the first place."

"Do you mean that Dr Singh caused the ultra pneumonia pandemic?"

"Well, maybe not, but he is the reason that Sophie is bobbing up and down in the North Atlantic, instead of being home with us."

"I want you to be nice to Matt, and be polite about his father. You know Matt and I are getting married, and that we are having a baby. I want you to be nice to the father of your grandchild. I know you went to that Astrological church, the Sunday before last. Didn't Patrick Quinn say that he was wrong previously, and that everyone on the island wherever they were from, or whatever their religion, were God's children and were being admitted to the new world?"

"Something like that, yes."

"And you don't want to cause any problems about seeing your grandchild, do you?"

Beryl reminded herself that she had decided that the child's skin tone would probably be okay. Maybe Patrick was right to change his tune, to say that really that we are all God's children. She concluded that any more hostility towards Matthew would be pointless. She said, "Sorry Emma. Sorry Matthew. Would you both like to come for dinner on Sunday?"

Emma was a bit taken aback. She said, "Yes that sounds nice. What do you think Matt?"

At that moment, her PC made noises to let Sophie join the online group. She clicked Sophie in, and everyone said hello. Matt noticed that Olivia wasn't on the screen. He said to Sophie, "Sophie, where is your pal Olivia? You haven't thrown her overboard have you?"

Sophie said, "No she is just checking out some of the other passengers. The sea was a bit rough today, and two didn't show up for dinner."

Suddenly, they could hear the cabin door open. Olivia was screaming, "We're going to die. I don't want to die. I want my Mum," and they could hear her crying.

Sophie went off screen, but the others could hear Sophie and Olivia talking loudly to each other.

Sophie asked, "What's happened? What have you found out?"

"The two who were missing, you know, two of the airline crew, Sylvia and Jimmy. She's in Jimmy's cabin. It's horrible, and it's going to happen to us," Olivia told her.

Sophie demanded, "What? What is it?"

Olivia blurted out, "Jimmy opened the door to me. He was breathing heavily. He didn't say anything, just took a big swig of whisky and laid down. Sylvia was on the other bed, white faced, cold, dead!"

Then both girls could be heard screaming.

Matt and Emma looked at each other. Matt felt terrible, and he could see tears running down Emma's face. She was saying, "Oh Sophie, please no. It might not be the virus!"

Matt thought it probably was ultra pneumonia, and decided that everyone needed the little help he could give. He muted the microphone on the PC, and said to Emma, "Your sister might not have long, but we have got to help her cope as best as possible. Does she believe in God?"

Emma replied, "Sort of. She goes to church at Easter and Christmas, and I think I have heard her saying to a friend that she would not want to be an atheist. But, I don't really believe in God myself. I only ever go to church to please Mum. This is terrible. We will never see her again."

Matt turned the microphone back on, and started talking loudly into it, "Sophie, are you there? Please answer me. It's Matt, we need to talk. Please talk to me."

He could hear a reply. "Hello, it's Olivia. What is the point of talking?" asked Olivia.

Matt told her, "Please we need to talk to her, to both of you, for the sake of her sister, and her parents, and your parents as well."

Olivia asked, "What difference would that make?"

Matt said, "Because they are suffering as well, and I think that you and Sophie must still care about people close to you."

There was the noise of the WC flushing, and then Sophie and Olivia were on the screen looking very scared. Sophie said, "Okay Matt, what do you want to talk about?"

Matt said, "God, Jesus, religion."

Sophie was sceptical, "What do you care about that? You don't believe in any of that, especially the Jesus bit, do you?"

Matt agreed, "Yes that is what I say, but what do I know? I want to know what you think?"

Sophie answered, "Normally I don't think about it much. But when I do, I feel that there is something. It is hard to explain. I am not great with words. I am only seventeen, and too young to die. But it feels real in church at Christmas, and on Good Friday, that there is a life or salvation after death."

Matt felt he was helping. He said, "Sophie, I want you to try to connect with those feelings. I can't pretend. If this is ultra pneumonia, you may not have any way out of your situation on Earth, but please try to find that belief in the afterlife again. Pray to God in other words, and believe that you will all be reunited in Heaven. You will find it a comfort, and it will help your sister and mother and father too, to know that you are waiting for them in Heaven."

Sophie agreed, "Okay I will do it. It's not much of a plan really, but I can't think of a better one."

Matt told her, "Well, we will all be praying for you here, as well."

Olivia spoke up, "What about me?"

Matt asked, "Do you have a religious faith?"

Olivia told him, "I am a bit like Sophie really. I don't think about it a lot, but I liked the hymns and prayers at school. It used to make me think maybe there is a God, looking down on us."

Matt urged her, "Well then, pray together with Sophie that you will rise to Heaven together, and that you will be there waiting for your parents. Do you have any brothers or sisters?"

Olivia told him, "No. but I would like to see my parents again, even if it is only on a screen like this."

Matt asked, "Don't they have a PC and the internet?"

Olivia replied, "Yes, they are just not technically minded."

Matt said, "Give me their phone number. I will arrange to go round their house, and set it all up, just before 8pm tomorrow. Let's hope that Zoom is still working then, and we can all talk again then. You will both pray together before then, and when we talk tomorrow it will be about happy events in the past. Okay?"

Olivia said, "It's 202150 the number. Thanks Matt."

Sophie said, "Thank you Matt. See you tomorrow Mum, Dad, Emma. I love you all."

Chapter 33, Thursday 29 April 2027

Emma and Matt had not slept very well the night before. Matt had been in to both his SITS office in the morning, and an Emergency Advisory Committee meeting in the afternoon, and no-one had said anything about the ship. He had not felt in the mood to mention it himself. At 7.40pm he set up his PC, so that Emma could link up with everyone at 8pm. Then he drove to Olivia's parents house at Strang, near the hospital. He set up the connection, and then got back to his house at 8.05pm. Emma and the two sets of parents were already connected, and then Olivia and Sophie connected in too.

Sophie said, "We prayed like you suggested Matt. We thought God had answered our prayers, because we found out that Sylvia and Jimmy had been doing some serious drug use. Sylvia had actually died of an overdose. I don't know, or care, whether Jimmy is still alive at the moment."

Matt was wondering what was coming next, but Olivia's dad said, "So you are going to be alright then. The ship hasn't got this virus..." He fell silent as he saw Olivia and Sophie's sombre expressions.

Olivia said, "No, that's not right Dad. There were a lot of staff and passengers missing at dinner. Some people who were there seemed to be breathing heavily. I would say about

40 people had not come out of their cabins. It is pretty obvious that we have the ultra pneumonia virus on the ship."

Sophie took over, "But we have prayed, and it has helped. We have convinced each other we are going to Heaven. Maybe it is you guys who will be in Hell, when your tobacco and coffee and wine and chocolate run out. We're thinking we will probably get the bad breathing at the same time, as Olivia and I have been together for 5 weeks now. When we get bad, we will come back in our cabin, put on some Shawn Mendes music really loud, and drink loads of gin with lemonade. It will be a race to see who passes out first!"

Amazingly, both Olivia and Sophie giggled at that point. They didn't see their families' reaction, as the link broke between everyone just then.

Matt looked at Emma. Tears were streaming down her face. He felt terrible. He said "I was worried the link might not continue to work. We probably won't get it back. But we could try just using a phone. It might not use the same servers as Zoom. The signal might just bounce okay between them and us, via a satellite."

Emma shook her head, "I'm not sure I could bear it. I don't even think it would help Sophie and Olivia, who seem to be helping each other. My poor sister. My poor Mum and Dad." Then she lashed out at Matt, with the cushion she had been holding. "It is your father's fault. Why all the stupid secrecy? Why didn't they decide on the embargo earlier, and give everyone a week's notice?"

Despite feeling desperately sad about Sophie and Olivia, and for Emma, and her parents even, Matt suddenly felt angry on behalf of his father. He said to Emma, "My poor old dad couldn't win could he? He is not responsible for public health. Somebody else should have rung the alarm, before he felt he had to. He didn't know Sophie was away. That repatriation plane was a real danger, but he didn't want Sophie to die. He was the one who persuaded the Governor to organise a ship for them. Nobody else had thought of that. He would have been delighted if that ship had been in the clear and had come sailing into Douglas in a few days time. And, if it had, people would have said, 'Why didn't you let the plane land? You nearly killed everyone on it. Look at all the heartache you've caused.' "

Then he looked at the abject misery on Emma's face, and felt guilty. He said, "I am sorry. Say what you like. I don't mind. Do you want me to hold you?"

She nodded her head, and he held her in his arms as she wept.

Chapter 34, Friday 30 April 2027

Vin was checking out reports on tissue samples at Nobles Hospital. He had heard from Matthew, at around 10pm the previous evening, about the video calls with the Senior Serenade. He was very disappointed, especially as he wanted everything to be well with Emma and Matthew, and he realised this distressing news could affect them badly for some time. He knew that billions of people would ultimately die across the world, but, when it is was someone as closely connected as Sophie, it seemed much more real. He was puzzled that the ultra pneumonia virus had manifested so late on the ship. He could not concentrate on the reports, so he decided to go and check personally on Peter Quinnel.

Vin checked the notes about Peter in the ward office, before he walked through to Peter's bed. He was sitting up and holding a book. Peter saw him and smiled. He said "Gosh Vin, this is twice you have come to see me, at least. I hope it is not because you are expecting to carry out a post mortem on me."

Vin told him, "Post mortems aren't that common after deaths in hospital. I think they don't think most doctors or hospital staff would be suspected of foul play."

Peter became serious and said, "Seriously though, do you know if I am going to be okay?"

"No, nobody is ever 100% certain after a head trauma case, but I took the liberty of looking at your notes just now, and the surgeon seems to think there is a very good chance of a full recovery. That is about as good a prognosis as you could hope for. Tell me, how do you feel?"

"A lot better than I was. I feel more alert, it's just I am still forgetting the odd word."

"But no general or specific amnesia? I don't mean 'Do you have perfect recall?' just that you can recall everything as well as you would expect? The name of your wife, where you live, what you were doing before you got injured."

"No, no amnesia like that. I just forget some words occasionally, like the thing above my head being a ceiling."

"But if you had forgotten a word like ceiling, and I said to you 'Look at the ceiling', you would understand wouldn't you?"

"Yes. I need to recover for Amanda's sake," Peter hesitated, and then said, "I think she is expecting."

Vin recalled that Peter had told him about his dead daughter. Vin said, "You think so?"

Peter said, "She thinks so. She was sure on Wednesday, and yesterday."

"Well some women understand their own bodies very well. That's great news. Just take it easy, and avoid any hard work or stress. You know that my wife and I are expecting a grandchild."

"Yes, but you look a bit subdued. What is up with you, doctor?"

"It seems that the Senior Serenade has probably got the ultra pneumonia virus." Vin went on to explain what Matthew had told him.

Peter thought about the young girls and their parents, and about James Quirk and his parents. He said, "No that is terrible. I didn't want to be proved right. I wanted them to live."

Vin assured him, "Well, I would have been to blame really, if we had been wrong. I helped persuade you to force the plane to divert. But I wanted our grandchild to have a living aunt, and a happy mother."

Just then Vin's bleeper bleeped. He went back to his office to take a call. It was from Nicola Kermode. She said, "Hello Dr Singh, it's Nicola Kermode. Do you remember me from the Emergency Advisory Committee?"

Vin remembered her saying how much he liked dead bodies, and how he wanted to murder people. He said, "Err, yes."

Nicola explained, "The Marine Control Centre have just had a radio call from the Senior Serenade. It's in the St George's Channel apparently, and requesting permission to berth and disembark at Douglas."

Vin was taken aback. He said, "Sorry, let me just check what you said. You said the Senior Serenade is requesting permission to berth and disembark at Douglas?"

Nicola confirmed, "Yes that's right. Poor bastards have been cast away for three weeks to lurch about in the Atlantic, having nearly been shot down before then, whilst approaching Ronaldsway in an aeroplane, and now they would all like to come home."

Vin told her, "I heard there was at least one person dead on board, and others who were definitely unwell. I don't think you should let it berth yet, if it all."

Nicola said, "If it was up to me I would have said yes straightaway. But I had quite firm instructions, given by the Council of Ministers, that you, Dr Singh, had to approve any berthing or disembarkation of this vessel."

Vin thought about Emma thinking about her sister, but felt his resolve stiffen. He said, "I would be delighted to let them disembark, but I need more information before I can do that."

There was a pause. Emma said, "We still have radio contact with the ship. Would you like to talk to the captain? I could probably get them to patch him through to your phone."

Vin agreed, "Yes, of course I will talk to him."

Emma told him, "Okay hang up now. If the phone rings again soon it will be our Control, trying to pass him through to you."

A few minutes later the telephone rang. Vin picked it up. A male voice said, "Marine Control Centre here. Putting Captain Kevin Tapsell through to you now."

Vin said, "Hello this is Dr Singh. Is that Captain Tapsell, master of the Senior Serenade?"

Captain Tapsell replied, "Yes I am Captain Tapsell. Hello Dr Singh. I suppose if it wasn't for you, I would have died by now, with my wife and children in Portsmouth. I am not sure I am grateful. It was just presented to me, as my duty, to master this ship for this voyage. But we have been at sea for three weeks, we are running out of supplies, some people are unwell with norovirus, and they all want to go home."

"Did you just say norovirus?"

"Pretty sure that's what it is. They couldn't persuade the medical officer to come on this voyage, but our nurse thinks that is what it is, and in my experience, I think she is right.

Nobody seems too desperate, but tossing about on a ship obviously doesn't help."

"How many people have it?"

"Last count it was 31 passengers and six crew."

"But I was told someone has died."

"I was going to tell you about that. I am not trying to conceal anything. One of the aircrew Sylvia Faragher has died. We are pretty sure it was a drugs overdose. She was found in the cabin of a male colleague, Jimmy Wilson. He admitted they had been taking amphetamines and whisky. He said they took them in the afternoon. After a while, he said she passed out. He got panicky and drank some more whisky, and he vaguely remembers a young girl Olivia knocking on his door. This girl, Olivia Cornell, actually came to tell us at around 9pm. She was very hysterical, saying we were all going to die. We checked Jimmy's cabin straightaway, and we found her dead on one of the beds. We found amphetamine tablets in his cabin. Jimmy was pretty drugged and drunk, so we didn't get much out of him until the next day. By that time our poor nurse was being kept busy with requests for diarrhoea tablets. You know that sort of thing."

"Hmm... deaths from straight amphetamine tablets are rare. What have you done with the body? Have you got the tablets?"

"Unusually for a fairly small ship, we have a refrigerated morgue. Just room for one. So, that is where she is. Yes, we do have the tablets. I have put them in my own safe."

"I would actually say wait at least another week, and then come in. And even then, I am not happy about the dead girl."

"So, can we can at least berth in Douglas, then you can come on board and check for yourself?"

"No I don't want you to berth in Douglas or even anchor off shore. I think ultra pneumonia is capable of carrying hundreds of metres in the air. That must be the reason it is so infectious. If we are going to let you berth, we need to get to you well out at sea first. Then we could check the body and the sick passengers before you berth, just in case you do have ultra pneumonia on board."

"So, could you get a helicopter flight? We have enough space on the top deck behind the bridge for it to land. I can't give you a pinpoint location, because our computer navigation aids have stopped working, but we are steaming at 15 knots and I would say we are pretty much 52 degrees North, and midchannel between Ireland and Wales. If you take off in 2 hours time you won't have to fly more than 100 nautical miles, well within return helicopter range."

"I would like you to slow right down, 5 knots will be plenty. We need a bit of time to get a helicopter if we can, to get to you, and be certain you don't have ultra pneumonia on board."

"Well, you seem to be in charge of whether we are allowed to get to the Isle of Man. But please try not to take too long. We have been three weeks at sea, fuel and supplies are getting low, and our very fearful passengers are now getting their hopes up. But some of them said to me 'Make sure you get permission to dock, we don't want to be shot at again, like we were in the plane.'"

"The version of events I have been told, which I am sure is true, attributes all the blame for shells being fired to the wilful recklessness of the pilot. Our Major Quinnel wanted no loss of life. I forgot to ask earlier, has your ship had any physical contact with anyone else at all, since leaving Liverpool three weeks ago?"

"No, none at all. We have been tossing about in the Atlantic, under the impression we were doomed. I gather everything in Britain is going down rapidly, and I am guessing elsewhere too, so we are fairly surprised to all still be alive, barring that poor girl. Most of the crew will be like me, losing their families and loved ones. Most of the waiters and cleaners are from the Philippines, so they will find it the hardest to adjust I think."

"I will do my best to get a helicopter to bring me to you. I presume I will be able to radio you to confirm that."

Vin finished the call, and put the phone down. He decided his best course of action would be to speak to Jack Coyle. He gave him a ring, and explained the situation. Jack said, "Well, I will check about authority and payment for the helicopter, but everyone is bound to agree to it. I will get on to the ambulance service who use helicopters during the TT races. And, if the firm the ambulance service use can't help, I will ask Gemma Cain, you know the Enterprise Minister, for contacts with Harrison Helicopters, who are a helicopter company based at Ronaldsway. They won't have flown anywhere for more than 3 weeks. I can see a problem though."

Vin asked, "Are you wondering about what happens, if I find they have ultra pneumonia on board?

Jack agreed, "That is the problem."

"I would just have to stay on board and die with them, or after them."

"And that would be tough on your son Matt, who I really like by the way, and your wife. But what about the helicopter

Mann Alone

pilot? Could he just land briefly, let you out, and then fly straight off again?"

"I hadn't thought about him. No, I wouldn't be happy with that. I was just saying to the ship's master, I think the ultra pneumonia virus spreads hundreds of metres in the air. So basically the pilot landing on the ship puts him at risk, and even more so when the door is opened for me to get out."

"So we need a pilot prepared to risk dying with you on the ship, maybe weeks after everyone else has died."

"That doesn't sound like a very attractive proposition does it? The obvious answer is to make the ship wait another week or two weeks, but that would be very hard on them and their relatives, after what they have gone through. I am thinking it is likely they haven't got ultra pneumonia. Whilst 84,000 people can't afford the risk of my hunch being wrong, I am willing to risk it personally by landing on the ship, and we just need one brave helicopter pilot to take the same risk."

"Okay let's see what we can do!"

Twenty-five minutes later Vin got another phone call. A male voice said, "Hello, is that Dr Singh? I gather you want a helicopter to fly you 100 miles or so down the Irish Sea, to see if we can find the Senior Serenade and land on her deck?"

Vin confirmed, "Yes, that's right I suppose. Sorry who are you?"

"I'm John Harrison but people call me Harry. I'm the owner of a company which has a small fleet of just 5 helicopters. It's called Harrison Helicopters. Can you be ready by the hospital helicopter field in 15 minutes?"

"I wasn't thinking you would be that quick."

"I was told you wanted to get there as soon as possible. Something about the passengers, and their relatives,

252

deserving an end to their anguish?"

Vin was wondering whether he had said that to Jack.

Harry went on, "And anyway it needs to be soon, before the pilot realises the risk of dying is not worth the pleasure of getting airborne again."

Vin asked, "Your helicopters aren't dangerous are they?"

"No not especially, when compared with driving on the road. It is just I was told that the pilot might have to stay on the ship with you, while he and you wait for two weeks to die from ultra pneumonia."

"Well, there is a body needs looking at, and I can't really expect the only other pathologist on the island to do this. He is not even at work today. But your pilot is taking a risk agreeing to this."

"Yes he is. So he will be with you in 15 minutes. If you are ready before the helicopter has arrived, wait by the vehicle entrance."

Vin started shoving useful items in his bag of equipment, including a camera, and evidence bags, which he would not normally have to use himself. He felt a bit rushed, but he did not want to turn the helicopter away. It was just landing as he got to the field, and he waited for the engine to stop and for the pilot to get out, before he approached the helicopter. He saw a fairly tall well-built chap aged about 60 years, and felt a bit surprised it was not someone younger.

The pilot said, "You must be Dr Singh, Vin is that right? I am Harry Harrison."

Vin said, "You never said you would be the pilot."

Harry told him, "Well, it didn't seem fair to put any of my employees at risk. And anyway, I want to see my daughter's partner, who is on the ship. My daughter Amie has been really worried about him. Right, let's get going."

With the noise of the engine before he got in, the actions of getting in with his bag and strapping himself in, and with Harry's own attention to take off and setting a course, Vin forgot to ask Harry anything about his daughter's partner.

Chapter 35, Friday 30 April 2027

Harry and Vin flew on a course of 205 degrees, for about an hour. Neither seemed to want to talk much. Harry had radio contact with the ship, but neither he nor Captain Tapsell were certain of their exact positions. Eventually, after some circling around, Harry found the ship slightly further west than expected, in terms of the ship's course, and slightly further away than expected, in terms of distance from Mann. He landed the helicopter, without great difficulty, on the main deck behing the bridge. A crew member came to lead them to the bridge, where they were introduced to Captain Tapsell. Captain Tapsell asked his crew member, "Would you be able to whistle up some coffee for the three of us?"

Harry guessed that Vin would rather talk privately. Harry said to the crew man, "Can you take me to the main lounge, I might surprise Jimmy, my girl's boyfriend." Harry wandered off with him.

Vin felt the name Jimmy had been mentioned before. Captain Tapsell said, "Dr Singh, We have one of the airline crew called James, but I think we only have one other man on board called James or Jimmy. That is the name of the man who had the cabin we found the dead woman in, Jimmy Wilson."

Vin asked, "Oh! So if it was Jimmy's cabin, does that mean the woman had her own cabin?"

"Yes, that's right. I am told the pair of them were pretty friendly, but all the airline crew had their own cabins. We had quite a few to spare, so it seemed sensible that people who wanted a cabin to themselves should have one," the Captain confirmed.

Vin said, "I really ought to have a look at her, as soon as possible. Her name is Sylvia Faragher, is that right?"

Captain Tapsell replied,"Yes"

Vin asked, "And her date of birth?"

Captain Tapsell looked at a notebook he kept, and said, "5 February 2005. What does it matter? Surely you just want to make sure she didn't die from ultra pneumonia?"

Vin replied, "Yes, it is the critical thing to do, but if it is not ultra pneumonia , her death would be called a "sudden death" by police. Age is an important factor in assessing the condition of a body, and the date of birth helps identify who the person is. There would have been a good argument for a police officer to have come with me, but obviously the risk to him or her could not be justified. Let's have a look at her now, and I will take it from there."

Captain Tapsell took Vin to the morgue. It was a fairly small room. The cabinet for the body was designed for it to open by pulling a drawer, so that the victim's head would appear first and the feet would be at the far end. Vin clipped a microphone to his lapel, and plugged the other end in his smartphone, so that he could record his own comments. He noted the date and time, the ship and its approximate location, and then referred to the body as being that of Sylvia Faragher, date of birth 5 February 2005, and the date and time and circumstances of her being found. He then started describing a visual examination of the body.

At the end of his visual examination, Vin was sure that Sylvia had been raped and strangled. He had noted injuries to the lips and petechiae (blood spotting) around the neck as well as two thumb marks on the neck. There were also two thumb marks on her inner thighs. He was not sure whether penetration had occurred before or after she had died. He was glad it was murder, rather than ultra pneumonia, but he still felt sad about the violent death of a young woman. He had taken a number of photographs. The mouth, neck, and vaginal swabs he had taken, he put in exhibit bags and labelled them. He decided to put the bags in the cabinet with the body.

There were still things that needed to be done about Sylvia, but Vin decided a higher priority was checking that the virus on the ship was norovirus, or at least definitely not ultra pneumonia. He spoke to the nurse, who had two patients in the medical bay, whilst most people feeling ill had remained in their cabins. Amongst other checks, he got his stethoscope out for the first time in years, and listened to ten peoples' breathing. He was satisfied that no-one had any serious respiratory problems, confirming the illness not to be ultra pneumonia. He decided that now he should speak to Captain Tapsell again.

Vin found Captain Tapsell on his bridge. He gave him a pair of latex gloves, and put on a fresh pair himself. He said, "Please, can you get the packet of amphetamine out and show them to me. No wait, let's minimise handling of the packet. Have you opened it yourself?

Captain Tapsell said, "Yes"

Vin asked, "Can you remember how many had been removed?"

"Yes, it was only 8 actually. I think the packet holds 28 or 30." He got the packet out of the fridge. It was clearly labelled Evekeo 30 tablets.

Vin said, "There is no need for me to touch it." He held open a plastic evidence bag and said, "Put it straight in here please, and then can you seal the bag, complete the label and sign and date it please."

Captain Tapsell said, "Yes alright, but please tell me what is going on."

Vin did not answer the request, but asked a question instead, "Do you know whether that is the only packet that was in Jimmy's cabin?"

Captain Tapsell replied, "No, not definitely. But. it was me who found the packet. I went to the cabin, as soon as I heard. I actually remember thinking, maybe there would be other packets or drugs about. I looked in the bin, and on the shelves. I asked Jimmy about it the next day when he was sober, and he said, 'Captain that's all there is. She took 4, I took 4. But she had some of my whisky as well.' Damn, I suppose we should have kept the whisky as well, but we left it in his cabin. I think you are saying that the drugs are not what killed her."

"Drugs are often used as a cover for deaths by strangulations. And strangulation is a common cause of death or injuries in domestic violence."

"So you are saying she was strangled?"

"Yes, and raped. But obviously I need to do a full post mortem, when we get her back to Douglas. I wish I had a police detective here. They would be making sure all the evidence is preserved, and everything is followed through.

Jimmy Wilson has to be interviewed and DNA taken, but the police can do that when we get back. Oh I have just thought, if we could photograph him. Ideally we should get him stripped off completely, but if we could take a photograph of his face, there might be defensive injuries there."

"Yes he had a scratch on his cheek, now you come to mention it."

"Was it recent?"

"Yes it looked it. Probably fading now. You talked about getting back to Douglas. Does that mean we are cleared to berth and disembark in Douglas?"

"Well, the people who are unwell, who I looked at, definitely haven't got ultra pneumonia. And I have concluded by its spread elsewhere, that you would have had it after two weeks. I am surprised you didn't get it, but there you are. So yes, I will confirm that you should be allowed to berth and disembark in Douglas."

"Well, that's great news. But have my sick passengers got norovirus?"

"Yes, probably I would say."

"You don't really care do you? You are much more interested in one dead body, than helping a much larger number of people who are unwell."

"I have been told something like that before, about my priorities. But it doesn't really matter what you call the passengers' illnesses. They need a very light diet with plenty of liquids, and they will be fine. I suspect most of them will feel a lot better once they get off this ship."

At that moment Harry Harrison tapped on the window by the door into the bridge. He came into the bridge. To Vin, he was looking a bit down. Harry said, "I have spoken to

Jimmy. Did you know he pulled the aircraft pilot Captain Smith out of his cockpit to let the other officer take over, just in time to avoid being hit by the artillery shell? So that makes him a bit of a hero. But now he has told me about the dead girl, Sylvia. Apparently she was in his cabin and they both took some amphetamine tablets, and both drank whisky as well. I am not happy about this. My Amie thinks he is wonderful, but he has got a woman in his cabin, and got her so drugged up she has died."

Vin told him, "It is worse than that I am afraid, Harry. Maybe Jimmy did save the plane and 128 lives, but I am pretty sure that he raped and murdered Sylvia."

Harry found an empty chair to sit on, feeling a bit stunned. He said, "Can you prove that Jimmy did that?"

Vin told him, "I am certain that she was raped and murdered, even though I still need to do a proper post-mortem in Douglas. And who else would it be, if not Jimmy? But I am not a lawyer."

Harry sat shaking his head, saying, "My poor Amie. I don't think I mentioned that I am a grandfather did I? She has a six month old son, and Jimmy is obviously the father."

Vin tried to show sympathy, "I am sorry. Look, are you okay to fly us back to Mann? You look a bit shaken."

Harry was cheered by thinking about flying, "Yes, I will be fine. I much prefer being in a helicopter to being on a ship, pitching about in the Irish Sea."

Vin said, "Okay, well I need to speak to people on the radio first, and then we can go."

Harry looked at Vin and the Captain, and said, "So no ultra pneumonia on the ship then?"

Vin replied, "No."

Harry smiled weakly, "Well that much is good news, anyway."

Chapter 36, Saturday 1 May 2027

Vin had agreed with the Marine Control Centre, and with Captain Tapsell, that Senior Serenade would berth at 10am. There were two police officers waiting to arrest Jimmy. Onchan and District Brass Band were ready to play. About 500 relatives, friends and well wishers were awaiting a reunion with passengers on the ship. An ambulance was waiting. It had been chosen as the best means of conveying Sylvia's body to the island morgue. Vin and Martha had decided to get the now well used, and relatively cheap, vintage electric railway into Douglas, from Baldrine. Part of the reason it was well used was because Vannin Buses had decided to cease all direct services from Douglas to Ramsey, to save their electric buses for all their other routes. Vin and Martha found that there were two main problems with this service. One was getting a seat on the train, as sometimes they were full with people travelling the whole route from Ramsey into Douglas. The other problem was that the terminus at the Douglas end was nowhere near the centre of town. It was too far to walk from there to the hospital for instance. But, when they used the train, they were saving on their electricity allowance. It was good weather that day, so the mile and a half walk along the promenade to Douglas Harbour, from the Derby Castle terminus, had been quite pleasant for them. They had met Emma and Matthew, and Beryl and Wayne O'Hara, on the quayside, where everyone had been allowed to gather. It was the first time that Vin and Martha had met Beryl and Wayne. Beryl's attitude towards Matthew had improved, since Emma had upbraided her three days earlier, and she was amiable towards Vin and Martha. Vin noticed Harry Harrison nearby, with a woman around his own age and a younger woman with a baby in a pram. He was surprised and worried to see Major Peter Quinnel in uniform, with Amanda. Vin did not even know that Peter had been discharged from hospital.

Before anyone disembarked, Vin saw the two police officers board the ship. Then the band struck up, and the passengers started disembarking. One of the first off was Flight Officer James Quirk. Major Peter Quinnel walked up to him, and offered his hand. "Hello James, I recognise you now. I am glad you made it," he said.

James replied angrily, "No thanks to you. You nearly killed us, even though we were an authorised flight, and we didn't have the ultra pneumonia virus. Everyone on the plane was terrified. Then we were condemned to three weeks tossing about in the Atlantic. Why should I shake your hand? You should be in prison."

James walked away. Peter felt himself fainting. When he revived, he found himself propped up on a bench, with Amanda sitting next to him looking very anxious. Vin was also looking at him. Peter said, "Sorry Amanda, I didn't mean to scare you. Did I fall?"

Amanda "No, Vin and another chap helped me prop you up and put you on this bench. Are you okay? I said we shouldn't come."

Peter replied, "You were right, of course. I just wanted to see the people I had nearly killed. Perhaps I was hoping for their forgiveness, or something."

Vin intervened, "Peter, it is not you who needs forgiveness. If anyone needs it, it is me. I didn't really know how likely it was that any of them would have the ultra pneumonia virus. I just wanted to play it safe for 84,000 people, and I encouraged you to think it was very likely. And anyway you probably have saved them."

Peter asked, "You mean the Russian yacht?"

Vin said, "We really will never know. Luckily their bodies are either trapped in the wreckage, or they have been carried away from the island by currents. But Peter, those Russians weren't coming here to do us any favours, were they? And you nearly got killed stopping them. That makes you a hero, not a villain."

Peter looked more alert, but he still felt glum. He said, "Maybe. But I am glad these people have made it. Look, that's Matt over there, and the girls must be Emma and her sister Sophie. They look so happy, and yet I nearly killed Sophie didn't I?"

Amanda gave Peter a hug. She said to him, "Well you are a hero to me. Do you feel okay to walk to the car park, and I will drive us home."

Vin said to them, "Just give me a moment with Matthew and the others, and I will walk with you back to your car."

Vin was only gone a couple of minutes, and then he and Martha walked with Peter and Amanda to Peter's old Jaguar. Vin wanted to go back to the quay again, so Martha went with him. The band had stopped playing, and most people had gone. Vin noticed that the ambulance was still there. Harry and the two women were still there. The younger woman was now holding the baby in her arms, and the baby was looking around curiously. Also still waiting was a middle-aged woman, standing on her own. The ambulance crew then emerged from the ship, wheeling a body, which they then loaded in the back of the ambulance. Vin saw the solitary woman crying, and assumed she was Sylvia's mother. Next the police officers emerged, with a young man in handcuffs. Vin had not taken a photograph of Jimmy Wilson, having left that to Captain Tapsell, but he assumed that the man in handcuffs was Jimmy. Vin saw Jimmy look towards Harry and the two women. The baby looked at his father and held his arm out, but Jimmy bowed his head, and he was led past them towards a police van without anything being said.

Chapter 37, Sunday 2 May 2027

Peter had a lie in, and left it to Amanda to worry about the farm. Being a Sunday they just had one hand in, mainly for milking. Peter was feeling fairly morose. Around 11am Amanda asked him to shower and get dressed, so that they could have a nice Sunday lunch together.

When lunch was ready, he carved a small leg of lamb, from a sheep raised on their upper fields. Amanda had been thinking about opening one of their last 4 bottles of wine, but wondered if that would be a good idea given his head injury. Anyway she decided, "I will save it for another day when he is feeling more cheerful."

During lunch, she mentioned the lambing season a few weeks earlier. That prompted him to say, "So you are definitely expecting then?"

She said, "Yes, my darling."

He said, without any obvious enthusiasm, "Okay, that's good I suppose."

After lunch she said, "Your Committee must have been working overtime without you. I have had several emails, which amazingly seems to work still, through a local SITS server. These include requests for information, and questionnaires about what sort of livestock or produce we could grow, under different circumstances. Also there is stuff from the Manx NFU. Would you like me to get them, and we could just talk about them, just so I know what you think? I am happy to deal with sending the replies."

Peter agreed, "Alright then."

Amanda went out of the room, and returned with several sheets of paper and letters. She handed one over to Peter and said, "This one is asking if we would consider growing sugar beet. In England they grow it mainly in East Anglia, where it is drier and warmer than here, with a harvest quite late in the year. But, accepting a smaller yield by weight, it should be viable here, and might be worth doing. People will still have a sweet tooth, and nowhere else to get sugar from. What do you think?

Peter just glanced at the sheet, without real interest. He said, "It's probably best if we just stick with the dairy cattle and the sheep."

Just then they heard a tap on the back door. Amanda went to see who it was. She was concerned when she saw James Quirk standing there. She said to him, "Please, I know you had a hard time, but Peter was only doing what he thought was right. Did you know he got badly concussed stopping a Russian yacht only 6 days ago, and he is still not right. Could you please leave us alone?"

James said, "Yes I heard about the yacht yesterday. I just want a few words please. I am not going to be unpleasant."

Amanda was reassured, and said, "Alright then, come through."

James was led into their lounge. He said to Peter, "Basically I have come to apologise. I talked to people yesterday. I have been to church this morning. And now I see things with a different perspective. Lots of people are so glad, that they have been given the chance to survive. It was wrong to jeopardise 84,000 people, by authorising a plane to bring 120 people back, when nobody could be certain that none of them were carrying the ultra pneumonia virus. You did your best to warn and direct Captain Smith, but he just wouldn't listen. He can be an extremely awkward and difficult colleague. And I have heard all about the Russian yacht, and how you got injured stopping that arriving. Most people think you are a hero, and now I agree with them. When you offered to shake my hand yesterday I refused. But I hope we can shake hands today?"

James held out his hand. Peter stood up and shook his hand. Peter said, "Thank you for coming to tell me that. I really appreciate it."

James felt he made amends. He said, "Okay, well I will leave you both alone now, and I very much hope your head injury recovers fully."

Amanda showed James out, and came back into the lounge.

Peter said, "That was nice of him to come here to say that."

Amanda was feeling a bit strained. She said, "Yes."

Peter looked at her and said, "I am sorry, I have been bit miserable since I got home. I was feeling bad about nearly shooting the plane down. Now I am just glad the passengers are all okay."

He stood up, and took Amanda in his arms, and said, "So you are definitely pregnant then? That's marvellous isn't it?"

Amanda told him, "Yes I am very happy about it."

Peter kissed her neck, and said, "So how did you get pregnant then?"

Amanda replied, "I have got a feeling you are about to remind me."

Chapter 38, Friday 21 May 2027

Vin was looking at his tiny runner bean plants in pots in his greenhouse. He had not grown them before, but he felt sure that he had seen some beans halfway up their 8 foot poles in Jersey in late May, about thirty years before. He had been there on a holiday with Martha, when they still lived in London. Still, he had definitely read that one should protect beans from frosts, and frosts could easily happen right up to the end of May, in Mann. So, he reflected, it is just as well they haven't outgrown their pots yet. His thoughts were broken by Martha saying, "They are here!"

Then he was aware of David Quayle standing next to him, saying, "They are a bit feeble aren't they?" referring to the beans, "but I am glad to see you have a trench ready. They should catch up with a bit of warmer weather, if you are lucky."

Vin said, "And it's great to see you too! Where is Amber?"

"She's inside talking to Martha," David told him.

Vin asked, "Do you think we have the right climate for growing beans?"

David looked quizzically at Vin, and said, "Well, we can't import them now can we? Maybe it would be better to grow other things instead, but I personally quite like them, you know with a bit of pepper and butter."

Vin commented, "I think I might miss rice, when that runs out. I will just have to get used to potatoes or mash, with everything. We could perhaps use pasta, if there is enough wheat to make it, but I prefer naan bread anyway."

David had been feeling his mood swing between optimism and pessimism several times since the embargo started. Suddenly, he felt the urge to express pessimistic sentiments. He responded, "Well, we have a flour mill, but do we have the capability to make pasta or naan bread? I'm not sure. And I think more than 50% of our flour and bread consumption had been met from imports. But, it's not just certain kinds of food we can't get though, is it? We are going to run out most things eventually, shampoo, car parts, surgical dressings, clothes, crockery, engineering parts, just name it! Even large countries, like Germany or the USA, didn't manufacture the full range of consumer and industrial goods that they used. We are a tiny island of 84,000 people, whose prosperity was based on selling services nobody really needs, like insurance and online gambling. We have a small engineering and manufacturing sector. By which I mean, it is a small number of businesses, and the individual businesses are generally fairly small in size. Some businesses are proving very resourceful and good at improvising, but this will only take us so far."

"Well on that cheerful note we ought to go indoors, and see if Martha has got any food she can spare for you to eat this evening," said Vin, sounding not particularly worried.

They were sitting around the dining table after the main course, and were relaxing. When they were ready, Martha was going to fetch some gooseberry fool desserts she had prepared and kept in the fridge. Amber said, "Vin, tell us a bit about that poor girl who died on the ship. You were going to do a post-mortem weren't you? What is the latest?"

David interjected, "Excuse my wife, but she does have a bit of a taste for reading about murders, and in this case she has the pathologist at hand to answer her questions."

Vin responded to Amber, "Well my evidence and findings will be in the public domain soon anyway. So, I will tell you and David, but I can't show you the gory photographs that were taken during the post mortem."

Amber's facial expression gave a slight hint of disappointment about not seeing photographs, but she did not say so.

Vin went on, "I got formal direction from the Coroner's Office to carry out a post mortem, and I was able to do that on the Tuesday after the ship docked, it being a bank holiday Monday in between. So, there were nearly six days between her death, and my formal post mortem examination. That is not ideal. Also, now we can only do very limited forensic toxicology and other tests, on blood and tissue samples. That is, obviously, because we can't send them off to England any more. All we have been able to do, was establish that there toxins in her system. Whilst I am talking about sampling, you may not know that we have a company Vannin Genomics Ltd, on the island, which does DNA testing. It used to do DNA testing for customers right across the UK. The point being that, since the post-mortem, the police have sent samples to this company's laboratory for DNA testing. They compared swabs I took on the ship from the girl, with a DNA sample from the suspect, who is in custody. I am told, unofficially by the Coroner's Office, that the results show a match of his DNA with the vaginal swabs, and with those I took from her neck.

But I haven't mentioned that, the result of my examinations of cross sections of the neck, showed pre-death damage to the carotid artery, and displacement of the hyoid bone. She died because of lack of oxygen to the brain, because she was strangled."

"Gosh, so it seems pretty clear, that the suspect Jimmy Wilson raped and strangled the poor girl?" said Amber, who had been listening carefully.

Vin answered, "Well you would think so. But I have been involved in several murders over the years, and I know what the suspect might say. He might say that intercourse was consensual, although the bruises on her inner thighs say otherwise. He might say that his DNA on her neck was just a kiss, from earlier. He might say someone else did it. He might say she was already dead from overdosing, despite my evidence that the injuries to the carotid artery and hyoid bone were while she was alive. He might even say it was consensual rough sex, that went wrong. Of course, we can't ask the unfortunate girl for her version of events. But I would be surprised if he gets off the murder charge."

David commented, "There is another issue I can think of. Do Isle of Man courts have any jurisdiction over events that occur on the high seas?"

Martha said, "I can't see that being allowed to be a problem. I mean, the suspect is a British citizen for passport purposes, so is the victim, and the ship is a British registered ship. The only British courts left are Isle of Man courts, and, if push came to shove, I reckon some sort of retrospective adjustment to the law could be made. It would be outrageous if he got off on a technicality, rather than some serious doubt about his guilt."

Vin responded, "I agree, it would be outrageous. People think I like seeing dead bodies. Well, when I do post-mortems, I try to do them with a dispassionate professional interest, but even so, when I first looked at this poor girl on the ship, I thought, 'What a waste of a young life'. And you know, I saw the suspect escorted off the ship in handcuffs, and I felt sympathy for his girlfriend and their baby, but I felt angry when I saw the mother of the victim standing alone, crying, whilst her daughter's body was loaded into the back of the ambulance."

Chapter 39, Tuesday 1 June 2027

Vin was at home in the evening, when the phone rang. It was David Quayle. David said, "Vin, various people on the Committee, or connected with Government, could have been asked to call you, but they picked on me as the senior official in the Department that covers Health, because some are seeing this as mainly a health issue. And even though, as you pointed out, I am only a jumped up social worker."

Vin responded, "Well you are quite a clued up social worker, but I am not quite with you. You have been asked to phone me in your official capacity, but I don't know what you are ringing about."

"Well we have this complete embargo of the island, thanks to you, and it looks like it has saved human life on Mann. I don't think you said that ultra pneumonia would necessarily wipe out everyone, everywhere, but you definitely said, or implied, that everyone on the mainland would die from it."

"I suppose that is, more or less, what I said. But I have had time to reflect. You know, it was a real surprise to me, that the people on the Senior Serenade didn't have it. I think we would have been justified in saying, 'stop the repatriation flight' even if it had been only one in a hundred chance of its carrying the infection, but I actually did think it very likely, possibly 80 or 90% chance. So, the rate of spread must have been slower than I originally guestimated. But you know, as people have said, I am not an epidemiologist. I think I was right, about the incubation period being around 2 weeks. As for it being completely lethal, I now think that probably isn't completely right, but it can't be far off. Say, maybe one person in fifty thousand survives initially, but what sort of life do they have afterwards, and would we ever hear from them?"

"Well, that is just it, actually."

"You mean that we have heard from someone?"

"Yes."

"And, you have rung me because the Committee, and the Government, want to know what I think we should do about it? So, therefore this person, or persons, is presumably somewhere not too remote from us?"

"Yes, you've got it."

"So tell me, what has happened."

"Telecoms, and all communications with mainland Britain, went down over approximately a two to three week period, starting around 22 April. By Tuesday 11 May 2027 all of our Government departments had lost all contact with all previous known contacts, anywhere in Britain. So we assumed that was it. We assumed that the electricity supply on the mainland would have ceased at the same time, so communication by phone would not be possible, even if anyone had survived. But we were wrong. A mobile phone battery can keep a charge for quite a time if it's not used, and our radio masts here can still pick up signals. I never realised it, but you can reach a mast up to 50 miles away from a mobile phone. Somebody has rung Manx Radio from Barrow in Furness, this morning."

"Well, that is interesting. Who are they? What did they say?"

"It was just one person. A young chap called Ben Roper rang the Radio Station, at 10.03 am. The conversation has been recorded, if you want to listen to it. Manx Radio can...could often be picked up on the mainland. Radio sets can work on replaceable batteries. Manx Radio often gives out a phone number for listeners to ring. Maybe, this chap Ben Roper had been fiddling with his radio, hoping to find a radio station still broadcasting. Lots of people must have known, anyway, about our embargo to try to keep ultra pneumonia out. Maybe, he had been specifically trying to pick up Manx Radio. Anyway, he tried ringing on his mobile, and he got through. It's not really clear how or why he survived. He said he is only 19 years old. He lived with his parents, but they died. He had a friend who also survived, but his friend has committed suicide. He says there is no one else alive in the whole town, as far as he can tell. He would like..."

Vin interrupted, "to come to live on the Isle of Man. And please will we come and fetch him?"

"Yes that's right. He would like to live here."

"And, what was he told?"

"Well, the person he spoke to told him that they would speak to the Government, and would he please ring back again, at 10am tomorrow. He was asked about his phone battery. He said both of his parents' mobile phones have still got charged batteries, as well as his own. He was told to keep listening to Manx Radio, at 10am every day, if the phones stopped working. And they told him that they would try to ensure that he would be able to pick up Manx Radio, in Barrow in Furness."

"Can they do that?"

"They can make it less directional, apparently, so that it is easier to hear further afield west to east, rather than mainly north to south."

"So, is it really up to me to decide what we do?"

"Well although Adrian Kelly is still Minister for Health and Social Services, Henry Smith has said quite plainly, that it should be your decision. Basically, Henry is terrified to let anyone in, without your say so. By the way, Adrian still resents you strongly. His sister never got on the ship. She went back to London, and presumably died with Keith in London."

"We shouldn't just let him come over, but I suppose we could learn from him, maybe. It could be useful to try to work out why he survived."

"Are you thinking that someone should go over there?"

"Yes, well maybe."

David had to ask, "But what if he is infectious?"

Vin told him, "That's a very good question."

Chapter 40, Wednesday 2 June 2027

Vin got to the Manx Radio building in Douglas at 9.45am. He had decided that he needed to talk to Ben Roper himself. He was invited into a studio and given a set of headphones, with the promise that he was not about to be broadcast. He was seated in front of a microphone, and told that if Ben phoned he would be put through, and he would hear Ben clearly. And Ben would hear him, via the microphone.

It had got to 10.12am, and Vin was thinking he should go to do something more useful at the hospital, when he heard a female voice in his headphones saying, "Dr Singh, I am putting Ben Roper through to you now."

Vin could hear him say, "Hello who is that? I spoke to someone called Mike yesterday."

Vin replied, "Hello my name is Vin Singh, but please just call me Vin. And you are Ben Roper, is that right?"

Ben said, "That's right. I'm sorry I am a bit late. I couldn't get through at first. I thought if I walked across the golf links, you know a bit nearer the sea, I might get through, and it worked."

"I can certainly hear you alright. I have been told what you told Mike yesterday. You are 19 years old, and you live in Barrow on Furness. Is that right?"

"Yes, I was 19 in January. I actually live on Walney Island, which is the part of Barrow nearest the open sea, although a lot of the houses on the island are nothing special."

"Sorry Ben, I don't know Barrow. Do you have to get a ferry to get to Walney Island?"

"No it's joined by a bridge. It's not very long, the bridge. It is supposed to lift up in the middle, you know like Tower Bridge, but it hardly ever does. Are you in the Isle Of Man Government, Vin?"

"I am not a Minister, or an official, more like a special adviser. Normally I am a pathologist, that is a doctor who checks why people have died."

"Everyone in Barrow seems to have died. I haven't seen anyone alive, other than Billy, for four weeks now."

"That must be awful."

"It's horrible. Do you think I could come and live on the Isle of Man? I would get a job, working on a farm or in a supermarket, or anything. I will go crazy if I have to stay here. If you could send a light plane, there is a little airfield on Walney Island near my house."

"We would have to check things out first. Look, in case we lose contact, can you give me your address now, please."

"Okay, its 79 Rubble Gardens, on Walney Island."

"Like I said, we need to check things, before we can let you come over here. Can you tell me who Billy was? Was he a friend?"

" Sort of. Not really close. I bumped in to him, after I thought everyone in Barrow was dead. But he's hung himself now."

Vin felt a bit uneasy. He suspected he was not being told the truth, or at least not the whole truth. He said, "Ben, can you tell us what happened, and what happened to your parents."

"I think it was about 5 weeks ago. I had gone down the pub, the Prince of Wales. I normally play darts on a Monday. There had been plenty of stuff on social media, about people dying down south, and some cases in Manchester and Leeds. I was trying to take no notice to be honest, but one of my older mates, a lorry driver, didn't show up at the pub. After a while I started feeling really breathless, and I decided to go home. It was about half past nine. My Mum and Dad had gone to bed, which was really early for them. I sort of assumed that this was it for them and me, and I went to bed too. When I woke up it was light. I can't remember the time, but it was pretty early. I felt really thirsty, so I went down to the kitchen, without really thinking too clearly, and had two glasses of water. I still wasn't breathing well, and I went back to bed. I woke up again, around midday. My breathing was better. I checked on my Mum and Dad, and they were both cold, dead."

Ben paused, and Vin thought he could hear a couple of sobs. Vin did not say anything, and after a while Ben went on, "I went out, and there were not many people about. The ones I saw all looked a bit spaced out. The baker's was open, and I bought a pie. Next day it wasn't open. After 2 or 3 days, there was no one about at all."

"So what about Billy?"

"Oh yeah, I did see him wandering about. He lives nearby, and I sometimes see...saw him in the Prince of Wales. So, since everyone died, we would go round each other's house for a chat. He helped me move my parents' bodies out. They are in the shed. I probably ought to have buried them, but I don't have a spade or any soft ground. It's funny, well actually it's shit, but I don't think I've seen any bodies, apart from my parents. Everyone must have had time to get home, and presumably get to bed."

"So, your parents are still where you left them, shoved in the shed. And where is Billy?"

"I think I said that he hung himself. I found him hanging from a rafter, in his garage."

"And is that where he is still, hanging from a rafter?"

"Umm, yes."

"So why do you suppose that you survived, and this friend Billy survived?"

"I don't know, I'm not an expert am I? Most people survive most illnesses don't they? Except for this ultra pneumonia, which seems to have killed everyone, except me, and someone else in Barrow, and you lot on the Isle of Man."

"Ben, you have just referred to Billy as someone else, not as your friend. Look, Ben tell me the truth, or we are not going to help you at all. You can stay in Barrow all by yourself."

"No, don't make me do that. I'll tell you. Billy was my dealer. I found out he was alive, because I had already found out where he lived by accident, and I thought he would probably be dead, but he might have a stash somewhere. So I went round his address to look for it, and he was still alive. He actually said, 'What are you doing here? Are you looking for my stash?' But I think he was glad to see another living person. He even let me have some more at first, but he uses …used it himself, so he stopped giving me any more, after a while."

"What sort of stash are we talking about, heroin?"

"Yes, you had sort of guessed hadn't you? How?"

"There was a verbal clue. Drug users sometimes talk about being spaced out. But I had been wondering if a powerful depressant, like heroin, could have helped you and Billy survive. So has the stash run out, and is that why Billy couldn't face going on, whereas you thought you would check out Manx Radio to rescue you?"

"As I said, Billy stopped letting me have any, but I reckon the stash has gone. I looked for it after I found him hanging, but couldn't find it."

"So, when did you last have some heroin?

"Five days ago. I felt bad for a while, but I reckon I am okay now. You wouldn't make me stay here, just because of the heroin use, would you? I will go mad. There's no electricity, there is no fresh food, nobody to talk to, nothing to do."

"Listen Ben I can't give you a definite plan yet, but we will try to help you. We will probably need to test your blood when we come. Would that be okay?

"I suppose so!"

"Good! So, what I want you to do is phone this Manx Radio number every day, at 10am okay. There must be other mobiles you can find, with live batteries if you need to. And keep listening to Manx Radio. If it is not me you speak to, I may have left a message for you, and anything you say will be passed on to me, alright?"

"Can't I have a number to speak to you direct?"

"No, we are not going to do that. And a word of warning. You might have been thinking you would make you own way, by boat or something, but don't do that. Armed police and the Army Reserve have orders to shoot anyone who tries to get onto the Isle of Man, and that includes people who have got ashore, before they find out." Vin could hear a few sniffs. He went on, "So chin up Ben, we will work something out in a few days, and take it from there."

Chapter 41, Wednesday 2 June 2027

David had agreed to meet Vin in his office at 11.30am, to hear about his conversation with Ben Roper, and to discuss what might be done. Vin was invited to go into David's office, and found Adrian Kelly was there with David. Adrian looked at Vin and said, "The hero of the island. You, and that Major Quinnel, who tried to shoot down the aeroplane with my sister in it. And now she is dead, because of the pair of you. And nobody gives any credit to the British, led by my fine brother in law, for giving us so much support. They flew in some vital supplies, and they carried on naval and air patrols for as long as they could. And, all Keith wanted in return was a safe haven for his wife, my twin sister Kathy, who was Manx born, not like you."

Vin replied, "Minister, I am really sorry. It must be terrible to lose a twin. I was wrong about the aeroplane, but I was only trying to help the people of Mann. I have lived here for nearly 30 years, and grown quite fond of them."

Adrian grunted and said, "I will leave you both to it. I hope you will do me the courtesy of informing me of any plans you come up with, to deal with this person in Barrow, so I at least know what is going on."

Adrian walked out of the room. David said, "He is as pompous as ever. But you were very diplomatic. Are you Vin's polite brother?"

Vin replied, "Seriously I do feel sympathy for him. We could have let the plane land, as it turned out. It is awful to lose someone you are close to, even if billions have died around the world. And he is struggling to cope with everything, like most of us, I suppose."

"Anyway, what did you find out from the man in Barrow?"

"It is strange. Two of them survived originally. And they are, or were, both heroin users. The one who hanged himself was called Billy. He was Ben's dealer. Ben is saying that the heroin ran out, so Billy hanged himself, and Ben hasn't had any for five days. But, I am just wondering, if they had both taken a big injection of heroin at a critical time, would it be that by suppressing their bodies' systems, it allowed them to survive the ultra pneumonia? Ben is only 19 years old, and lived at home with his parents, who are both dead now, like everyone else in Barrow. It sounds like he didn't have a job, but I neglected to ask."

"Wouldn't it be best if we don't go near him, nor let him come here? Ideally we would help him, but adopting the utilitarian approach again, would it really make sense to jeopardise everything?"

"I certainly wouldn't advocate his being brought here, without being sure it would be safe. But it could be dangerous just to wash our hands of him. There must be some boats around in Barrow, that he could try to navigate over to us, if he felt desperate enough. We might not find out, until he has got here. And anyway, if two people go over to Barrow for a while, they could make sure it was safe for him to come here."

"How would they do that?"

"Inject some of his blood into themselves. The least likely thing is that Ben has not been infected. If, more likely, he has been infected and recovered the virus should be dead, and I would definitely expect there to be antibodies in his blood..."

David interrupted, "So, with antibodies, you could develop a vaccine?"

"Ultimately, that might be possible. But, I don't think we have the technology, at the moment, to develop a vaccine from his blood, on the Isle of Man. If you think back to the Covid 19 pandemic, it took competing teams, with big specialised resources and facilities, a year to come up with a vaccine. So, if he hasn't been infected, or he has been infected and he has recovered, they will all be fine to come back three weeks later."

"And, is there another possibility?"

"He might be a carrier, or still infected and still alive in other words. In which case, being anywhere near him would probably ensure the death of his two visitors, within two weeks or so, but being injected with his blood would make absolutely sure. Especially if the sample size is two people, not just one."

"So, the main reason, for injecting our two guinea pigs with Ben's blood, is to be certain whether or not it is safe for them to come back with him?"

"It is the only way I can think of, that gives us real certainty."

"So, if our two volunteers are dead, we would then know not to let Ben come over. But, if they are okay, it is safe for them and Ben to come here. What about different blood groups? Couldn't having an injection of the wrong blood group be dangerous, even if he is not infectious?"

"Well, I didn't ask him his blood group, but, even if he knows, I wouldn't want to rely on what he says. There is a way round that problem though. We could send two people who are in the universal recipient group, which is AB rhesus positive. Generally it doesn't matter what blood you give to people in that group. The trouble is, not many Manx people are in that group."

"Is it different for different racial or ethnic groups?"

"Yes the percentages vary quite a lot. With Asian people, it is around 10% of people who are in the AB positive blood group. With your average Manxman or woman, it is probably only 2 or 3%"

"Vin, you're Asian, what blood group are you?"

"I sort of wish I wasn't, but the truth is that I am actually AB positive. So, that is one volunteer found. But it will be a lot more tricky to find a pilot of a helicopter or a light plane, whose blood group is also AB positive, and who is willing to risk his life, and remain with me and a junkie in Barrow, for three weeks."

"Are you sure we need to do this?"

"David, do you remember we had a little chat recently, about running out of lots of things eventually? It seems pretty clear that, sooner or later, we will need to go over to the mainland, and basically scavenge for those things. Well, Barrow might actually be a good place to start. I don't know too much about Barrow. I never knew it was joined to an island called Walney Island, for example. But, doesn't it...didn't it have a population about the same size as Mann? And it does have industries doesn't it? It must have warehouses and stores full of useful items. Probably there is diesel or petrol storage. It sounds like it has a little airfield, as well as docks. If we assume that ultra pneumonia won't survive indefinitely outside a live human body, the main risk is other humans. So if we can prove Ben is safe, or eliminate him as a danger, and confirm the absence of other human life in Barrow, that will be a good place to start scavenging."

Chapter 42 Wednesday 2 June 2027

Vin and Martha were sitting at home having supper together, at around 7pm. Vin saw the worried look on her face. He asked, "Martha are you worrying about something in particular?"

Martha told him, "Vin, the trouble is that you still don't really let me in on things you are up to, until it is too late. I had sort of hoped that had changed, after you nearly left Matthew and Emma in London, but I'm sure you are planning something now I won't like. You have said almost nothing, about this chap in Barrow. You haven't told me what happened at Manx Radio, or what you have discussed with anyone else since."

"You're right. I should be more open with you. You deserve better. Mainly I haven't told you because I know you won't like it, but I don't think there is much choice."

"Please Vin, just tell me."

"Someone, no two people, need to go to Barrow for three weeks. They need to be certain that it is safe to bring this Ben Roper chap back to the Isle of Man."

"It is pretty obvious that you have decided, that one of the two people should be you. Why does it have to be you? Isn't it very risky?"

"It is not that risky. It sounds like this Ben has survived infection from the virus. Possibly because he was doped up on heroin, and his whole system's response was depressed. I don't really know."

"You don't really know? So you are taking a huge gamble, that he, or someone, or something won't infect you."

"It's not that big a gamble. This virus might be able to carry in the air, but it must still depend on human hosts, to carry on 'living'. There has been no sign of any animals becoming sick, or dying from it. If it attacked Ben, Ben won. If it bypassed him somehow, the virus is not around anymore, anyway."

"So if he is okay, why not just bring him over here?"

"Well, it is just possible that Ben is infected, even though he is still alive. We can't expose 84,000 people to that risk."

"But it is okay to expose yourself to that risk? And you haven't said why it has to be you."

"Henry Smith trusts me. That is one reason. And I am Asian."

"I had noticed, but I don't think Asians should be discriminated against, by being sent on dangerous missions."

Vin had noticed a hint of a smile from Martha. He said, "The point about my being Asian is that 10% of us are in the AB positive blood group."

Martha stopped smiling, and said, "Don't tell me. You've already told me before, that AB positive is the universal recipient blood group. You are going to inject yourself with his blood aren't you? And you want to be sure, when you get ill, that it is ultra pneumonia that has caused it?"

"I don't want anyone to get ill, or to die. We just need to be completely sure that it is safe for Ben to come here. Someone has to do this, and I am the obvious person."

Martha looked at Vin, now with tears in her eyes. She said, "I can't stop you can I? But please come back to me. Your son, and your future grandchild, might manage alright, but I need you to cut the grass, and to make me a decent curry occasionally."

Chapter 43, Friday 4 June 2027

Vin was at home in the evening, when his phone rang. Martha was listening, as he talked. He heard the caller say, "Is that Dr Singh? I am phoning about a trip to Barrow."

Vin said, "That sounds a lot like Major Quinnel to me. How are you Peter? We haven't spoken for a while. How is your head injury?"

"My head seems much better, thank you Vin, even without a neurosurgeon to look after me. Actually, Amanda has looked after me really well. She is not very happy with me just now though. How are you and Martha?"

"Oh, we are fine. Actually snap, Martha is not very happy with me."

"Would that be because you have some mad plan to go over to Barrow in Furness, for three weeks?"

"Yes that's right. David Quayle must have told you. Have you rung to try to talk me out of it?"

"No, not at all. I was wondering if I could join you?"

"I really need someone who can fly a helicopter or a small plane, who is willing to stay three weeks with me and this chap Ben, who you have probably been told about. We won't need a third person."

"What about a boat and a skipper instead? One of my Reservists, her dad has got a decent sized private boat which has been sitting unused, like all the others in Douglas Marina, since the embargo began. He is willing to let me take you over to Barrow in it, and not come back for 3 weeks."

"I am not sure that this is a good idea. You may have heard that Ben lives on Walney Island. There is a small airfield very close to his house, which would be ideal for a plane or a helicopter. And do you know how to pilot a boat? And where would we moor? The sea might get rough."

"We could moor in Walney Channel, right next to the Promenade on Walney Island. I have found out that Walney Island is not wide, and its length runs parallel with the coast of the mainland. The Channel is only two to three hundred yards wide and very sheltered. Wherever this Ben lives, we could probably moor quite close to his house. We could wait to go, if the weather was not very good. I have piloted boats before on holidays on waterways. The owner is quite willing to show me the ropes tomorrow, assuming we will have permission to leave Douglas for a demo."

"What blood group are you Peter?"

"I am in Group A positive. I know you wanted someone in Group AB positive, but I have read up a bit. Groups A and O are the most common. I only can't take blood from Groups AB and B, the two rarest groups. You could even test Ben first, couldn't you?"

"Yes, we have fairly simple kits we can use. If Ben shows up as AB or B, I would not inject you with his blood. So you would not get agglutination of your blood. Then, I would have to ask you to ingest his saliva instead."

"So, we are on then?"

"Why do you want to do this? Isn't Amanda expecting? Haven't you put yourself on the line enough already?"

"What about you, you have stuck your head above the parapet a few times, haven't you?"

"I suppose so. But I was pretty sure there was something odd about the death on the ship, before I agreed to fly out to it."

"And, aren't you pretty sure this chap Ben won't be infectious?"

"Yes, but 84,000 people need me to be 100% sure, so we will be taking some risk."

"Well, I want to come, because I think you deserve support. My support in particular. You have shown concern and practical support to Amanda and me, several times. I also think you might need somebody with you, who will make Ben think twice about any nonsense. And I have absolutely promised Amanda that, when I get back, I will leave the Army Reserve and stop taking any more risks of any kind."

"Well, it looks like you and I are on our way to Barrow soon then."

Chapter 44, Tuesday 8 June 2027

Vin looked around him, as they went north along the Walney Channel, and passed under the bridge linking Walney Island with the main part of Barrow in Furness. It was only around 9.30am, and they had left Douglas at mid tide at 6.30am, to get to Barrow just after high tide. They had only 20 cms clearance under the bridge. After that, Peter was keeping well to the left only, about 20 yards away from Walney Island. Vin said, "This looks tricky to me. I wish I had found a helicopter pilot to bring me instead."

Peter replied, "I don't think you would have found anyone gullible enough. Just look out for a couple of spare mooring rings close together. I should be able to hold the bow against the bank, while you tie the mooring rope. Then you can jump off, and I will throw you the rope at the stern, to tie that one as well. And, before we walk off we should put some slack in both ropes, so the boat can settle on the creek bed at low tide, and rise again at high tide."

Vin responded, "Whatever you say, captain. Look we have just gone past two rings close enough together."

Peter told him, "Right I will circle round, and put the bow near the upstream ring."

After a short while, they had tied up and unloaded everything, except two bicycles. They had each brought a lightweight postman's trolley, in which they put everything. Peter said, "Right let's slacken the rear rope, and slacken the front one. Trouble is the boat will rest at an angle at low tide, but still drift about a bit at high tide. But, with any luck, we should still have the boat here undamaged to take us home again."

They looked around. Vin said, "This is creepy, isn't it. Birds are singing, but no traffic or human activity at all. Wait, what's that? Oh it's a fox. Animal life; that is a good sign."

Peter commented, "I presume you mean, because it shows that ultra pneumonia hasn't spread to other species. Hmm, I might have been foolish to do this, but I am relying on you for finding our way to Ben's house, from here."

Vin was looking at his Ordnance Survey 1:25,000 scale map. He said, "Let me see, according to this map, there is a road to the left, after about 200 metres along this Promenade Road. That should be Mill Lane, and then it's along there, about another 1200 metres."

After about 25 minutes, they were standing outside 79 Rubble Gardens. They had seen various animals on the way, including a couple of dogs, that had growled at them. They had noticed one car parked outside a fire station, with two bodies showing signs of beginning to decompose in the front seats, but they had seen no bodies in the open air. There was no answer to banging on the front door, so Peter went around the side, and found the back door unlocked. He walked through to the front door, and let Vin in. The house downstairs was in a very odious and dirty condition, with food wrappers and discarded tins and bottles lying around. There were lots of cigarette ends, in a couple of ashtrays. As

Vin walked in, a black and white cat walked in with him. Vin called out, "Ben, are you upstairs?"

There was no answer. Vin went upstairs, and found a young man asleep in a single bed. Vin shook him gently, and said, "Ben wake up!"

Ben opened his eyes, and saw Vin looking at him. He said, "Jesus, what the fuck?... Oh yes, I remember. You must be Vin. Sorry, you startled me."

Vin said, "Well you knew we were coming today. I thought maybe you would have made the house ready for us. Is the water still running?"

Ben sat up, and said, "Yes, just cold water. The gas cooker still works, but it seems to need electricity, to make the gas boiler come on."

"Well, that's not so bad. I want you to wash your hands and face, brush your teeth, put on the cleanest clothes you can find, and come downstairs; and then we can discuss what happens next," Vin told him.

Ben was not pleased to be told what to do. He told Vin, "This is my house. I don't have to do what you say."

At that point Peter entered the room. He was wearing his army uniform. He said to Ben, "Listen son, you are going to do exactly whatever Vin or I say. If you don't, we will do whatever we need to do anyway, and we will make sure you don't come, and aren't ever able to come, over to the Isle of Man. Do you understand?"

Ben muttered, "Yes I suppose so."

Peter told him, "Right, we will see you downstairs in five minutes." Peter walked into the bathroom, and checked that the shower still worked with cold water. He checked the WC, and saw that it was relatively clean. He pulled the lever on it, and was pleased to note that it flushed as normal, and the cistern refilled. He thought to himself, 'Well, I don't know how far the waste is going but we seem to be on a slight rise here. With any luck it won't back up to here, before we leave.' He checked the other two rooms upstairs. He found that one contained a double bed, but that the sheets had obviously not been changed, presumably since Ben's parents had died in it. The smallest room contained a single bed, made up with apparently clean linen.

Downstairs, about ten minutes later, Ben walked into the kitchen-diner, where Peter and Vin were waiting for him. Vin said to Ben, "Right the most urgent thing is to take a small amount of blood from you. If you sit there, and roll your sleeve up please."

Ben told Vin, "I'm fine, apart from feeling a bit hungover. No need to check my blood." Then he saw Peter glaring at him. He said, "Oh, okay." and he sat down, and offered his arm.

Vin said, "First we need to test your blood group, so I will make a small prick in your thumb for that, and then we will draw two small amounts from your upper arm, to inject Major Quinnel and myself."

Vin tested Ben's blood with an easy to use kit, which just required 8 circles to have a smear of blood placed in each. Each circle represented a discrete blood group. One circle changed colour. Vin said to Peter, "It's O positive, so you will be fine."

Peter replied, "Well, for the time being anyway." He looked at Vin.

Vin told him, "The risk is as I said. It's probably too late already, just by you being in the same street as Ben. But, if you don't want to go ahead with the injection, I'm not going to be able to force you, am I." Vin said, and smiled. It was obvious that he was referring to Peter being younger, taller, fitter, and stronger than himself.

Peter shrugged, remembering that he had volunteered for the trip. He said, "No, let's both be in the same position."

Ben commented, "I think I get it. You want to be sure that I am not going to infect people, so you are going to make sure by injecting yourselves with my blood." He added with a smile, "Let's hope you both survive then!"

After Vin had finished taking blood from Ben, and injecting himself and Peter, Vin said to Ben, "We need to talk about quite a lot of things, but firstly I am curious about the cat."

Ben replied, "What, Sam? It's not even our cat. He started visiting, after everyone else had died. I fed him once, and he came back the next day. So, now I have to forage for him, as well as myself. Tins of catfood haven't been a problem, but I am having to use powdered milk for him and me. He usually hangs around in here, dozing during the day. I let him out late each evening, and he comes back the next day, when I get up and can hear him scratching at the door."

Peter was not impressed with Ben. He decided that he compared badly with the younger men in his Army Reserve, and with his youngest farmhand. He said to him, "Okay that is one mark out of ten then, for taking care of the cat. But the house is a state. You need to tidy it up. You need to wash your clothes, and have a shower. And what about your parents?"

Ben replied, "What about my parents! They died like everyone else. It wasn't my fault. My two sisters, and their husbands, and their children, and my mates, and most people around the world are dead too."

Peter was not satisfied. He said, "Yes, lots of people are dead, but your parents gave you life, and looked after you. You lived in their house. You can't worry about all the other bodies I know, but just to shove your parents in the shed wasn't respectful, was it? Don't you think you should bury them, and say a few words afterwards?"

"Well I do feel badly about that...um Major, but I have noticed a few flies buzzing round the shed. I don't really want to look at them."

"Did you and the other chap carry them in anything?"

"A couple of old blankets."

"How about if we find you a pick and a spade, somewhere. Some of the ground at the back looks like it would easily break up. You can dig one big hole, or two not so big. When the holes are big enough, I will help you get your parents out of the shed, and lower them in. When you have covered them over, if you like, Vin and I will come and listen, if you want to say a prayer or a few words in their memory. I am not going to try to force you to do that, but I think you would feel better for it."

"Yes I think it would be better."

Chapter 45, Wednesday 9 June 2027

Ben was standing at one end of the two parallel graves containing his parents. The cat, Sam, was standing next to him. Vin and Peter were standing at the other end, facing Ben.

Ben said, "Mum and Dad, I am sorry about the delay in burying you. I am sorry it is not a proper graveyard, but at least it is at the back of the house, where you brought my sisters and me up. Thank you for giving me life, and for looking after me. The disease that has killed you and nearly everyone else is a terrible thing, and I am not sure why I am still alive. I hope you wouldn't mind me going to live on the Isle of Man soon. We had a nice holiday there when I was young, didn't we? I remember we all went up Snaefell on the electric train one day, and we could see back across to the mountains in the Lake District. I hope there is a Heaven, and that you are there with Sarah and Louise, and their children. And if I am lucky, I will join you one day."

Ben stopped speaking, as tears rolled down his cheeks. Peter walked over to him, put his arm around Ben's shoulder, and said, "Well done lad."

Chapter 46, Thursday 24 June 2027

Vin, Ben, and Peter were sitting around the table around the table in the kitchen diner having breakfast. Vin said to Peter, "How are you feeling?"

Peter replied, "Since we ran out of the fresh eggs we brought with us, I am feeling completely fed up with our diet, which seems to involve a lot of powdered milk and tinned food, and the occasional undergrown vegetable, taken from someone's back garden. I am feeling fed up with cycling around Barrow, and finding the occasional decomposing body. I suppose I am feeling a bit fitter. I am feeling a bit surprised we are still getting running water on this rise, and I think the water pressure has dropped a bit. I am feeling like I wish I was at home with my wife. How are you feeling?"

Vin told him, "Much the same as you, plus I am feeling pleased and hopeful, because you and I are still alive. So, you don't feel unwell in any way?"

Peter was suddenly feeling more cheerful. He answered, "No, I don't feel unwell at all."

They both looked at Ben. Vin said to Ben, "I am a bit surprised my stern friend here hasn't mentioned it, but you might feel more lively in the mornings, if you went easier on the booze. And also cut down on the fags. You won't get either for nothing on Mann, and supplies of booze and fags will be limited. You should find cutting down on booze very easy, compared with coming off heroin. How long have you been 'clean' now?"

Ben coloured slightly. He said, "Since when I said before, so that's about 4 weeks. Look, I want to be straight with both of you. Billy's stash did run out, but I searched other places desperately for more before you came, and if I had found some, I would have taken it. But you have both helped me pull myself together. You have given me hope. I don't want to touch H ever again, and I will cut down on the booze and fags. It sounds like I won't have much choice."

Vin smiled. He said, "Okay, shall we have a recap on things? I think I am 12 to 6 ahead on games of chess with Peter, and I reckon I am about 25 to 10 ahead on Chinese patience with Ben. It's a shame neither of you like Scrabble, so I will have to wait until we get back to play David Quayle at that."

Peter commented, "Moving on from your prowess at pointless games, I think we have pretty much established that there is no one else alive in Barrow. We have found various stores, and other places where we can send people to scavenge; we have seen diesel and oil depots, apart from regular petrol stations, but someone will need to figure out how to work pumps without mains electricity. We have seen that there is room in the main dock for us to get some decent sized boats in. The airfield, a mile from here, will be okay for helicopters and light planes. The main point is, that we reckon it would be safe and profitable for organised groups to come here. So, when do we go home?"

Vin said, "Next Tuesday, it will be three weeks since we got here, and injected ourselves with Ben's blood. That will allow a margin of error of 7 days over what I am confident is the incubation period for ultra pneumonia, the period between getting infected and seeming to be well, and then rapidly deteriorating and dying from it. That is, with the exception of Ben and Billy, and probably about one in a hundred thousand other people. And I really don't know whether a heroin dose would have anything to do with preventing that deterioration leading to death, and allowing recovery instead."

Peter asked, "So at 9.30am today, we will call up the Marine Control Centre and tell them we would like an aeroplane or helicopter organised to pick us up on Tuesday?"

Vin was puzzled. He said, "Aren't we going back on the boat we came on?"

Peter had an admission to make. He told them, "There is a slight problem. I went to check up on it yesterday, and the tide was in. It was only attached by one of the mooring ropes. It was floating, but listing to one side. I think it must have taken a bit of a battering. It doesn't look seaworthy. It probably wasn't the best mooring place we could have chosen. I hope Jack and Adrian don't mind the Government paying Mr Walker compensation. I don't think I could afford it personally."

Vin had been frowning about the boat. He said, "Let's hope they don't decide we can stay here, instead."

Peter assumed he was joking, but he was never quite sure with Vin.

At 9.40am Peter and Vin had been on the radio for a while, when Vin asked to be patched through to Martha his wife. He said to Ben and Peter, "I am sorry, but would you both just give me five minutes please?"

Ben and Peter left Vin alone in the kitchen diner. Vin was put through to Martha. After a short while he said, "Martha, we have talked about Ben haven't we? I feel quite sorry for him really, and wonder how he will manage if he just gets dumped in a hostel. I was wondering..."

Martha interrupted, "No Vin. You are going to say, 'let's put him up with us.' I don't want to do that. As a social worker, from time to time, I have thought that some young man, or young woman, would benefit from living with us. And I have then told myself, it wouldn't be fair on you. Isn't the only reason Ben is off heroin, is because he can't find any more to take? Well, there is still some to be found on this island, I can tell you."

Vin thought about what Ben had said a short while earlier, about looking for more heroin. Vin said, "Yes, he admitted he looked for more, but he seems clear now, he doen't want to take it ever again."

"Sorry Vin, but no. We have a grandchild on the way. I don't want Emma and Matthew worrying about a junkie being in the house, when they bring her here," Martha told him.

Vin asked, "Did you say 'her'? Is it going to be a girl then?"

"Yes, they told me yesterday."

"Well that's wonderful. I mean a grandson would have been fine, but girls are sometimes cuter aren't they?"

"Maybe. So, I will look forward to seeing you again on Tuesday. But come through to me again before then, if you like. Take care Vin."

Vin "Yes I will. You take care too."

Chapter 47, Tuesday 29 June 2027

Vin, Peter and Ben had walked out of the front door of Ben's house. The two post office carts now included some of Ben's stuff. Ben said to the other two, "Sorry, can you just give me a moment, please?"

He went back indoors. He opened the back door, and looked at the two mounds he had made. He whispered "Bye Dad, bye Mum." and tears formed in his eyes. He turned again, and rejoined Peter and Vin.

Vin said to him, "Alright then?"

Ben replied, "Yes fine."

Peter said to Ben, "That's good, because these carts seem pretty heavy, and I think you should push this one for a bit."

Ben agreed, "Yes old man, I can do that. Can you manage to walk, do you think?"

Peter told him, "Well, I could ride my bike, but I don't think there is going to be room in the helicopter for it."

A short while later they were at the airfield. A helicopter landed soon after, and Vin recognised the pilot when he stopped the engine, and got out. Vin said to him, "Hello Harry, I wasn't expecting it to be you again."

Harry answered, "How could I refuse? The only time we are allowed to fly is when Dr Singh needs a ride to or from some exotic location. Like to a ship off course in the Irish Sea, or to a windswept Walney Island."

Peter said to Harry, "You must be Harry Harrison. Well I think there might be some more flights out to here from now, although boats and ships can carry more."

Harry said, "We shall see, I suppose. You are the famous Major Peter Quinnel aren't you? Is it right, you've wrecked a motor boat? Or should I say, another one?"

Peter replied, "Well this second one is still floating, but I wasn't sure it was seaworthy, after bashing about on its moorings."

About half an hour later they landed at the helicopter field next to Nobles Hospital, on the outskirts of Douglas. Peter could see his old Jag parked nearby. Then he was out of the helicopter, and Amanda was hugging him. Vin looked around, and saw Martha coming up. They hugged. Ben was standing nearby. Martha broke her embrace, and said to him, "You must be Ben, and is that Sam you're holding under your jacket? I heard that you have adopted him."

Ben replied, "Yes, I am hoping they will let me keep him in the hostel. Do you know how to get there? I think they have got a place for me."

Martha asked him, "Ben, would you like to stay with us for a while instead, to help you settle in? We are a bit out of town, but there are occasional vintage electric trains into Douglas."

Ben looked at Vin, and saw that he was smiling. Ben said, "Can I bring Sam?"

Martha pretended a frown, and said, "Will he be any good at chasing off pigeons and squirrels, from our vegetable patch?"

Ben replied, "To be honest, he only prowls at night. He generally takes it easy during the day. But I have brought plenty of tins of catfood I took from the local supermarket, to keep him going."

Vin chipped in, "I was wondering what was in that heavy cardboard box."

Martha smiled again, and said, "So, both you and Sam are coming to live with us then, okay?"

Ben answered, "Yes please. That's very kind of you and Vin."

Epilogue by David Quayle, dated Wednesday 5 April 2028

Exactly a year has gone by Dr Vahin Singh (Vin) came into my office, and demanded that the Isle of Man Government embargo the rest of the world from it straightaway. Luckily for us we followed his advice, albeit with that repatriation flight saga thrown in. So I think it is down to him, and to Major Peter Quinnel, that most people who were living on the Isle of Man at that time are still alive now.

There have been big changes in everyone's lives, though. Lots of people lost their livelihoods, but farming, manufacturing, and engineering businesses are all employing a lot more people. Everyone has had to adapt. People's diets have changed. Most non-perishable food and drink from warmer countries has not completely disappeared yet, but the fresh fruit and vegetables that we eat, are all Manx produce now. Surprisingly, our fish diet has become more varied. People have developed a taste for the scallops and crabs that used to be exported.

Rationing is still in force for some things, but I think people would rather decide their own priorities. For example some people would like more petrol or electricity allowances for driving round the island, and do not need their butter and milk rations if they don't like dairy produce.

Our adaptation to a digital and telecommunications world, without the rest of the world, has been remarkable. We still have the Internet and telecomms; it just all starts and ends in Mann. There are no regular TV stations, but podcasts and video downloads were becoming the norm anyway. Strangely people do listen still to Manx radio. I personally swear by it for reliable news updates, and random light music.

Pubs and restaurants are very popular, and there is no shortage of Manx brewed beer or cider, and other alcoholic fruit drinks. Incidentally Ben, who arrived from Barrow in Furness, works behind the bar in a pub in Douglas, having moved into a shared flat with a couple of ex waiters from the Senior Serenade ship. Sam, Ben's adopted cat, still lives with Vin and Martha, but he is always pleased to see Ben when he pays a visit.

You can still see a production at the Gaiety Theatre in Douglas, albeit with amateur actors, singers and musicians. You can still take part in sports or outdoor activities. Life goes on.

I had been worried that we would just not be able to replace or repair all the many things, that we don't manufacture on Mann. But, since Vin and Peter returned from Barrow in Furness, there have been organised authorised groups visiting the mainland, and retrieving from various locations a huge variety of items. These include clothing, crockery, cosmetics, sanitary products, tools, engineering parts, fuel, microprocessors, even bottles of wine. At the same time our manufacturing and engineering companies have become very adaptive. For example, they have figured out how to rig up tanks, pipes, and valves to convert some petrol cars to run on Liquid Petroleum Gas. LPG is readily available as a byproduct from the gas, that is piped from our gas field.

It is difficult to predict what the future holds, but I am feeling optimistic. Perhaps, ultimately, we will set up permanent bases on the mainland, or even further afield. Call it colonisation if you like, but without any indigenous people to repress. This will require a decent birth rate to achieve. As a final note, I can report on two recent contributions to that birth rate. 20 years old Emma Singh gave birth to a girl in October 2027; and 39 years old Amanda Quinnel gave birth to twins, a boy and a girl, in January 2028. All are doing well.